GALLOWS RECKONING

Gallows Reckoning: A Tale of an Infamous Bandit in the American Southwest
By Doug White

Published by Creative Texts Publishers, LLC
PO Box 50
Barto, PA 19504
www.creativetexts.com

Kindle Edition

GALLOWS RECKONING

A Tale of an Infamous Bandit in the American Southwest

DOUG WHITE

TABLE OF CONTENTS

PROLOGUE

Greetings, kind reader; please allow me to introduce myself. My name is Robert Dunbar, an author from New York City. Perhaps you've read or heard of my last two books, *The Execution of Billy the Kid* and *The Execution of Jesse James*? True crime sagas are the genre in which I find myself carving a niche in the writing world, particularly in the world of the outlaw. Billy the Kid was shot and killed in 1881 and Jesse James the same in 1882, but here I am, telling this tale of a man who swung at the end of a noose in 1852.

While traveling by rail through extreme South Mississippi two years ago in 1886, a fortuitous stop spurred the beginnings of this story. In the following pages you will become acquainted with Bill Campbell—an otherwise-unknown outlaw anywhere outside of a few counties in South Mississippi—but just as ruthless, cunning, inventive, and successful as any famous outlaw. Campbell was active in the 1830s and '40s in a section of the country not only thinly populated but practically devoid of both newspapers and those capable of reading the news. It is because of these factors that Campbell's exploits remained hidden from the outside world for over thirty years. Through the pure lucky happenstance of my discovering his would-be biographer—who would not write his tale for private reasons—it became available to my pen and allowed for the story that follows. Please understand: the story, for reasons of clarity, is written from the viewpoint of Sheriff Larry Bacot, the source of the information on the infamous villain Bill Campbell. I stand in as merely your storyteller. As I present this outlaw's adventures and demise, I also sincerely pray this story could be useful for any parents of a wayward teenage boy and serve as a true-to-life cautionary tale, instrumental in returning him to a good and righteous path. So, for clarification, beginning with the paragraph below, when you read the word "I", it's not from the mouth of Robert Dunbar, but the words and thoughts of Sheriff Bacot.

CHAPTER ONE

The Backward Beginning

The sound was one I'd heard a thousand times over, but in this instance, it was different. Very different. I took a moment to think on it; here I was, a mere day short of my forty-fourth birthday, and in all those forty-four years, never had my ears heard a sweeter, more satisfying sound. It was the sound of freedom. It was the sound of redemption. It was the sound of what was, but never should have been.

My ears took in the "ka-chunk-chunk" of the iron-barred cell door slamming, the firm noise of the locking mechanism sliding into place. A very familiar sound, yet right now, it was different—I was on the other side, the free side, of that damned door, that cold cage, and more importantly, it was the last time I'd ever hear that sound. The jailer walked me to the front gate and pushed the door open for me. The bright sun blinded my eyes and my ears picked up the song of a mockingbird singing its heart out in the nearest tree. I could have sworn the air smelled sweeter on this side of the wall, even though physically it was the same, but just crossing the stone barrier made it so. Finally, the nightmare was over. Freedom.

Some dates cloud the mind and cannot be precisely recalled. Other important ones, such as the birthdates of loved ones, are readily available. This is a milestone date I won't soon forget. August 1, 1855, the date of my release from jail when I, Larry Bacot, became a free man again, a truly precious and dear state of life mostly taken for granted until it is stolen away.

DOUG WHITE

After two years and serving half of my sentence, the new governor of Mississippi had read my letters, listened to my former employer's widowed wife, Mrs. Smith, and granted my attorney's plea to pardon me for a crime I did not commit. Thank you, dear governor. In the same breath, a fervent "damn you!" to the previous governor, Governor W.J. Matthews, a pawn of the rich and a crook in his own right, who waved his high hand and had me railroaded into the Jackson County jail after a sham trial three years ago for an alleged crime of libel. My largest debt of gratitude will always go to the widow, Mrs. Junious Smith, who possesses the determination of a bulldog behind the face of an angel. Without her, I would not be smelling the sweet air of freedom.

This is my story, and it is not my story, as well. I was yet the messenger, the one the old axiom says "do not kill." While not killed, I was shamefully locked up as punishment for speaking the truth, my written words threatening a certain group of the high and mighty in my state, those who would have much to lose should my words of truth make it to the outside world. And make it to the outside world they almost did. The eye-opening experience that followed engulfed my very soul. Never in a million years did I harbor the slightest inkling that men I and others of my station admired could be, in reality, such low-down, belly-crawling snakes in the grass who had no problem running roughshod over the laws of man, of God, and also just basic right and wrong. Besides Governor Matthews, there were a couple of state judges, a handful of politicians, a few prominent attorneys, and quite a large number of successful businessmen, all in South Mississippi. Who would have dreamed that such a group held strong and secret ties to a murderous gang of bandits that preyed on the good folk of the American South from 1835 to 1851? Yet, when I uncovered the truth and the names of at least two dozen of these highly esteemed men who were in bed with the Devil, I was silenced; first, they went after my pen and then my physical safety, stashing me away in a filthy, damp cell underneath the courthouse of Jackson County, Mississippi. No doubt hoping disease and illness would eventually infect my mind and body, effectively silencing me for good.

It was approximately four years ago when I was told a fantastic tale by the leader of the outlaw gang as he awaited his execution, a true deathbed confession. The human mind is not only wondrous in its creations but a thing of darkness capable of unspeakable atrocities. The outlaw bared his soul to me for four straight days, admitting every crime he'd ever committed and even ones he simply knew of. At the very end, just minutes before the noose was to be slipped around his thick neck, he began revealing the identities of corrupt men who protected the criminal operation in exchange for bribe money, all the while staying hidden behind a cloak of respectability and sharing in their ill-gotten gains.

As I was the second son of my father, knowing the farm would one day belong to my older brother, I had to go my own way. After an unsuccessful stint as a merchant, I had gone into the Word of the Lord with moderate success until a plague of Yellow Fever wiped out most of my flock, and in much too soon a time left me nearly penniless. It was the same Yellow Fever that took my wife, infant son, and three-year-old daughter. It was then that Sheriff J. P. Smith, once a member of my congregation, rescued my livelihood by taking me in as deputy with a steady source of income. He assured me going from a man of God to a man of Law was an easy transition, one he'd previously made himself. My dear Mother, in my younger days, knowing my status as the second son, insisted I receive a proper education. I was one of the few in my station at the time who could read and write. And so, the outlaw's confession was transcribed into my notebook, later into a draft for a manuscript, and then still later into a finished book printed by a bookbinding and publishing firm in New Orleans. Five thousand copies, to be sold for one dollar apiece, of which my share was twenty cents a copy. This would serve as a windfall and allow me to finally shift from a boardinghouse renter into a homeowner, for myself and quite possibly the second chance of a family. Those were my plans. However, sometimes life has other ideas. My five thousand books, stored in a warehouse while arrangements were made to distribute them to bookstores across the Deep South, never saw a bookshelf. An arsonist made sure the books never left the warehouse and my hard work, as well as the efforts of the publishing house, was reduced to ashes.

I can only assume those men in power—in league with the outlaw gang—had connections to someone at the publisher in New Orleans and did not approve of the information contained in my book. Not long after the fiery incident at the warehouse, an attempt was made on my life as I made my rounds about Perrine County delivering a subpoena to one secluded village. On my ride home, I had my horse shot out from under me. I returned fire in the general direction of the shot's origin and then from behind a bank of large bushes, I heard horse's hooves retreating; the assassin must not have been one for confrontation. Their next attempt on my life proved more successful, as I was served with papers accusing me of libel. The lawsuit was filed in Americus, the county seat of Jackson, but the prosecuting attorney filed for, and received, a change of venue. The trial was moved far from my residence in Batson, and from my hometown of Westville to Rodney, an old river town flush with cotton cash and powerful men of great wealth. I was charged, held, and a court date was set on the docket in record time. With hardly any funds to my name, I could only afford a young attorney from Vicksburg who was completely overmatched. It was then I discovered at least one copy of my book survived the blaze—it was entered into evidence against me. A day and a half after it began, the trial was over. The jury took an hour of deliberation and I was found guilty. The next day, the judge pronounced his sentencing. The following day, under guard, I was taken to Vicksburg and Jackson via rail, then down toward Mobile, where the train stopped at Ellisville, and I was removed in shackles. Deputy Sheriff Bob Daniels had papers drawn up with the circuit judge, ordering me to be handed over to him while I awaited appeal, but the appointed marshal from Jackson decided to ignore that. After a tense standoff between county and state officials, I was whisked down into solitary confinement under the Jackson County Courthouse where I remained for the next two years. It wasn't until a new governor's election and the widow of my former mentor, Sheriff Smith, championing my release that I walked out of the jail, up the stairs, and into the bright sunlight of freedom. A renewed freedom to once again try to tell the outlaw's confession and reveal the names of corrupt individuals. More astute now, and wary of my enemies after my hard-learned two-year lesson, I used the services of a ghostwriter. This ghostwriter wasn't from Mississippi but from the great masses of humanity inhabiting our northeast, one who goes under a clever pen name. And so it is: I can only deduce, if you're reading this today, you know I, Lawrence Bacot, have succeeded. Pay close attention, as what follows is the mighty truth.

The outlaw went by more than one name during his career but he was born William Wallace Campbell. He was called Billy by his parents and three brothers during his childhood, and then answered to Bill from his thirteenth birthday on; a very significant year to him and those in his world. And as it was in 1852, the last year of Bill Campbell's life, I was one of two deputies charged with the transfer of this outlaw from Jackson to Perrine County. Campbell had dark hair, vivid blue eyes, and wore a short full beard. He appeared of average height and build until one's eyes focused on his upper torso. He seemed to bear the skeletal structure and musculature of a much larger, athletic man; thick upper arms, large sloping shoulders—almost bear-like—and a big neck with prominent bulging veins. Thankfully, the journey was unremarkable, as he lay prone and in shackles in a farm wagon and thus gave no trouble to Deputy Daniels or me.

So began the first full day of Bill Campbell's incarceration at my jail. I delivered his breakfast and sat down with him, the iron bars between us. He studied me with his sharp, piercing eyes, and even though he was only thirty-two and had lived a hardscrabble life, his eyes were alight with the precociousness of a young child. I ambled through some small talk—giving him my name, asking how he liked his breakfast, and things of that nature—but he ignored my banter. In the mid-afternoon, breaking his silence, he asked who was really in charge of the jail and, after I told him of Sheriff J. P. Smith, asked if he might converse with him. After I relayed the word that the sheriff was in Jackson for some legal business until later in the week, he seemed to lighten his demeanor toward me.

"So, deputy, uh…I forgot your name," Campbell said in a low voice as if he didn't want anyone else to hear him ask.

I raised up from behind the sheriff's desk and moved a couple of steps closer to the cell but kept my distance. "Lawrence Bacot, most call me Larry."

"Well okay, Deputy Bacot," the outlaw said, even quieter.

"Just Larry please, and if you don't mind, I'll just go with Bill for you?"

We both nodded in silent agreement, but I noted how his near whisper might be a trick to draw me closer to grab me. I retreated to the desk, atop which my new 1851 Colt revolver rested, and pointed it in the direction of the cell. My move prompted his retreat to the single-slat chair in his eight-by-eight-foot cell and the conversation ended there. Campbell didn't speak to me the rest of the week. All I could guess was he was waiting for Sheriff Smith's return.

At the end of the week, upon Sheriff J. P. Smith's return, Campbell was immediately all over him, firing questions constantly. The sheriff reminded him that he wasn't a lawyer, that Campbell had one, as did the state of Mississippi, and to shut up or lose tobacco and coffee privileges. Campbell took the advice to heart and then began to slowly build bonds with me, but only when we were alone. I had an idea of what he was doing but saw no harm or danger in his actions, taking note that after he figured out I was not a simpleton jailer in which he could trick, we both relaxed at a comfortable distance from each other.

Toward the end of that week an official looking letter arrived at our little post office in Batson, Mississippi. The sheriff read the letter in silence and motioned for me to accompany him to the back door of the jail, keeping the prisoner out of earshot but still in our line of sight. The sheriff asked me to read the letter and give my opinion.

"Something seems a little bit strange," I replied as the sheriff lit his pipe and stretched. "What is this with a circuit judge and an exact schedule? Never heard of such."

"Me neither," said J.P. as he took back the letter. "The rest seems legitimate, there's even a raised seal at the bottom. Except for the precise date of arrival and the fact the timing seems much faster than normal, too. All our courts are backed up with cases to try, and small 'burgs like ours have to wait on the circuit-riding judge to come to town. Sure, the judge knows an approximation of his schedule, but things happen. I mean, a case that should've taken two days might end up taking four. A circuit judge can't predict any exact day he'll show up. T'ain't possible."

"He gets here when he gets here, we all know that," I nodded.

"And the most suspicious part is he didn't mention sending a rider ahead by a day or two that'll let us know. Don't see nothing like that in this letter," the sheriff stated matter-of-factly. "I'm hard to believe this is some kind of escape attempt for Bill Campbell's benefit. What do you think?"

"I wouldn't put it past him. He did put together a big gang, so some rescue attempt isn't at all out of the question. What are you going to do, sir?"

"Come by my place for supper when Deputy Daniels relieves you at six. Ella is going to visit her baby sister down to Biloxi the day after tomorrow, so she's making fried chicken tonight to make up for not being here on Sunday. We'll discuss this letter and our prisoner after we eat."

"Much obliged sir, I'll be there."

It turned out Sheriff J.P. Smith was every bit as skillful of a liar as the members of the Campbell Gang. J.P. decided to let the ruse play out but kept himself and both deputies fully armed during every second of their time with the visiting "judge". The new circuit judge said he was on loan from the Second District, headquartered in Columbus, because the regular circuit judge had a bad case of gout and was on leave. J.P. said nothing, but nodded and awaited the interloper's next move, which of course involved a private meeting with Campbell. J.P. shook his head and said it was impossible, that the prisoner had been removed to Biloxi for a new trial about a murder there six years ago, and even produced a receipt from the stagecoach line, showing travel for three from Batson to Biloxi three days prior. The frustrated "judge" seemed upset and asked many questions, of which J.P. offered no help.

GALLOWS RECKONING

The sheriff simply informed the judge that the Hotel Batson served a good meal at midday, and every night, and he should wait out Campbell's return there, although it could take many weeks or even a month.

Together, we watched the "judge" ride north out of Batson, never to be seen again. All the while my fellow deputy held Campbell prisoner in shackles, gagged, and tightly bound in ropes at Sheriff Smith's home, inside his carriage house. We felt good about deterring the rescue attempt, but both agreed we hoped the appeal's trial would begin soon, so we could stop worrying about other possibly dangerous attempts from Campbell and his minions.

We got word the following day that our district circuit-rider judge would be in Batson the day after tomorrow. J.P. looked my way, smiled, and said, "can't wait to ask him how his gout is doing."

I acknowledged his comment with a laugh and immediately looked over at Campbell to see if he knew anything about the fake judge and story but saw nothing in his face that made anything clearer. Later that afternoon, Campbell's lawyer came in from Jackson, but he was well-known to Sheriff Smith, and there was no reason to suspect anything but above-board legal proceedings. The state's prosecuting attorney, also from Jackson, rode in on the same stagecoach. The attorney told J.P. he was retiring to the hotel and would be by in the morning to discuss Bill Campbell. The next day, one witness for the defense, a young woman, rode into town, as did three prosecution witnesses.

Thus began Bill Campbell's appeal for his murder conviction, and on a Friday the thirteenth no less. The trial moved quickly, as Judge Wilson was always in a hurry and therefore, allowed no drama in his courtroom. Campbell did not take the stand in his own defense, and his sole witness, a young widow named Janie McTimmons, had no hard facts, just her opinion. Janie claimed that Bill Campbell didn't gun down Harvey Mays, because Campbell said he had not. Mays's son and a family friend in the employment of Mr. Mays, servings as eyewitnesses, all testified they saw Campbell blast Harvey Mays with a shotgun from four feet away in an ambush at Mays's farm. Campbell's attorney made an impassioned plea to the jury, composed of merchants from Batson and farmers from around Perrine County, but his effort was of no avail. The jury took less than half an hour to announce the verdict, upholding the guilty charge and denying the appeal. After a brief recess, Judge Wilson pronounced that William Wallace Campbell would suffer his penalty at noon the day after suitable gallows could be erected in the town square of Batson, to be hanged by the neck until dead.

The next day I visited the sawmill and was told that sufficient lumber was in inventory to erect proper gallows. Next, I employed the services of two of Batson's better-known carpenters and gave the go-ahead to begin building. Sheriff Smith has always wanted to have sturdy and permanent gallows built in the town square, both to skip the wait time for future hangings and to serve as a physical reminder of what happens to those who stray outside the law. The carpenters measured and sawed for two days began hammering on the morning of day three, not twenty-five yards from the jail.

It was then Bill Campbell took me into his confidence, told me he wanted to confess the clear facts and events of his life, and swore on the lives of his parents that it would be nothing but the truth. He had less than three days to live and a lot to say. He drew his chair close to the bars of his cell; I moved the small desk I shared with the other deputy to within four feet of it, brought out my pencil and notebook, and his purging began.

CHAPTER TWO

A Bad Beginning

William Wallace Campbell was born in Jackson County, Mississippi outside Brewer's Bluff on Cedar Creek, a tributary of the Pascagoula River. His mother remembered his birth as the last day in February of 1820, but his father insisted it was the first day of March. The family Bible bore this out, he said, as his birthday had been written in and scratched out at least four times. Campbell told me personally that March 1st was easier to remember and used it once he left home. He reflected on his home life as a youth, and said his father, Isaac, did better than most, as he'd learned to make pitch and turpentine growing up in North Carolina. Isaac saw the great forests of the Carolinas being felled. In 1815, when he heard of the untapped riches and great yellow pine forests of the southern end of the Mississippi Territory, he packed up and moved.

That first year, Isaac and his wife, Mary, bought land, built a homestead, and planted a few essential food crops. By year two, he purchased two large copper kettles, a pair of oxen, and a flatbed wagon, and started his business. The pines had the bark removed from the bottom three feet, a practice called slashing, and collection buckets were attached to collect the resin or sap. The sap was taken to the kettles and, depending on the amount of time and heat applied, would produce two products. One was turpentine, used as a solvent and as an ingredient chemists used for medicinal purposes. The lesser-heat byproduct was pitch, used for protecting the ropes and lines on sailing vessels and for waterproofing wooden ship hulls. Mary, when not producing children, continued a craft she'd learned from her father, that of making barrels, which proved a godsend by saving Ike the expense of transporting his barrels to the small flatboats which plied the Pascagoula River, where Isaac would sell his goods to middlemen that eventually would end up in the larger markets of New Orleans and Mobile. With thousands of trees to harvest sap, and enough children to work their operation, Isaac and Mary Campbell were, while not rich, better off than two-thirds of the other families in Jackson County. In addition to his turpentine and pitch factory, Isaac later began to raise hogs, sheep, and a few cattle.

With success and some money came responsibility, and at about the time of William Wallace Campbell's birth, Isaac was elected mayor of Brewer's Bluff. Two years later he ran for and won the County Commissioner position for central Jackson County. There was little monetary compensation for either job, but it gave Ike powerful sway in their local business economy and political discussions. Those duties, in addition to his livestock and main business, meant Isaac was not around the house very much for young Billy. Mary became Billy's main influence and, likewise, he was hers. His mother won the argument over Billy going to school instead of slashing and collecting resin, and by the age of ten, Billy could not only read and write better than his parents, but his teacher discovered and encouraged his natural-born artistic instincts.

With two older brothers and one slightly younger than her son, and with the purchase of one male slave, Mary Campbell believed Isaac had all the hands necessary to run his growing business and farm. She wanted her brightest son to follow in the footsteps of her male ancestors and become a Presbyterian minister. Thus, Billy was spared from participating in outdoor labor and kept inside to read the Bible and practice not just writing sermons, but delivering them aloud, as if in front of a congregation. His mother would beam proudly and praise Billy as a "prodigy of the pulpit."

Billy's mostly-absent father might have played a role in what happened next, or maybe it was just the way a young male's brain begins to work as those thirteen-year-old hormones take over. He'd overheard one of his older brothers complain their hogs had contracted some disease, that five had died that day and seventeen more seemed to be sick. What's more, those hogs were due at the Mobile market on the first day of December, less than a week away. Seizing a chance to do more to help the family than read and preach to an empty table and array of chairs, Billy hatched a plan. Under the cover of darkness, he would make his way southeast, stop by Mr. Hurlbert's hog farm, relieve him of two dozen pigs, and then continue onto Mobile for the sale. All went according to plan until just after the sale when the market organizer, a longtime friend of Mr. Hurlbert, noticed the pigs bore his friend's tiny, dyed brand behind their left ear. When confronted, the fast-thinking Billy said yes, these were not his pigs, but he'd been hired by Hurlbert, who was ill, to deliver them to the market. The foreman sent a man along with Billy to see that the sale money was indeed delivered to the rightful owner.

The ruse did not work, and Mr. Hurlbert not only got his money, but the satisfaction of seeing the arrest of Billy Campbell on a charge of larceny. With Mr. Campbell's connections, Billy was allowed to stay home until the trial, which would take place early the next year. In the meantime, Billy concocted a story that he'd been used by an older man who'd forced him at knifepoint to steal the pigs and sell them. Mary, believing in her seemingly pious and religious boy, took the story as gospel and started to devise some way to keep her young preaching prodigy out of jail.

DOUG WHITE

Mary knew of a flatboat man that used the Pascagoula, by the name of James Harmon. She and others had been warned to steer clear of Harmon, as he was a bad man, just recently released from the state penitentiary in Jackson for kidnapping. It was said he'd caught an easy break, as he was suspected of, but never tried for, at least five counts of first-degree murder during his life. She sent word to the ferryman at Cedar Creek for him to stop Harmon the next time he was there so she could speak to him. A few days later, they met behind the ferryman's house and discussed Billy's situation. Harmon's first response was that he could kill Hurlbert and thus there would be no plaintiff, but Mary could not agree to such a drastic measure. His next idea was to destroy the lawsuit and evidence. The easiest, most efficient, and safest way to do this would be by burning down the Jackson County Courthouse. The idea was acceptable to Mary, and she paid him twenty-five dollars, with another fifty due after the deed. He had one stipulation; she must provide him someone to assist with his arson. Harmon's twisted logic demanded only one person, Billy, and Mary was at a loss to offer anyone else.

"So, we did. Well, I did. Harmon and I waited until after midnight and the town was completely deserted. We took a few gallons of my daddy's turpentine and broke in through the back door. He covered the first floor and I the second, and then we lit our torches, set fire, and ran like the Dickens. I paid him the other fifty dollars, and he took off south and me north. Mama had a horse ready for me, and rations, and I took off to hide for a couple of weeks in the dense woods between the small communities of Cross Roads and Howell," Campbell said as he moved, and his chest swelled a bit.

"So, Harmon left after he got his money?" I asked.

"I thought so, but darned if he didn't show up where I was hiding two days later. He said he'd never seen such audacity from a mere thirteen-year-old boy, and he was wanting to talk," continued the outlaw. "He asked me if I was a dupe or a fool and naturally, I replied in the negative. Harmon said only fools farm and work outdoors from sunup to sundown, and men that use their brain not only have it much easier and live longer, but they make much more money, too, and have a better life."

I paused in my writing and told Campbell to wait a minute, as I had a feeling he was about to say something I needed to be sure I recorded correctly. He did, and said, "yes, take this down just as I say."

Campbell said that Harmon's only issue was his age, that thirteen was too young. However, if he was fifteen, he'd ask Bill to join their gang.

"Harmon asked me if I was willing to skirt some issues with the law, said he could see me in positions to make as much as $100[1] or more in a day, instead of in a whole year. Right then and there, he had me," the outlaw said, as a smile crossed his lips and he stepped back from the bars and gave a nod. "When I didn't say anything immediately, Harmon said, 'hey you already crossed the line. *You* burned down the courthouse. Did you happen to notice after I lit your torch, I never lit mine? Don't mean to be nasty about it, but it was you who burnt it down, not me.'"

"How did you take that?" I asked.

"I was angry, I stood up and took a swing at Harmon, but Harmon was a grown man, fifteen years older, and blocked my punch but did not retaliate. He told me he admired my spunky fire, said that kind of attitude would make me a rich man at an early age if I'd join up with him and his gang," Campbell explained. "That did it for me. Being a

---

[1] $100 in 1840 would be $3000 today

rich man at an early age? Who wouldn't want that? Hell, we all do, even you, deputy," Campbell said with a big laugh and then paused to light a cigar stub.

I knew he was right but couldn't let him know that so I kept a straight face. Campbell mentioned his throat was parched, so I pushed the water bucket over with my foot so he could reach through the bars with his tin cup. He reminded both of us that we'd been so caught up in his speaking, and my writing, we'd completely skipped breakfast, and with that I laid my pencil and paper aside, went out back to the cooking shed, and started cooking our bacon, grits and eggs.

Meanwhile, the carpenters continued to hammer away.

CHAPTER THREE

Another Kind of Prodigy

After a break for food, Bill Campbell continued the history lesson on his life. He started from the night he burned down the courthouse. He had been eighteen months shy of his fifteenth birthday, just a *hobbadehoy*[2], as he put it. Mary Campbell did not want to implicate any other family members in Billy's bad deed, so she used Harmon as her hired go-between in communications between the family home and Billy's camp in the woods. Harmon agreed with Mary that removing Billy from the area was a good idea. She had two brothers living in Port Gibson, Mississippi, about 150 miles to the west. One had a hog farm, the other was a general store owner in town, so surely one of them could use some free labor in exchange for room and board. It had crossed her mind to send her boy to boarding school, but the expense would surely upset Isaac. Billy would live in Port Gibson until his fifteenth birthday, upon which time Harmon told her he'd not only deliver the boy to his uncles but would bring him back home to Brewer's Bluff at the appointed time. Campbell's story skipped over his year and a half in Port Gibson without many details, other than that he was ready to leave from the moment he arrived.

Harmon liked Billy Campbell and saw him as the little brother he'd never had. He quizzed Billy over and over on their ride back to

---

[2] hobbadehoy is a nineteenth century term for a boy who calls himself a

man

Brewer's Bluff, mainly about if he going to go to seminary and become a preacher, or if he wished to live like Harmon and eventually join their gang. Billy's decision never wavered, nor was there any hesitation, as he parroted back Harmon's words from a year and a half earlier; he was not a fool, but working on a hog farm convinced him he'd never, ever be a fool. No, Billy Campbell wanted to be a rich man at a young age.

However, he could only help so much. If Bill, as he now went by at Harmon's encouragement, was to share in the profits of the gang, he'd have to share in the risks and dangers, too. The first step was initiation into the Harmon Gang, also known as the Beaver Creek Clan. They were about a dozen strong in number and about half used fictitious names. Rule number one was loyalty to the gang, and that meant total silence if ever captured by the law. Breaking of this rule not only meant death for the gang member, but death to his immediate family as well. Strangely enough, this oath was sworn on a Bible with a bloody knife wedged between the palm of the hand and the Good Book. The second rule was that Harmon was the undisputed leader, and the Irishman, McTimmons, was his first lieutenant. Strict following of their orders was mandatory. There was some democracy, however, and all the gang's actions were put to a vote. For example, if there was an idea to rob a certain person or business, the gang voted, but Harmon's vote counted double, and he was careful to always keep an even number of members. Harmon used the vote count as his barometer to get a feel on any gang action, and with McTimmons feeding him inside knowledge on the gang's feelings on an issue, there was rarely ever a close vote.

Bill's gang initiation was in four parts. First, he had to prove he could fire a single-shot pistol, hit a target at ten paces, and reload in under half a minute. Second, with blunt, wooden practice knives, he had to prove he could handle himself in a knife fight. Third, he'd need the courage to run the gauntlet of gang members armed with wooden clubs, prove he could handle the pain, and then have the courage to do so twice. Finally, he'd have to memorize the gang's mystic alphabet, which instead of letters, used symbols. These symbols could be carved in a tree trunk to call a meeting, or even used on paper to communicate over long distance without fear of detection by the authorities. Bill was given six days to master these tasks and would be tested at next week's meeting. Harmon and McTimmons both assisted young Bill and he successfully passed all four tests. He was admitted into the gang with a rowdy cheer and the opening of several bottles of whiskey and rum.

"That was the first time my lips touched alcohol, and doggone, I'll tell you, I loved it, loved the damned stuff," the outlaw confessed as he paused and probably hoped his jailer would slip him a few drams. "The whole damn gang got fallin' down drunk, especially our Irish member Mr. McTimmons. All got drunk except for Harmon, who'd I come to learn did drink, just sparingly. Unless there was some sort of legitimate celebration, then he'd have a few more."

It was then I noticed Campbell had paused. He stared at me as if he wanted something, but I did not know what. A condemned man had no reason to hold his tongue, he should just say whatever needed saying. He was smacking his lips and moving his tongue around them, but stayed silent for another couple of minutes.

When he started back, Campbell said, "after I was in the gang, Harmon said it was time to lay out and hide, so we visited his father's farm right near the little village known as Krebs on the road to Mobile. McTimmons went too, and upon learning I could read and write, they insisted I record their grand scheme on paper. They wanted to study the plan, especially the timeline of planned events. Later, after revisions, it'd be my job to transfer the plan to paper, but in a code only the gang knew."

It was quite the ambitious plan they'd hatched. The city of Mobile had hired four night watchmen to guard their city, from an hour after sundown until dawn. Little did the officials in Mobile know, these four were Beaver Creek gang members. Campbell admitted he learned a lot from Harmon over the years, but the Mobile plot was probably the best thing he saw him do. All the watchmen had been hired well over a year before the heist, so they were trusted. Trusted so much, in fact, a few shop owners had given them an emergency key to the front door. On this appointed night, all but one member of the gang came into downtown Mobile around 1:00 in the morning. That lone member was stationed out in the bay, on deserted Blakeley Island, to start huge fires in the hay fields and distract any curious townspeople. Harmon came in with four large covered-wagons and then calmly, quietly, and methodically opened the stores and relieved them of their finest wares, including fine silks and muslins, food stuffs, jewelry, liquor, cash, and anything else of value. Harmon had done his homework; with a copy of the newspaper, the *Mobile Commercial Register and Patriot,* he'd perused the back page of merchant ads and was virtually handed an inventory of each store. In a little more than one hour the fully laden wagons were on the western edge of Mobile, heading south for a meeting Harmon had arranged on the Dog River with two cargo sailing vessels. After off-loading at St. Marks in the Florida panhandle, the wagon train would travel north into Georgia, thereby putting almost two entire states between the scene of his heist and where his goods could safely be sold to an unsuspecting public. After their first stop in Tallahassee, they crossed the state line and stopped in Bainbridge, Newton, and Albany. These folk of the wiregrass region were starved for any amenities. Among their goods for sale were ginger, cloves, soap, candles, champagne, port, claret, lard, linseed oil, snuff, waffle irons, sad irons, fire dogs, tin kettles, anvils, frying pans, washboards, wood screws, bourbon, and rye whiskey. After that, they went east toward Irwinville, and south to Troupsville, Thomasville, and Duncanville.

"Yep, was quite the operation. Naturally, all I was good for was muscle. I was just a kid, of course. We traveled up, I'd guess went about a hundred miles up into the state of Georgia before we sold the last of our goods, then we traded the mules and wagon for horses and started back to South Mississippi. Our haul netted the gang around $20,000, if memory serves me. It was divided up more or less equally between the fourteen of us, with Harmon getting about 50% more and McTimmons about 25% more, because of rank. The four watchmen got a $150 bonus. But all in all, it was a smash of a winner, and I saw $1300 for roughly four weeks work. That was winter of 1835, if'n you want to put that in your journal, and I was on my way to being a rich man at an early age," the outlaw said with smug satisfaction.

I paused as he said those last words. Something bothered me. Was it the lack of morals in a fifteen-year-old boy? Maybe, or was it his path to being a Presbyterian minister being waylaid by one simple stumble of larceny, then compounded by the arson? If he and his mother had just taken the consequences of his stealing, he'd likely have gotten off with a fine and short prison sentence, and his life could have returned to normal. But it hadn't, and time only knows one direction. Bill had been taken in by the promise of an easy life. He'd seen how hard-working his parents were, and instead of emulating them, rejected their work ethic as foolish. But here and now, who was the fool? An infamous outlaw due to hang in seventy-two hours, or his hardworking kinfolk who earned life's joy of sweet freedom with their sweat and toil.

Campbell continued. "Here again, Harmon taught me a lesson on being on the outer limits of the law. Once home, it was time to lay out and hide. On the journey back from Georgia, he'd instructed all in the gang to lay out, and that there would not be another meeting at gang headquarters for a full calendar year. People and lawmen have a knack for putting two and two together in that, 'hey, you're not around and some big crime happens and then poof, here you are back home again.' The solution is hiding out and pretending the law is always on your back. You don't relax. You can't relax, but you can disappear. It means disappearing from friends, women, and especially family. Harmon preached it, 'those that don't follow these guides are soon for the jail cell.' Smart man, that Harmon," Campbell said with immense admiration.

We looked at each other for a moment and he started back, "I'll tell of the hideout, but might I...Mr. Bacot, kind sir, possibly have a few drams of whiskey to sooth my aches and mental pains?"

"I'll tell you Bill, if things were different, then sure I'd give you a drink, but they ain't. You're a prisoner. Actually, my prisoner, and why, if I gave alcohol to any prisoner, it'd not only be my job, but I could end up on your side of the bars. Sorry, can't risk it...Mr. Campbell, sir," I countered with the formal salutation, taking notice of his.

Unwilling to take my answer as final, he merely addressed it as temporary, something to be discussed again in the future. I shook my head and silently acknowledged his perseverance. He told of Harmon's hideout between the town of Americus and the state line, on the west side of the Escatawpa River. "He'd chosen a place far from any main road, and in what was actually an old abandoned small Choctaw Indian village. Most locals knew the Indians all died off from disease and considered the few remaining huts as off-limits, for their own health. Harmon had no such fear and gave me a log hut of my own upon arriving back from Georgia. Another trick of the outlaw trade was to appear to be gainfully employed, as was his ruse of a job as a flatboat man on the Pascagoula. He suggested a couple of "jobs" I could use as a front, should the authorities ever question me about how I may have come into some money. The everyday appearance of being an everyday working fool was required when laying out. One job Harmon suggested was firewood supply to homes of widows or the elderly. All one needed to do was keep a decent amount of wood always chopped and visible to any prying eyes and make an occasional sale for legitimacy's sake. He also suggested claiming to be a fisherman and supplier to the larger towns downriver like Scranton, Belle Fountain, Krebs, and Biloxi. One just had to know the names of the buyers and their location, and again, make the occasional sale. Another false legitimacy was the job of producing charcoal. It was relatively easy by stacking burning hardwood and then smothering it slowly with a mixture of sand and dirt to leave only the flammable carbon. Have a few pits visible, and a supply of charcoal at the ready, and one is set."

As I wrote down Campbell's deceitful words, it occurred to me that I was not only hearing what amounted to a deathbed confession but learning insider tools of the outlaw trade, which could come in handy in my future plans and secret goal, to one day return home to Westville as Sheriff of Simpson County. The hammering outside stopped, and Campbell retreated to the opposite side of his cell and peered out the small, barred window. But before he could maneuver to see his gallows being built, Sheriff Smith walked by, toward the door. "Here comes Smith, deputy. I'm gonna rest my voice box and take a lay down for a few, all right by you?" he said, without waiting on my response, and was on his cot, facing the blank brick wall. I took the hint and placed my notebook in the bottom left drawer of my desk just as Smith entered.

"Hello deputy," Smith said upon entering, "how's our prisoner holding up? Them carpenters banging away...that bothering him as you can tell?" Sheriff Smith got behind his desk, removed his pistol from his belt and sat down.

"Far as I can tell it ain't. See him right now just laying there? He's got a good appetite because he ate four eggs and four strips of bacon, oh, and a mug full of grits. Oh, hey Sheriff, now that you're here is a good time for me to empty out his piss bucket," I said, realizing with other prisoners it was usually a one-man job, but Smith, knowing of Campbell's deadly reputation, insisted we deputies wait until two men were present. I unlocked the cell, grabbed the bucket quickly and shut it. All the while, Campbell never moved a muscle. Going out the front door, I made a sharp turn around the side of the jail and walked out a good ten yards past our cooking shed. The other deputy had dug a new hole a few days back, and I deposited the waste there, grabbed the nearby shovel, pushed a spadesful of dirt over it, and returned to my post.

No sooner had I sat back down, the carpenters returned to hammering. I looked over at Campbell and then at the sheriff. Campbell raised his head, then laid it back on his mattress. The sheriff smiled and then spoke to me, "some fellow over to the hotel told me he'd seen a *New Orleans Picayune* paper last week and there's another big gold rush on, 'cepting this one is in Australia, but he's hearing lots of Americans are booking passage and going to try and strike it rich, just like a few did in California a couple of years back."

"Oh yes, never forget that big California strike. There was a lot of gold but so many fellows rushed in that it petered out in a few years. I had a friend who had a brother who tried his luck out there and came back busted flat. He said the only one making money were the ones mining the miners. Ha!" I interjected.

"I could see that, sure could, a man's out in the middle of nowhere and needs supplies, ain't a stretch to see the merchants can command any price they wanna set," said Smith as he opened his mail and started reading to himself. After about ten minutes, he was done. He rose from his chair and announced he'd be at the hotel for an early dinner. He explained Ella was still in Biloxi visiting her sister and all he had for breakfast was a stale hoecake and was now starving to death.

With the sheriff's leaving, I expected Campbell to rise from his tiny bed, take up his stance by the cell bars, and continue his life's story. Instead, I heard slight snoring. Normally, when there weren't any prisoners, or prisoners of a tamer variety, I'd use this time to walk the town and visit the merchants, the school, and the church, to check on everyone and see if anybody had my need to investigate any kind of the unusual, or even criminal. Sheriff Smith had changed all that with Campbell's arrival. A minimum of one set of eyes were to be on the outlaw at all times, no exception. There was another nugget for me to use, should a similar situation arise for me, in my hypothetical future job as Simpson County Sheriff. I retrieved my Bible from the drawer and began reading silently from whichever passage happened to open.

CHAPTER FOUR

The Pupil's Work Begins

I left the room that I rented at Widow Batson's Boarding House just before 6:00 a.m. and began the 100-yard walk to the sheriff's office. Main street held little foot traffic and there were three or four farm wagons coming into town from the surrounding countryside. The day had started with light fog, but by this hour it was already dissipating. I noticed the dampness on the lumber and base of the gallows, still under construction, as I passed by, and deduced it would delay the carpenters at least until the sun rose high enough to dry their serious project. Batson was not much of a town, but it was the largest in Perrine County with a population of around 1,200 souls. The chief occupation was logging. Batson, being the only town in the county with a sawmill, drove up population numbers and it became the county seat. We also had a tannery, two blacksmiths, two doctors, a dry goods store, two general stores, a bank, a livery stable, three churches, the courthouse, a cobbler, two saloons, and even a barber. After logging, raising hogs, cattle, and sheep were about equally divided. As good as the South Mississippi soil was for growing pine trees, it was as poor for large-scale crop production. Most could skimp by with a family garden, but the local soil could not support cotton, which in turn kept the bottom third of the state less affluent and with less clout than in the capital city. There were not many rich men in South Mississippi, but in my line of work, cotton and cash were of no consequence. My job was keeping the peace and protecting the people, if the need arose.

GALLOWS RECKONING

I was briefed by my counterpart, Deputy Daniels, the next morning. He said Campbell had slept entirely through night, but he did say the outlaw had a fitful sleep and he'd talked on and off in his sleep about half the evening. He said it was mostly incoherent mumbles, although he did hear him mumbling "sorry, Mama, sorry" two or three times. I noticed the outlaw was beginning to stir, and he'd be using his piss bucket shortly. I offered to empty it and said I'd go ahead and start breakfast for Daniels, Campbell, Sheriff Smith, and myself. After I returned the bucket, I crossed the street to the nearest general store and, after charging a dozen eggs, two pounds of bacon, a pound of coffee, and a loaf of bread to the county, went back and started cooking. Sheriff Smith showed up just as it was all ready, and the four of us ate our hearty morning meal mostly in silence. Well, three of us did. The sheriff ate his bread and that was all, stating he just wasn't up for bacon and eggs. I gave Campbell the extras and he gobbled it down in a hurry. Daniels left to grab some sleep and the sheriff said he was off to a sheep rancher's spread out on Leakesville Road who'd sent word of a recent theft. And like that, Bill Campbell and I were alone. I pulled out my writing supplies. The outlaw lit another cigar stub and took his stance at the cell door.

"Harmon and me laid out in the old Indian village," Campbell began, cutting straight to the point, and I recorded. "True to his instructions, we cut firewood and stacked it, and made some charcoal so we'd look gainfully employed as regular fools if anyone came a'snoopin'. After about three months, McTimmons showed up one day and said he had an idea."

The outlaw continued his story, explaining that over a venison meal that night, the Irishman unfolded his plan. He wanted to head west into Mexican Texas and steal horses. As they returned east toward home, they could sell them off in north Louisiana and central

Mississippi. With that announcement, McTimmons produced a small leather pouch full of chewing tobacco and offered to Harmon and Bill. Bill didn't know exactly how it was done but watched the two older men take the leaves and stuff them on one side of their mouth, chew, and spit into the fire. Bill took a small amount and shoved it in his mouth but was hesitant to chew. McTimmons strengthened his case by telling them of his days as a lad in Galway, Ireland, and about his father and uncle's occupation of breeding, raising, and training racehorses. He said that he himself had a fine eye for horseflesh. Harmon seemed pleased and agreed to the venture but said the trip west should first include a stop at Louisiana State Bank in New Orleans to deposit the majority of the gold and silver coins earned from the Mobile robbery.

The three of them used Harmon's small flatboat to float down the Leaf River, then into the Pascagoula to the Gulf. There in Scranton, they stored the rig and made passage on a small sailboat for their trip to New Orleans. McTimmons and Harmon slept most of the trip, but Bill was wide-eyed at the sights of the offshore islands, the surfacing dolphins, the trek up the Mississippi River and past the two great military forts the government built to protect New Orleans. It was only the beginning. He had no idea the world had so many people. Never in his life had he seen so many humans in such a small area as he did in New Orleans. Harmon told Bill it was the fourth largest city in all the United States.

He marveled at the huge houses and buildings, the fine clothes the people wore, and the expensive carriages they traveled inside. Bill had never been in a bank before, much less opened an account, so he followed their lead to deposit all but $200, to be kept for expenses on the Texas trip and for emergencies, if needed. Then they took a small paddle wheeler up the Mississippi, past Baton Rouge, into the Red River until they were finally thwarted by the rapids of Alexandria,

GALLOWS RECKONING

Louisiana and forced to purchase horses. In addition, McTimmons brought along a Kentucky long-rifle with the recently invented percussion cap firing mechanism. They rode due west through Natchitoches, a thriving cotton port town. After resupplying, they trekked west and continued into the Mexican state of Texas.

Taking a long drag and exhaling a copious stream of blue smoke, Campbell moved about his cell and said, "yep, we didn't realize it at the time, but we were in Texas at the same time Crockett, Bowie, and Travis were putting up their famous Alamo fight. We were up north and knew nothing of it, of course. Anyway, and here's why I'd joined such a good team. Harmon was the creative part of the team, but McTimmons had the connections. He was about twenty years older than Harmon and spent most of his American years traveling the South, stealing and such, but making friends and contacts to use when needed. We'd picked up a guide in Natchitoches who led us into Texas and began to see great cotton plantations and pockets of wealth in towns like San Augustine, Teran, and Bevil. We were planning on going further south, but the guide said he'd go no more, and now that we knew how to get back to Natchitoches, he was out. He left. Shoot, we were in a quandary, but then Lady Luck provided. We'd turned back north and were out in the wilderness when we saw a huge dust cloud behind us. We veered off and waited in the woods to see what caused it. Lo and behold, sweet providence it was.

Three Mexican drivers had a herd of nearly eighty fine horses with them. They said they were headed up to Fort Towson to deliver the horses their boss had sold to the US Cavalry. Harmon quickly told them the plan, where they'd approach and offer food for a night's rest with them for protection, and that they'd take the Mexicans out as they slept and be off with the herd, and of course McTimmons and Bill agreed with his plan.

Campbell's mood darkened and he started pacing like a caged tiger in the tiny cell.

They ate with the Mexicans and McTimmons produced a small bottle of whiskey, with implicit orders for Harmon and Bill not to touch it, as he'd laced it with a small amount laudanum to drug the *vaqueros* and put them in a deep sleep. Harmon would later come back to camp with three stones the size of horse apples, instructing them to smash out the brains of the Mexicans and have a knife ready in case it was needed to finalize the deed.

I paused in my writing and looked him in the face. He immediately broke off eye contact, turned his back to me, and with disgust, flung his cigar through the bars of the window of his cell. Still with his back to me, he said, "time slowed down for me. I knew better. I'd been raised better, and I wavered, but then I remembered walking out of that New Orleans bank with that tiny little book that said I had nearly one thousand dollars in there. One thousand dollars saved up! And I remembered what Harmon said about being a rich man at a young age and I wanted more...so I took...took the stone to the Mexican's head and did it again to be sure he was dead. Next morning, McTimmons went to work altering the brand of the hindquarters of each and every horse, and after two days we were ready to head back east."

"So that was number one for you?" I asked as Campbell finally turned back around, but his head hung down and his whiskered chin was buried in his chest. "Your first murder, I mean."

With an unexpected burst of fire and energy, Campbell leaped up, then grabbed the bars violently and tried to shake them, yelling, "Hell yes, oh Hell yes, that was my first! The thought tortured my nightly realm for a week. Over and over, I kept seeing that rock shatter that young Mexican's forehead. Shoot, he was probably just about my age, too, and I'd snuffed him out for good in an unfair advantage where he had no chance." Then he plopped down on his cot and turned his back to me, but to my surprise, did not quit talking. "After that, for the next few weeks, I knew the nights of MacBeth. I had a hard time sleeping, and I saw the Mexican's face in my dreams when I did manage to sleep, just like MacBeth saw the ghost of Banquo."

CHAPTER FIVE

Learning From the Master

About fifteen minutes after his outburst, Bill Campbell had calmed down and was ready to resume his life story. If I had doubts that his story was being falsified or embellished, his reaction to the word murder quelled all that. I was hearing an elongated deathbed confession and could rest assured he was only dealing in the truth. Before he got started, Ella Smith, the sheriff's wife, came into the office, greeted me, and kept her eyes averted from the jail cell.

"Hello and good morning, so is Junius around? Out back or somewhere in town?" she said.

"No ma'am, Mrs. Smith, he had to see a sheep herder out on Leakesville Road about some matter. I'd guess he'll be back in two or three hours," I said, now standing. "Can I get you anything? That coffee isn't too old, or at least old for what we call old around here."

She declined and smiled, and I remembered back six years ago when I was first hired, had just moved to Batson, and met her. My first thought was their marriage had to be some kind of arrangement. She was twenty years younger and much too pretty for a skinny, old, weathered-bird dog like the sheriff. She prepared to leave, and I mentioned I'd relay word to him she was back home and that it was obvious that the sheriff had been missing her cooking, and in her absence, hadn't been eating like he should. It made her smile and she retreated across the street to the general store for something to cook for him later. I think the scene touched something in the outlaw. Here was normal life. A man with a job, keeping his nose clean, doing his work, and missing his wife. The wife, anxious to reunite with her husband, comfort him, and cook him a fine meal as reward. These were things a famous outlaw wasn't allowed, and I saw him take a mental rewind of events that he could have had, if he'd not crossed paths with the likes of Harmon and his false promises of an easy life.

"That's a big herd of horses for only three men, Bill," I said.

"You're tellin' me. The Mexicans *vaqueros* could do it cause they'd done it all their life, but I'd never been around more than maybe four horses at a time, and neither had Harmon. McTimmons had growed up with them and used ropes to keep them on a short leash, and those horses that had a wild streak, well, McTimmons used his knife and fashioned kind of caps to drop over the horses's eyes. So, then we knew why he'd had me strip the Mexicans of their clothes and blankets before we dropped them into shallow graves."

Harmon held a belief to never travel the same road twice in a short period of time, because you don't know if people recognized you and are awaiting your return. He preferred a more southern route back through Louisiana. McTimmons said he was also of the school of thought to not travel the same road but nixed a southern Louisiana route. The land was populated with bad men, just as bad or worse than the clan to which these outlaws belonged.

McTimmons told Harmon and Bill that remnants of the pirate band that sailed with Jean Laffitte had settled the area and were notorious for way-laying travelers. He also knew personally of a bad man named Doc Yokum who ran a very large gang, and Yokum had ridden with one of the most infamous killers of the wilderness, John Murrell, back in his younger days. McTimmons's tale seemed to be working on Harmon. Then he said the whole area went by the name of the Neutral Strip, or sometimes No Man's Land, and on some maps it was part of Louisiana and some it was Mexican Texas. The US government even offered to *give* it to Mexico, but they refused. And so, it was off to the north with the group and their stolen horses, but too far north would take them dangerously close to Fort Towson, so as much as neither of them wanted to retrace their steps through Natchitoches and Alexandria, they had to go it again.

I paused from my writing while Campbell took a sip of water and it dawned on me. I'd never really considered the amount of thought and planning that goes through the outlaw's mind to avoid capture. The ones good at being bad had sharp minds, indeed; they just used them for the wrong purpose. *Great Scott*, what if these nimble brains had put their power to use for the lawful side of life? What greatness might they have accomplished?

"Well, we did what we had to and found plenty of buyers in the Natchitoches area," Campbell said. "It seemed a severe case of The Strangles had hit the area about a year before and decimated the horse population locally. We were left with less than twenty horses when we got to Alexandria and sold them there within a week's time, clearing over $4800 in profit. Harmon, said it was time to split up, that word of two men and a teenage boy traveling and selling horses was bound to cause talk. McTimmons would take a boat down the Red River to the Mississippi, down to New Orleans, and wait for our arrival at the home of a Mr. Benny, who had ties with our clan. Harmon and I would go over land to Natchez, Mississippi, and take a few days of rest before continuing our eventual trip to New Orleans and the Louisiana State Bank, again."

Once more I was a little awed at the outlaw's insight into how a lawman would think, deduct, and reason about suspicious behavior.

"I spy a gold band on your left hand there, Mr. Bacot. You a married fella?" the outlaw continued.

GALLOWS RECKONING

"Was, 'til Yellow Fever outbreak of 1846 took my wife and family, leaving me a widower. I still wear our wedding band as a reminder. Why are you asking?"

"Well, just wanted to be sure I was all right telling you about my time in Natchez. Harmon, remember, wasn't big on drinking the spirits, but he did have a weakness, I learned: women. I guess when his life was all about becoming a rich man at a young age, he was too busy for them. He rented us a room for a week in the Pearl Street Hotel and purchased the services of a soiled dove. She went by the strange name of Little Lost Bet, so I spent most of the week just walking the streets and going down Silver Street to watch the giant steamboats load and off-load cotton and people. A good bit of time was spent drinking beer in what was called "Nasty Natchez," the saloons under the hill. Then on the next-to-last day in town, Harmon said for me to stay in the room all day with Little Lost Bet and he'd skedaddle. It was a *most* memorable day, and you being a gentleman, I won't go into details, suffice it to say Little Lost Bet's most intriguing nickname was well-earned, and she left me with more knowledge of the female body than most grown men know. Oh...and sorry about the fever and your wife and kids, meant to say that a minute ago."

He stared at me with neither a grin nor a scowl. I could tell he was testing me, wanting to see how'd I react to his bawdy little tale. I gave him nothing, affixed a look of boredom on my face, and after an appropriate pause, said, "thank you for them kind words, Bill, I sure miss my family."

"Oh, forgot this part, on our journey over to Natchez, Harmon told me to think up a false name as we'd both be registering at the hotel under assumed names. Well, I thought on it for two days and we were just about to Natchez when I told him I didn't have one. He said go simple; you're Bill, Bill for William, right? Just repeat it around and be Bill Williams, okay? Harmon went as Benjamin Luckney, said it stood for Been Lucky."

I moved my pencil over to the paper's margins and wrote down both the false names. After the hanging, I would get with Sheriff Smith and reveal the names, see if he wanted to get the word out that they were used by Harmon and Campbell years back, see if they were wanted for crimes under their aliases.

"We picked up McT in New Orleans, did our banking business, and decided to ride back to our hideout," Campbell said, slipping into the informal nickname for his former associate. "Harmon said it would be safer and besides, we had gang members living all around south Mississippi where we could sleep at night. Three days later we were back in the old, abandoned Choctaw village. We were dog-tired from the long journey and roasted potatoes over a flame as we sat around and drank rum. Even Harmon indulged, to celebrate another $1600 gain to all our bank accounts. The rum loosened his tongue evidently, and he openly began to tease me about spending all day in bed with a Natchez whore, much to McT's enjoyment," the outlaw said in reflective thought. "We all drank more, and when McT disappeared into the woods to relieve himself, Harmon pulled me over close, looped his arm around my neck, and said he guessed I had $2500 in the bank now, but not to get lazy. The way he'd figured it a man needed $30,000 saved up to quit the life, so I had a good way to go. Then he released me and moved back to his log around the fire. I did some quick math in my head. I'd been with Harmon and McTimmons almost a year. If all the years were as good as this, I'd be at that $30,000 mark in twelve years."

I had to inquire, "did he say why or how he came across such a specific number as thirty-thousand?"

GALLOWS RECKONING

"No, he didn't, and I didn't ask him in front of McT but waited until the next day when McTimmons rode back to his own camp. And Harmon ignored me, so I asked again. He just said, 'that's the number and that's all there is to it.' He added that I should never discuss it with anyone in the gang because even if the gang will work together on jobs, 'don't ever think you can trust any of them, especially when cash money is at stake'."

I didn't press the outlaw on the matter of trusting a thief and he kept on with his story, saying they had laid out in secluded hiding for five months after their Texas trip.

"Then one day, Harmon announced it was safe to go out. He was going to his father's farm near the Krebs community, east of Scranton, and I should go see my family at Brewer's Bluff. We rode together the first day, south on the Chickasawhay Trading Road, but he didn't want to go anywhere near Americus, where the burned courthouse used to be, and so he cut due east. As he left he said he'd be calling a gang meeting sometime within a month or so and for me to watch for tree trunks on main roads with the date carved in them in our secret mystic alphabet of course.

"My family's greeting was warm on the first evening I arrived. Then my two older brothers started asking questions. Paw would have too, but he had business in Mobile and left at daybreak on my second day at home. At first, I deflected all their inquiries with little more than vague answers. Sure, it made them mad that I wouldn't answer them, but I had not thought this out. How should I answer? I couldn't tell them the truth: that I'd just gotten back from killing a Mexican, stealing a herd of horses, and before that, cleaning out half the merchants in Mobile! So, I went with Harmon's advice and told them I was now making charcoal and selling firewood to folks in the communities of Tatum, McManus, Jacksonboro, and the like. My brothers were all too concerned with their own lives to worry about me after I answered, and I said I had been secretive because I knew that they'd laugh at me doing such simple jobs, so I tried to hide the truth," Campbell said, and then a smile crossed his face. "Yep, I knew if I could fool my brothers, that I was on my way to being a first-class liar, which was necessary in my chosen line of work."

I raised my pencil and waited until Campbell made eye contact with me. "What about your mother? Did she believe you?"

"As I recall...I wouldn't let myself ask that question. I wanted her to believe I was managing on my own selling firewood and such, but every time I thought hard on it, well...I made myself stop. But here, today, and you being my confessor, I'll say it. No, she knew I was lying."

"Did she confront you at all about how you were earning a living?"

"She did in her own subtle way, and I told her Harmon was my partner in the charcoal and firewood business. She stopped asking then, and just said she was glad I was home and looked to be in fine health. Looking back, she didn't want to know the truth as much as I didn't want to tell it. She knew what kind of business Harmon dealt. It was mother that woke me in the middle of the night of my third day visiting and said it was probably best for me to keep moving, that I should be getting on. So, yes, she knew the kind of life I'd chosen. She gave me rations and grain for my horse and told me to be off before my three brothers woke."

Something made my hand move into the margin and I scribbled the word 'sad' there. Choices. Our lives are made of choices, and Bill Campbell's choice to be an outlaw meant he'd never have the same relationship with his family. Greed it was, one of the seven deadly. I had to ponder the actions of Mrs. Campbell. Why did she not try and convince her prodigal son to return to the road of righteousness?

Surely, she knew the teachings of Luke, 15:11. It would help her son to see the light in God's forgiveness. We all make mistakes. God knows we do, and his salvation gives us a second chance of His mercy to correct our errors and get back on that righteous road.

The hammering outside stopped. I could have known the time without looking, as it was the carpenters's mid-morning break. I couldn't resist and looked at my pocket watch; it read 9:31. I took stock of the outlaw's remaining time; he was now almost down to his last forty-eight hours on earth, and I wondered if he was counting the hours, the minutes, the seconds. It dawned on me if our stations were reversed, I'd probably be counting them.

Campbell continued his story, saying he left the old homestead uncertain on what to do and where to go. His heart was heavy with the realization he'd never be a member of his family again, but a mere visitor. He thought of his mother and how much he would miss her love and then recalled a part of his youth he'd tried to block from his memory. He recalled this incident as much for my narrative of his life, and equally as a cautionary tale for the youth of our state.

"A few months before I stole the two dozen hogs from our neighbor, Mr. Hurlbert, I was walking past the Hurlbert's home, coming back from an unsuccessful fishing trip on Cedar Creek," Campbell said. "Mrs. Hurlbert hailed me and asked if I would be interested in making a nickel for some work, and I said yes. Her crop of squash was ready to be picked, but her lumbago was causing her too much pain to bend over. She said there were probably forty plants to harvest and loaned me a knife to sever the squash off the vine. I was quite taken with the little folding knife, learned to like it the more I cut squash, liking it so much that when I was done, I told Mrs. Hurlbert I'd dropped it somewhere in the dirt of her garden and it was lost, but I'd really slipped it into my boot.

"She went to look for her favorite little knife in the garden, but no luck. Back home, I played with my new knife, and when my mother saw me throwing at a stump and asked, I told her I'd found it at the creek where I was fishing. The next day Mrs. Hurlbert came calling on mother, accused me of stealing her knife. I watched as my mother vigorously defended me, told Mrs. Hurlbert that her son would never break the Seventh Commandment. She was insulted at the accusation. Mrs. Hurlbert left without the knife.

"Yep, me stealing the knife would have been my first crime, but it wouldn't be the last, would it?" Campbell said, as he took a seat on the chair in his cell.

Campbell kept on talking, revealing what happened after his mother advised him to leave the house. The road north would take him past Americus and to the old Indian village. The road south would intersect with Mobile Road. He went south, and after about a half-day's ride, he spotted a large pine by the side of the road with fresh carving in the trunk, about eye level for a man atop a horse's back. Easily deciphered, the cryptic abbreviation said "June the second, two weeks from today" and so Bill wheeled his horse north toward the old Indian village to ride out the time until the gang meeting.

Campbell said he was a little apprehensive of riding alone to the Beaver Creek Clan meeting house. He'd only been there once, and Harmon led the way; he had not been paying as close attention as he wished he had. He did recall it was off Mobile Road and that he needed to turn north just past the old, abandoned settlement of French Colony. It was roughly ten miles past the Mississippi state boundary, and mostly a collection of rotten log cabins, maybe twelve in total, that had been inhabited forty years earlier. When the Great Terror of the French Revolution was in full swing, an alarmed group of aristocrats fled France. They had no farming knowledge and attempted to make olive oil and wine to subsist. But with their limited agricultural experience, sandy soil, and excruciating summers, they could not grow olive trees or sustain a vineyard. All that was left was a settlement of pine log cabins, rotting and being overtaken by the vines and creepers. Well-hidden was a sandy, small trail that led north and to the hideout just 100 yards past the last log cabin.

He missed it at first but saw it on his second pass. A purposefully placed low wall of briars helped guard the entrance. The trail zigged and zagged back and forth for about half a mile until there in the small clearing was the meeting house, made of wattle and daub and some pine logs. There were ten horses already tied up to the post when he approached. He entered the house, and where before all the chairs were pushed in the middle of the one-room structure, today they were divided across two opposite walls. McTimmons welcomed him in and said he was the last to arrive, explained the missing member was Charles McGraffin who had been arrested, tried, and convicted of arson of a Jewish synagogue on St. Emanuel Street in Mobile and was currently serving his sentence.

He looked about and saw seven members on the far wall and three on the near, including McTimmons and Harmon, so he joined the nearer group. A discussion began, and it quickly became clear that the reason the chairs were divided was that there was a split in the gang. The group of seven wanted to raid Mobile again, like they'd done a year prior. Harmon was vehemently against the idea, saying it was too soon, that they did not have night watchmen in place as before. Harmon explained the reason their Mobile raid was so successful was that they had used patience to allow the night watchmen to become a trusted part of the business community of Mobile's downtown.

The larger group had D. J. Doty as their spokesman. He stated that money was tight and there wasn't time to wait for the next crew of watchmen to build up trust. He produced a page from the latest *Mobile Commercial Register and Patriot*, citing the advertisement page and how flush the stores were brimming with merchandise. Doty then made sure all in attendance could see how a vote on the subject would result, even with Harmon's two vote privilege, the motion to hit Mobile would pass. For good measure, he threw in if they didn't hit the stores, some other gang probably would. Doty told them if things didn't change soon more to his liking, it might be time to hold a new election for clan leader and first lieutenant.

Harmon then rose to counter. He must've been boiling inside, but he kept his cool. First, he pointed out that Doty was in violation of Rule Two of the gang's oath, of strict obedience to the leader. Doty said the financial crisis he and the others were in took precedent to Rule Two right now.

"Knowing a vote to raid Mobile would pass even over his veto, Harmon tried diplomacy, with an idea to put in one or two watchmen and give them three months to build trust and then hit the stores," Campbell explained, saying, "he declared the meeting adjourned and for everyone to watch for signs of the next meeting, as it would not be too far into the future. With that he, McTimmons, and me announced we were off for Mobile to find a good meal and soft bed, and we left."

Instead of heading toward Mobile, Harmon knew Doty's hideout was in the Egerton community of the central Mississippi Coast. They rode past the French Colony and waited on Doty. About a half an hour later, Doty came riding along. With McTimmons and Bill on the south side of the road and Harmon the north, they trapped Doty between them and knocked him off his steed. McTimmons pulled his four-inch knife and made a deep cut on Doty's right forearm, his shooting hand. Bill jumped on the downed man, using his weight to help neutralize his attempts to escape, while Harmon slipped a roped garrote around

Doty's neck. McTimmons then removed Doty's pistol from his sash and tossed it in a bank of bushes. He stuffed a bandanna into Doty's mouth to muffle any screams for help, but he wasn't giving up, him being a true *dash-fire man*.[3] With his left hand, Doty belted Harmon's face and neck and pushed him off. Bill was helping, but not enough in Harmon's eyes, and Harmon yelled for him to get in and fight. Doty wheeled and gave Harmon a bunch of fives[4] and Bill saw Harmon lose the tension on the garrote's handle, so he took over and with all his might, twisted the handle on the rope, causing it to grip tighter and tighter. McTimmons had enough and raised his knife high, but the blade fell out rendering the weapon useless. Instead, he just punched Doty's stomach. Harmon was back in the game and pulled his small knife, too, and shot three stabs into Doty's upper torso. Bill's garrote strangle was working and he put all his might into the struggle. All three of them sat on Doty's torso and legs; they all watched as his eyes turned blood-red, grossly bulged from their sockets, and his face went purple. After a few more assists by all of them, the traitor went limp and there was no more fight. McTimmons and Bill pulled the body back a good 100 yards off the road, rounded up Doty's horse, and stripped the corpse.

"Then—and I hated this part of the outlaw life," Campbell promised, "McT borrowed my knife and split Doty's torso wide open."

They began filling his body with rocks, dirt, and mud, anything to add weight. They couldn't have the corpse attracting buzzards and attention, so they needed to sink the body in the bayou. They heard Harmon yell at that point that he'd found a water source and went toward his voice. They took the body out as deep as they could stand

---

[3] dash-fire man is a manly man full of strength and vigor
[4] bunch of fives is a fist for fighting

up and pushed him toward the middle. McTimmons and Bill watched until they were sure it had sunk to the bottom. Harmon took his pistol out and shot the horse in the brain, stating it was too dangerous to keep the horse, as they were close to Doty's home ground. And with that task behind them, the three outlaws mounted and rode toward New Orleans after dividing up the $20 in coins Doty had.

Curious, as he'd just described his second murder, I paused from writing. "So, Bill, with your two friends helping, you dispatch of a fellow gang member, Doty. Murder number two for you. How did that make you feel?" I asked the outlaw.

"The killing didn't bother me as much as the first one. Really, Doty brought in on himself for violating Rule Two. That, and he was not asleep in a drug stupor. He was a grown man, a big man to boot, that put up a fight. Doty cut Harmon over the eye with his fist, and I recalled in my initiation that Doty probably hit me the hardest when I ran the gauntlet. Doty was like Cassius, in Shakespeare's *Julius Caesar*. A treacherous mind, bent on the betrayal of Harmon. Doty got what he deserved. Still, I had a hard time sleeping that night. You know, a man's life was over and of the three of us, I figured I had the major role in the death of the man. Disposing of the body works hard on a man's brain, I'll admit that."

Quickly, I jotted down the outlaw's last words on the murder. No real remorse for killing a member of his own gang, and not nearly such as killing a young, sleeping Mexican. Pausing, it made me think how, as of now, Campbell had used Shakespeare references in his murder explanations twice. Those two don't fit.

CHAPTER SIX

Up North

"Sometimes after a job we'd lay out and disappear, as if the earth had opened and swallowed us up whole," Bill Campbell said after the carpenters's mid-day break was over and the hammering resumed. "This time, knowing most of the gang knew where we'd sometimes lay out, we did the opposite and left the area, and I mean in a big way."

The outlaw went on with his tale.

They arrived in New Orleans and made withdrawals from their bank of $100 apiece. Their city consort, Mr. Benny, put them up until there was a steamboat scheduled to make the trip north up the Mississippi, then the Ohio until it reached Cincinnati. This trip was Harmon's idea. He'd spoken to a flatboat man from Kentucky on his last trip to New Orleans. The Kentuckian had the criminal ideas, but not the nerve. He explained that each spring after the ice melt, many men in Cincinnati load their flatboats with stores such as flour, salt, whiskey, nails, paint, tools, cloth, and the like, and would be in need of deckhands to pole the boat downriver, selling their goods along the way. Some just cruise the Ohio, but others use the Ohio to get to the Mississippi. The Kentuckian said it was a situation to take advantage of, where the boat owner could be overpowered, and bold criminals could take $2000 or more worth of supplies.

The three changed their appearance while staying at Mr. Benny's. Harmon went clean-shaven, McTimmons, who had worn long hair on the Texas trip, now wore it short. Bill grew a mustache and, for the first time in his life, began wearing a hat—a medium-brim straw one with a bright-green extra-wide cloth band. McTimmons and Harmon pretended to not know each other while on the steamboat traveling upriver, while Harmon and Bill kept up the ruse that Harmon was the older brother. Bill mentioned that although he was fifteen at this point could easily pass for twenty. They made the trip to Cincinnati in a little more than eight days, without incident. Harmon instructed Bill they'd be using their alias names in the city. They all booked rooms at the Burnet House for headquarters while Harmon visited the waterfront to find the right flatboat for their real purpose. On day number three, he decided on one. It was a very large boat, probably sixty-five feet long and eighteen feet wide, and the owner stated he had purchased such a large volume of supplies that their final destination could be as far west as Evansville, Indiana, or possibly even all the way to the confluence and the small village of Cairo, Illinois.

At the appointed time, the three met the boat owner, an Irish immigrant named McSween, who promptly put them to work loading the boat with barrel after barrel of supplies to sell. McSween had a thick accent and was older, probably in his midsixties. The loading took most of the day, and they shoved off from the Cincinnati piers just before dark with four lanterns lit, one on each corner of the boat. Harmon had studied a map of the Ohio River in the hotel's lobby to choose the least populated area when it was time to overpower McSween. He chose a spot between Cincinnati and Louisville, Kentucky. First, it was secluded; second, it would be before McSween had sold too much of his goods; and third, it wouldn't give the owner much time to figure out his crew was not what they appeared to be.

The river was swift, and Bill and McTimmons tried to learn as much as they could from the boat's owner on how to handle her. McSween being from Ireland was keen to keep company with McTimmons every night and did a good job depleting the boat's whiskey supply. During the early afternoon of their third day aboard, McSween asked Bill if he'd ever seen a gunboat. Bill responded in the negative, saying he didn't ever have the chance to see any naval vessels. This brought a huge laugh from the others.

Bill didn't know it at the time, but a gunboat was a reference to a floating brothel, and they'd likely see their share of those on this trip. On the evening of their fourth day on the Ohio, Harmon gave McTimmons the signal. Once again, McTimmons laced his drinking partner's cup with a small shot of laudanum. McSween was a true *Admiral of the Red*[5] and after about his fourth cup, announced he was suddenly tired and headed off to his bed. After about half an hour, Harmon and McTimmons went to him and spoke loudly in his presence, then poked his arm with a finger. The boat owner had not the slightest reaction to either stimulus. Bill stood guard and took a lookout position to be sure no other boats came near. McTimmons grabbed a small hatchet by the cook stove and handed it to Harmon, stating he didn't have the stomach to take out a fellow son of Ireland. Harmon wasted no time, first hitting McSween atop his gray head with great force, using the blunt end of the hatchet, then flipping it around to the bladed side and handing it to Bill, who he instructed to hit McSween twice more in the forehead. All three stood around and looked down, trying to see any signs of life, and when they were convinced of none, Harmon ordered them to strip the old man and weigh the body down with scrap iron and one of the smaller anchors around his neck and feet. Bill and McTimmons did as they were told and then pulled him to the stern and nonchalantly kicked him off the deck. Bill stared at the white foam area from the splash as long as his eyes could see it in the dark.

---

[5] "Admiral of the Red" is a perpetual red face, like that of a heavy drinker

Harmon then told Bill to remove the two small flags McSween had raised on either side of the bow, one a green harp flag of Ireland, the other an American flag. Harmon explained they had to alter the boat's appearance, and fast, so Bill removed the flags, tied a small piece of iron to each and tossed them overboard. In addition, McSween had his flatboat's name, *The Sea Gull,* painted on her stern. Harmon and McTimmons discussed what to do and McTimmons offered an idea to change to *Galway*, after his old home in Ireland. McTimmons started to get the paint, but Harmon stopped him. He'd seen Bill doodle on paper while they hid out and said he had artistic talent. Harmon also wanted an American flag painted on both sides of the living quarters of the boat. While Bill painted, McTimmons was to go through the entire boat and get rid of all McSween's belongings as well as the bloody straw mattress. The cabin of the boat was rather distinctive, in Harmon's mind, and so with a saw, he set about making a window where there was none before. He also shortened the length of the stove's external chimney pipe. Painting the cabin door would help, so Harmon had Bill change it from its natural hue to a bright blue. Finally, Harmon would take the tiller and try to keep the boat center stream to make the best time and put miles between them and Cincinnati. He then divulged his plan of not stopping anywhere on the Ohio, as someone still might recognize McSween's boat, so they'd not begin selling his goods at least until they were in waters off southern Missouri. McTimmons and Bill liked the idea and told their leader so.

Their first day on their own, the boat probably floated downstream backward as much as it did correctly, but with practice and a slower current, they eventually mastered the art of keeping the boat's bow in the lead. Three days later, in a driving rainstorm, they reached Cairo. They were tempted to dock and go buy a hot meal but resisted the urge and within five minutes found themselves in the Father of Waters. A day later they made their first landing at New Madrid. Bill and Harmon stayed aboard as McTimmons went ashore and started spreading the word a boat from Louisville had docked with fine goods and wares for sale. Before landing, Harmon had set prices on all the goods on board for the benefit of McTimmons and Bill. The locals told them they were the first supply boat of the season, and that they were very low on everything. They stayed tied up for two days, and by the time a large group of farmers from the surrounding area showed up, they'd sold between a quarter and a third of everything on the boat. They made a few other landings on the muddy banks when they saw signs of habitation, before realizing it wasn't worth the effort. The outlaws continued, setting their sights on Memphis.

They tied up on the Memphis docks and McTimmons quickly made his way around the waterfront, telling all they had a great selection of wares. He also mentioned that one member of their group had an upcoming wedding, and they were running late. He assured the people that the wares were not only first-class quality, but they'd be sold, for the sake of speed, at a discount. Oh yes, even the flatboat was for sale. They had arrived on a Monday, and by the end of the week they had sold roughly half of all their remaining goods. Harmon found out the upcoming Saturday was Memphis's monthly market day, so he made arrangements to rent a horse and wagon and had everything transported to the center of the town's market, next to the fairgrounds racetrack, and with that move the last of everything was sold. The total tally came up just over $3000 for the stolen goods and in addition they profited $200 for the flatboat. Not a bad gain for roughly four weeks of work. For continuity's sake about their lie of the impending wedding, Harmon forced them to move on quickly. The proceeds for the flatboat were in the form of a ninety-day promissory note drawn on the Bank of Orleans, so they knew they'd eventually be in New Orleans to collect that, but what to do in the meantime?

Harmon had an idea, and it all hinged on Bill's young and artistic hand. He told Bill that McTimmons, McGraffin, and himself had made slave raids on the German Coast of Louisiana. Seeing confusion on Bill's face, Harmon backed up and gave the boy a little history lesson. In the early 1700s, investors lured Germans to an area of unsettled land between New Orleans and Baton Rouge with the promise of cheap farmland. The Germans came in sizable numbers and built plantations for growing cotton, rice, and sugarcane. Many became fabulously wealthy, and the slave population grew and grew. The three gang members raided the area around 1828 and made off with six fine slaves, that they then transported to the Tuscaloosa area of Alabama and sold to a large cotton plantation owner by the name of York. McGraffin had been raised in Pennsylvania and could deftly recall his Yankee accent when needed. He told the slaves he and his companions were all abolitionists, here to help them flee to freedom above the Mason-Dixon Line. Mr. York believed Harmon's made-up story that the six slaves were actually captured runaways and thus had no bill of sale nor registry of ownership on them. York said without legal papers he'd only pay a portion of their collective worth and thus gave over a total of $1100 for all, instead of $4000. The gang accepted the money and gained a valuable lesson in the transaction. Harmon would use Bill's talented hand to produce the false legal documentation for their next batch of stolen slaves.

With freshly purchased horses, the three left Memphis and headed for Natchez, where they would ride to the area of Louisiana south of Baton Rouge known as the German Coast. When McTimmons questioned why they were riding half their journey on horseback instead of fully by riverboat, Harmon said it was to give Bill time to perfect his craft of counterfeiting bill of sales. What McTimmons lacked in the creativity department of criminal ingenuity, he made up for in boldness. As they rode south and discussed the intricacies of getting this theft of slaves right, McTimmons volunteered to go, alone, into the Adams County Courthouse and find an example of slave registry and proof of ownership. After cleaning up and donning his best suit, he waited for the most inexperienced looking clerk to wait on him, took the deed book to a secluded area of the courthouse, ripped out a page, and quickly hid it in his boot.

At night around the campfire, Bill would practice his hand, not only on the correct legal wording, but the style and flair associated with a handwritten bill of sale. Still, they would need a wood cutter to complete the counterfeit. The top left corner had a small rendition of a bald eagle, and bottom right had a cotton wagon, with three giant bales aboard, in miniature print on the form. These could only be reproduced by a skilled hand, carving negative opposites into a block of wood, applying ink, and pressing the form onto the document. Harmon understood the need for authenticity and relieved Bill from duties like hunting for game or gathering firewood while on the ride down. Instead, Bill was to master the difficult task of producing two official-looking wood-cut squares. After experimenting with many varieties of wood, Bill settled on the cottonwood tree as his best source, but even the sharpest hone on his knife blade could not produce the desired results. It wasn't until they reached Baton Rouge and located a few graver tools at a general store, and after a solid three days of practice, that Bill's handiwork passed the keen eye necessary to pull off counterfeiting. His outlaw accomplices were satisfied. They were ready, and Harmon predicted their haul would make the Mobile job look paltry. After buying a covered wagon and two mules to transport their stolen slaves, they continued their ride south.

When the riders saw a road sign proclaiming New Orleans to be twenty-five miles distant, Harmon knew he was in the right area. His plan was for him and Bill to work together and McTimmons to work alone. They would meet here at this road sign in three days at the midnight hour. Before they split up, Harmon advised that they should strive for a total number of stolen slaves to be ten at most, so to garner five apiece, and of that number try for two teenage girls, two teenage males, and one male of any age, but with skills such as blacksmithing or carpentry. This was, of course, a wish list, acquiring the slaves was the priority, so they were instructed to not decline any that agree to flee north to freedom with their new abolitionist friends.

Bill was doing as Harmon instructed, which was mostly following his lead. When he was aboard McSween's flatboat, Bill had found a single-shot pistol, a leather bag of gunpowder, and supply of shot. He also began wearing a baggy overcoat of McSween's to hide this gun. They spent most of their first day hiding in bushes by a small trail leading to a main road that led to a sugarcane plantation. The only passersby were three old slave women with baskets of laundry balanced upon their heads. Their white-haired heads told Harmon to wait for more desirable subjects. None came, and they camped in the same place without benefit of a revealing campfire. The next day, just before noon, a teenage slave girl came walking up the trail, heavily ladened with two large, covered baskets in hand. Harmon and Bill came out of hiding and stopped her. Answering Harmon, she replied that she was taking lunch to the fieldhands who were weeding and tending the plantation's vegetable patch. Without asking, Harmon grabbed off two large handfuls of bread, then revealed he and Bill were abolitionists, there to help. The girl, probably fifteen or sixteen, was overjoyed, saying she knew this day was coming. The girl, who said her name was Weegie, told them she had a two-year-old son and would not leave without him. Harmon agreed and added that he had room in his wagon for three or four other like-minded slaves, but theirs would be a difficult journey to Illinois and instructed her not to invite any over the age of forty, for the sake of survivability. Harmon told her to bring her group an hour before midnight to the twenty-mile New Orleans road sign, and to be discreet. She promised she would and then went on up the trail to deliver the lunch.

The next day, Bill went out hunting, but had no luck until he saw a large rattlesnake sunning in the morning shine. Placing his hand on the pistol, he recalled Harmon's warning to stay quiet and not arouse attention. Releasing the gun, Bill found a five-foot-tall heavy stick and unsheathed his knife. Coming up from behind the snake, he was able to club the reptile with the stick and quickly remove its head. Arriving back at camp, Harmon was pleased with the huge size of the snake. He instructed Bill to round up a large number of small dry twigs and a handful of dry leaves, as he would make a smokeless fire to cook their meal. Harmon began gutting the snake while Bill searched. He'd learned from Harmon that to keep a fire from smoking, one feeds it just enough quick-burning fuel to keep it alive; too much and it smokes. Twenty minutes after his return, Bill was shoveling dirt over the small fire and they both had full stomachs. They took turns napping the morning and afternoon away, waiting on Weegie to arrive at 11:00. McTimmons showed up around nine that night with a big, strapping fieldhand, about twenty years of age, and two teenage boys, both very slight of build and light skinned. They were twins, McTimmons announced, which had been obvious to everyone else. Harmon gave the three slaves some smoked snake meat he'd made and instructed them to talk in whispers and only when necessary. The big buck gobbled down his jerky and took the uneaten portions away from the twins, who dared not object. Weegie showed up around half past ten with her young boy, two women likely in their mid-to-late thirties, and an older cotton-top woman probably pushing seventy. It occurred to Harmon to scold Weegie about the *gunpowder*[6], but this was not the time or place for an argument. Harmon greeted them and repeated his abolitionist tale for their benefit. McTimmons loaded all the slaves in the wagon back and covered them with horse blankets before he took the reins and headed the mule north. Harmon took the lead and Bill fell back to watch the rear. Harmon figured they'd have a seven-hour head start on the overseer and his trackers. They would head due east to reach the western shore of Lake Pontchartrain, where a clan member lived and owned a flatboat, which could whisk them away to Mississippi. No trackers would think to look for escaped slaves in a wagon, on a boat, or in the middle of a huge lake.

Two days later, they were at the home of another clan member by the name of Bradish Allen, who ran a flatboat up and down the Pearl River as his legitimate job. He took Bill and the group to the river's headwaters and to a small village called Edinburg, where they replenished supplies. McTimmons, Bill, and the eight slaves had stayed in the woods and out of sight while Harmon went into town for coffee, sugar, whiskey, bacon, grits, dried meat, and grain for the horses. It was Harmon's plan to head due east from there, and once more be among the cotton plantations surrounding Tuscaloosa, Alabama, 100 miles away. The first night out of Edinburg, with Bill on watch as all slept, the big buck slave, Timothy, quietly came out of the wagon and presented his physically imposing form to Bill. He had to be almost seven feet tall and easily 275 pounds. Timothy knew Illinois was due north of the plantation he'd grown up on and could

---

[6] gunpowder was a nineteenth century derogatory term for an old woman

tell from the position of the sun that the group had been heading northeast, now due east. Bill placed his hand on his pistol grip under his overcoat, in case it was needed. He deflected the question, saying Timothy should realize Harmon, their leader, could not head due north because his Underground Railroad connections did not follow a true north heading on a map. Bill assured him they'd probably take a more northerly path soon, on the way to Illinois. Timothy gave Bill a hard stare, then nodded in agreement and went back to the wagon.

The next morning as Weegie and the old lady made breakfast, Bill took McTimmons and Harmon aside and revealed his conversation with Timothy. Harmon sent Bill back to the group and conversed in private with his lieutenant. First, Timothy would be taken off alone and drugged with laudanum. He would have to be shackled on the wrists and ankles. Lasty, he had to have his tongue cut out.

After stopping for a midday rest, McTimmons switched places with Bill. Nonchalantly, McTimmons poured a tin cup of water that had been laced with laudanum for the slaves, allowed Timothy to drink it, and then took boy with him. When the wagon was far enough away and around a blind bend, McTimmons hit Timothy in the head with the butt of his rifle, dropping him and immediately shackling him. He quickly built a fire from surrounding sticks, leaves, and limbs. Then, with a pair of old rusty clamps, he pulled Timothy's tongue out, and with his other hand, quickly sliced off an inch from the tip and cast it aside. McTimmons carried an iron rod about a foot long and had inserted it into fire to heat the tip. He flipped Timothy onto his back, opened his mouth, and cauterized the stump of the tongue to stop the bleeding. Then, he tied the slave's wrist shackles to his saddle horn and slowly began to ride, dragging the big slave as he made his way back to the group.

Two days later, they were among a line of cotton plantations. Their first two stops came up empty, but their third was a grand palace just past a village called Mesopotamia. The owner's grown son wanted the two twenty-five-year-old girls and twin boys. Harmon conducted the negotiations, starting at $1500 apiece, but agreed on $1000 for each of the twins and $2000 for both girls. Bill completed his four separate bills of sales as Harmon pocketed $2000 in gold and a ninety-day note for the other $2000, drawn on the State Bank of Alabama in Mobile. McTimmons had retrieved each slave for presentation one by one as to not arouse suspicion of those slaves not being bought.

Following the main road to Tuscaloosa, Harmon started to see familiar landmarks and could recognize he was near Mr. York's plantation. Not wanting to arouse the possibility of any potential problems, as they had not cut out the tongues of the stolen slaves ten years ago, Harmon asked directions from a yeoman farmer on how to get to Columbus, Mississippi. Timothy had figured out they were not going to Illinois but being sold to a different plantation. Tried as he could, he could not get Weegie or the old woman to understand. While they were stopped, Timothy jumped from the back of the wagon and took off, best he could with leg irons, for the woods. With Harmon, McTimmons, and Bill all facing the wrong way, Timothy might have made it had the farmer not alerted them. McTimmons took off on his horse and quickly had a rope around the slave's neck. Led back to the wagon, Timothy was again the victim of McTimmons' rifle butt and fell over into the wagon. Weegie let out a scream, and Bill took the reins and moved the wagon north. Three days later, as they neared Columbus, McTimmons had an idea. He took the old woman off the wagon and, first with clippers and then with a straight razor, removed all the hair off her head. In his opinion, it worked, taking fifteen years off her age. When she asked why, McTimmons explained it was customary on the Underground Railroad for the oldest party member to have their head shaven, to reach freedom with a new crop of hair for their new life. As they walked back to the wagon, Timothy sprang out from behind a tree trunk and, even with his wrists bound by iron, delivered a tremendous blow to McTimmons neck, knocking him out. The sound of the hit was so vicious it drew Harmon's attention, and he rushed back to help. Timothy shuffled off through the thick brush to make his getaway. Bill heard a call for help from Harmon and ran to his side. Suddenly, the old woman sensed something wrong, and she took off running into the woods on the opposite side of the road. Harmon instructed to let her go; she had no real value, but the big buck could fetch $1500 at least. After about two minutes, they caught up with Timothy, who turned into them like a wounded bear and took wild swings at them with his cuffed hands.

Suddenly, Bill could hear Weegie urging the mule to get up. Both his and Harmon's horses were tethered to the wagon. She was getting away and leaving them stranded. Bill quickly yelled for her to stop and told Harmon he was going after her. Harmon had his hands full with the big angry man who now had leaned over and had a hickory stick in his hands. Bill ran as fast as he could, caught up to the mule, and then twisted its neck into stopping. Weegie had a frightened look as she clutched her little boy. The fight in the woods continued as Harmon cursed and yelled each time the hickory stick found its mark. Bill pulled his pistol and marched Weegie and her son back toward the sounds of the fight. Grabbing the boy away, he took him toward Harmon and Timothy, knowing Weegie would not flee, leaving him. By now, Harmon had picked up his own stick and was using it as a shield. From six feet away, Bill pointed his pistol at Timothy's face and told him to drop the stick. It worked, and he marched him out of the woods to where Weegie was waiting. Harmon's attention turned to

McTimmons who was awake, but groggy. After all the slaves were back in the wagon, except for the old woman, Harmon told McTimmons the tongue of Weegie had to go. Bill was sent to the opposite woods to try and find the old woman but had no luck. Later that night, McTimmons took Weegie off alone and knocked her out. He pulled her tongue out, cut off about a third of it and pressed a hot poker to her tongue to cauterize the wound and stop the bleeding. He picked her up and threw her in the wagon while Harmon kept the little boy with him as a hostage, should she wake and try to flee. Harmon had run a chain through Timothy's leg irons and secured it to the interior of the wagon. There would be no more escape attempts. Later, when McTimmons felt better, he went into the wagon and punched Timothy in the gut with all his might and gave him a mighty rap across the nose, causing the slave great pain.

The next morning, the troupe rode up on a fine mansion surrounded by acres and acres of cotton plants. Harmon had everyone hang back while he approached and asked to see the owner. To his surprise, a stylish middle-aged woman came out on the veranda and asked his business. Harmon said he wished to speak with the master of the plantation about buying some slaves. She introduced herself as Mrs. G. M. James, she was the lady of the house, and he could deal with her. Ever astute, Harmon, knowing slaveholders had an affinity for families—they tended to care for each other and therefore did not cause trouble—said he had a twenty-year-old fieldhand who was strong as an ox, the sixteen-year-old wife of his, and a two-year-old little boy. Mrs. James said she was interested and wanted an inspection, and with that Harmon rode back and told McTimmons and to bring the slaves up to the house.

Mrs. James instructed them all to get down from the wagon. She started with Timothy, looked him up and down, and thankfully didn't have him open his mouth. After doing the same for Weegie and her son, she said she'd offer $2000 for all three. Harmon gave a jolly laugh and said that was an excellent down payment, but $3000 was the going rate. They continued to haggle until a happy medium was met at $2500 for the lot. Campbell interjected that he needed to know an individual price for them to fill out his bills of sale. Mrs. James understood why, and priced Timothy at $1500, Weegie at $900, and the boy, whose name Campbell made up, as Weegie could no longer speak, at $100. Campbell had named him Eltee, which stood for L.T., as in Little Timothy. Mrs. James produced $1000 in gold and silver coins and a ninety-day promissory note, also drawn on the State Bank of Alabama, Mobile.

Harmon added that he no longer needed the mule and wagon and asked Mrs. James if she was an interested buyer. She quickly threw out a $35 offer to which Harmon agreed. As soon as she paid, the three rode off west toward the town of Columbus to find a hot meal and a soft bed. The venture was profitable, and as Harmon predicted, more so than the Mobile robbery. Divided three ways, each outlaw would have $2200 apiece for selling the slaves. Plus, there was the $1000 apiece they made selling McSween's goods off his flatboat and $66 apiece to collect in New Orleans for their share of the boat itself. Campbell was now an equal partner in the Harmon Gang and felt immense pride.

CHAPTER SEVEN

The Easy Life

Mrs. Smith, the sheriff's wife, came into the jailhouse, leading a man I'd never seen in with her. "Is Junius around?" she asked, scanning the room. "This gentleman just arrived from Jackson on official state business. I happened to be walking by the Widow Batson's Boarding House, and she told him that I could help locate the sheriff."

The man with her was around twenty-five years old, wore a Colt pistol in a holster, and was garbed in all black, except for his straw hat, which he removed upon entering the jailhouse. The man was slight of build and almost looked like a teen wearing his father's clothes, as they were easily much too big. Campbell would later call him poor as Job's turkey[7].

I explained the sheriff was out making rounds but expected back within the half hour. Mrs. Smith then left, and I exchanged introductions with Sgt. Micah Bailey of the Mississippi State Militia. He was interested in checking over my shoulder and looking at Campbell in his cell. Campbell was taking a break from all his talking and was napping. Sgt. Bailey moved with me as far away from the cell as we could go before speaking lowly. "I'm here to do the state's business. I'm the hangman. Would I be correct to assume that's William W. Campbell?"

---

[7] "As poor as Job's turkey" means an extremely thin man

GALLOWS RECKONING

I nodded an affirmative and said, "That's him. Judge Wilson's orders are he's to be...be uh...hanged...at noon the day after the gallows are built. I spoke to the carpenters this morning and they say they'll be through by dark tomorrow." I noticed my hesitation in saying the word and supposed listening to Campbell's talking the last twenty-four hours had softened me a bit on his coming demise.

"So, we'll be looking to do business at noon the day after tomorrow," Bailey said, once more trying to get a look at Campbell through the bars. "Well, I guess it's better to show up early rather than late. Don't want the condemned to have too much time to ponder the fate of their soul. I'd rather it be the gallows are ready, I show up, and the next day we do the deed. Oh, and this is a letter from the governor's desk, it's very important."

I motioned with my eyes and head that he should place the letter on the sheriff's desk, four feet away. "I'm presuming you have a room at the Hotel Batson?" I asked as we moved closer to the door. "I'll let Sheriff Smith know you're there and he'll come down the street and introduce himself, I'm sure."

Sgt. Bailey nodded, said goodbye, and left.

Much to my surprise, Campbell's voice rang out. "So, he's Jack Ketch[8]. That's the man who is going to kill me?" He began pacing his tiny cell as I searched for an appropriate response. "I think I could take him easily in a fair fight, like a knife fight, or pistols at ten paces. Heck fire, I know I could beat him in a bear wrestling match or a good ole fist fight."

"I'd have to agree with you on all counts, Bill," was all I could find. I didn't mean to preach, but it just kind of came gushing out.

---

[8] Jack Ketch was a common nineteenth century nickname for the hangman

"We're a land of rules now. Knife-fighting and shootings have consequences beyond just the two men involved. Things are different now; we've got money coming into the state. I know the lines have been expanding our stage routes about the state, and I've heard they're already building a railroad from New Orleans up to Canton. Things like that mean men with money are behind them, and they want their investment protected. Those same men want a safe society for their wives and families."

Bill obviously didn't want to hear my sermon and turned his back to me. After a few moments of silence, he spoke. "Well, I imagine there'd be some truth to what you just said, but a man still has to know how to take care of himself when the situation calls for it. Just because you got railroad tracks in your town, doesn't mean if another man challenges you or does you wrong that you don't take action. Besides, the very first rule of human nature is self-preservation, you know that to be true, deputy. A real man has to be able to break into fightin' and punish the offender...or kill him if he needs killing."

My pious background almost came out in verbal form, but I held back. I wanted so bad to quote him all ten Commandments, but especially, "thou shalt not kill". He'd been bad so long it was all he knew, and it made me question his long confession. Was he confessing for his own sake, or mine? Did he just want to have me tell his tale as the Baddest Badman in Mississippi? What if it was some form of "honor among thieves" to release all his stories of ill-gotten gains and murder? Was he confessing, or bragging? It was at that precise moment I knew I wasn't just taking down his words for the sake of practice. Then and there, I knew there would be a book about Bill Campbell's criminal life, and I'd author that book. The public could decide if he was confessing his many sins or boastfully telling of his actions.

GALLOWS RECKONING

Sheriff Smith came back and announced he'd be heading to his home for dinner. I told him his wife had dropped by and that there was an agent from the state staying at the hotel by the name of Sgt. Micah Bailey who had requested a meeting with the sheriff. Sheriff Smith quickly sorted through two pieces of mail on his desk, said he was off, and went out the door.

Bill was practically hanging on the cell bars when I looked over his way. "'Agent of the state'? Deputy Bacot, you are too kind. You can say the word 'executioner' in front of me. Won't change anything. I would not think less of you for saying, 'Hey Sheriff, the hangman needs to see you before we drop this accursed wretch off the gallows.' Not too long until I lay down the knife and fork[9], you know."

"Well, I heard of gallows…" I let it trail off without a complete response. Bill Campbell was in a surly mood today.

Once more, I was tempted to review the Ten Commandments with him, but with his current state of mind, knew it was a waste of time. "It's time to eat, Bill. I can't leave the jail, can't even go out back and put some fresh meat on a fire. I'll have to use the little stove and reheat a little spot of bacon and grits we didn't finish this morning, maybe break into a fresh loaf of bread we didn't get to earlier. Shoot, I'll even brew us up a fresh pot of coffee."

"Much obliged, deputy," Bill said.

"The county will make it up to you at supper tonight. What sounds good? When Sheriff Smith gets back, I'll walk across the street and see if the butcher's got any fresh rabbit or deer meat. After that, I'll go next door and see if they've got any mustard or collard greens left."

---

[9] "Lay down the knife & fork" means to die

"Sounds like a good meal. Say, you don't suppose your sheriff would let me wash it down, you know, with an elbow bender, you know, a few drams of whiskey?"

"I can't stop you from asking the sheriff, Bill. It's his call about the whiskey, not mine," I said as I moved to my small desk and picked up my pencil, anticipating his life story to continue.

"All right Larry, let me see. Harmon, McTimmons and me had just sold our last three slaves outside of Columbus, yea that's where we were. We rode back south and laid out until our bank notes came due in Mobile and New Orleans. Harmon said it would attract less attention if he went alone and McTimmons and me agreed. Harmon said he was of the opinion not to put those funds in the bank, but to bring them back to our hideout. From there, he said we should consider stashing some coins in the ground nearby, as it is too far to go over to New Orleans every time we need money."

"Seems like a good idea. How did that work for you?"

Campbell said it made him nervous to have $3500 in coins on his person, and we were back in the story. He went along with Harmon's suggestion to stash it nearby. Afterall, just because they were outlaws didn't prevent them from being robbed by highwaymen. Harmon had come back from Mobile with a well-stocked wagon, full of coffee, sugar, salt, fatback, salted pork, flour, potatoes, and corn, so he was not intending on any of them leaving camp for a while. Bill said his parents have a stockpile of empty barrels, and he could go home and obtain one for their burial purpose. Harmon overruled his idea, saying it was too soon to visit relatives and that he recommends all three of them lay low for two years minimum. The law would not be as keen on looking for the slave snatchers or killers of a flatboat owner after two years. McTimmons gave a weak argument that one year should suffice, but Harmon overruled and pulled clan rank on the Irishman, firmly insisting on two. Besides, they'd done hard work and much traveling and deserved to rest. He stressed the outlaw's greed as the lawman's greatest assistant, and McTimmons reluctantly agreed with the plan. Harmon did make one concession. He said at one year's time, the three of them would trek to a spot he'd previously noted that would be a perfect hiding spot for their cash. It was halfway between New Orleans and Mobile, the two prime banking centers of the region. The spot was eight to ten miles north of Handsboro, Mississippi, up the Biloxi River. They should all three go; one, for the reason of their collective memory and two, if something should happen to one of them, the other two could share in his portion.

A year is a long time, especially to a seventeen-year-old like Bill. When they returned from Columbus and sold the slaves, he looked forward to leaving their camp and to some travel. All three took every gun and knife they owned for protection on the route. It was nearly a two-day ride to Handsboro, but Harmon was adamant that only he should go into town to restock any supplies they'd run out of in a year's time. The meat, naturally, had gone first; they had to substitute with any turkey, deer, ducks, and fish they had caught themselves. Bill said he was looking forward to eating a pound of bacon soon. It was slow-going following the river north of Handsboro. The dirt trail was sporadic at best, with some portions hundreds of yards long where the creepers, vines, and small bushes had taken over. Hauling a wagon full of supplies only took longer. Late into the second day, Harmon announced they'd reached the perfect spot. They had just passed the sharpest bend in the river and a twenty-foot bluff. Harmon pointed out the three gigantic cypress trees on the opposite bank. They had seen other huge cypress trees on the river, but not three together arranged in an equal triangle. Harmon produced a two-foot-wide and one-foot-high wooden box with metal straps and a locking mechanism. Placing the box on the bed of the wagon, he opened it and instructed everyone to place $3000 each into a leather pouch, keeping $500 each in coins. After counting out the allotted amount for each person, to make sure no one was slighting the till, Harmon also placed a scrap of paper with the number written by each man's last name.

Harmon told McTimmons to stay with the horses while he and Bill swam across the river with the money and a long rope. It was upon arriving at the sandbar across the river that Harmon told Bill that since he was the youngest, and most nimble, he'd be climbing up the center cypress tree and finding an empty hole large enough to hide the box. Navigating around a big cypress tree is not an easy task. Unlike most trees, with their root system underground, these had long, knobby roots above the ground, and periodically, part of the root went vertical, straight up in the air a foot or two. These were called *cypress knees*. Making their way past those obstacles, Harmon threw the rope over the lowest limb, which was about twenty-five-feet high. Looping a leather strap Harmon had made for the box, Bill looped it on his foot and, using both hands, began climbing the tree, using the ropes for balance. Bill made it up after about ten minutes of hard climbing and two near-falls. Peering into the hole in the trunk, Bill was wary for snakes and kept his hand back as he pushed the box inside. To finish, Bill pulled a wad of Spanish Moss that Harmon had told him stuff into his pockets over the box for camouflage. Harmon retreated to the sandbar and yelled over to McTimmons, asking if he could see anything suspicious in the tree. He replied that he could not, and Harmon said it was okay for Bill to climb down. Bill eventually made it down, tearing his pants and getting a good scrape on his thigh in the process, but nevertheless made it safely down on the ground. After a return swim, McTimmons said the success needed to be toasted, and produced a bottle of whiskey. Harmon took a deep swig and handed the bottle to Bill for his turn. McTimmons took his second swig and returned the bottle to his pile of sleeping blankets in the wagon bed.

Harmon, always cautious, said they were returning to their lay out camp by following their northern route, as no bridges existed, and the next crossing was a ferry at a little village named Nugent, probably half a day's ride on a good road, but more likely a full one on this one. All three felt good about their work of accomplishing a mission, one that would keep their money safe without the long travel to New Orleans and Mobile. Later that day, Bill admitted his joy had turned to sorrow, realizing this was his last outing for another year. Another thought crossed his mind, too. What if Harmon or McTimmons went rogue? What if one of them decided to come back to the three cypress trees and steal the box and contents for themselves? The more he thought about it, the more he thought there was nothing he could do about it. He decided it was the promise of a lucrative future that kept each man honest. Why break up a successful partnership over a gain of $6000 when, if they stayed together, they could produce much more than that amount each year and into an unlimited future. It also struck home that Harmon, after taking his celebratory swig of whiskey, mentioned that climbing that particular tree would be impossible for one man. Two men were necessary to climb that cypress, with its big trunk that no man's arms could encircle.

He paused his story to light a new cigar, and I spoke. "Never really thought about hiding a treasure, so to speak, least not since I was a wee chap. High up in a cypress tree, on the opposite shore from the road, ten miles from the nearest settlement sure sounds like a good spot."

"It was a good spot," Campbell said as he spewed a fresh spout of blue smoke from his mouth. "Later, after a couple of years, we had to give it up. We moved our laying out place further west for a couple of reasons. McTimmons, like I said, was older, probably in his midfifties, and he found a young wife to take care of him. She had a sister that Harmon fell for, but neither wanted to move very far off from their mother who homesteaded on the Jourdan River, north of Shieldsboro, over to Hancock County, near the Louisiana line. They were both daughters of Bradish Allen, the Clan member who had taken us up the Pearl River to sell our stolen slaves. Another reason we moved our gold was because of me. At seventeen, I was a wiry thing, but by the time I'd hit nineteen, I'd filled out, and carried more weight and look about then as I do now. I was too heavy to climb trees with no limbs. In the end, we had a hurricane that next fall after hiding the gold and Harmon started to worry a big, strong wind might take the tree down and leave our hard-fought treasure there on the ground for anyone just passing by to steal."

Things settled in for a while. A short rain shower came over Batson and forced the carpenters to briefly quit their solemn job, so Bill Campbell continued to talk.

He was now in the second year of his forced quarantine from the outside world, per Harmon's instructions and orders. Rusticating, Harmon called it, the act of the long wait. There was no escaping Harmon's keen, watchful eye. Hunting for hogs, deer, rabbit, and squirrel now took up his days, as did fishing the tannic, shallow waters of the Red Creek or the Black Creek. Harmon, not to be outdone by his lieutenant, had likewise purchased a percussion cap firing rifle from a gunsmith in New Orleans on his last visit. He did not mind Bill borrowing it for hunting expeditions, to put fresh meat on their small community table. During his first year of laying out, Bill had made copious mounds of charcoal and firewood, so those were unnecessary tasks of year two. Bill took great delight in retelling a particular hunting story where he caught a fish.

GALLOWS RECKONING

One spring day, Bill had Harmon's rifle and went wading up Red Creek looking for game. After many hours of not having any luck, he came around a bend in the creek and heard a great thrashing in the water. Up ahead was a sandbar, separating the main channel of the twenty-foot- wide creek, that probably was about three-feet-deep, from the sandy shore on the north side. The side channel was less than half of one foot in depth and harbored a great fish, an alligator gar, easily close to a hundred pounds and five feet long. His great size made it impossible to escape the shallows. Bill drew his knife and decided to try and dispatch the fish with a gash to its brain. Kneeling close by, he changed his mind. The gar had a vicious row of sharp teeth, all white and shiny, and it was throwing his head violently back and forth in an effort to slash the human, who was all too close. Not worth the risking of losing a finger, Bill stepped back, took aim with the rifle, and blasted the great fish's brains out. He cut the head and tail off to lessen the weight, threw the remaining meat into his dampened burlap sack, and headed back to the hideout. This fish should easily supply McTimmons, Harmon, and Bill with two or three meals a piece.

Later that day, as the sun was setting and the fire was hot enough to liquefy the bacon grease in the iron skillet they dropped the cleaned portions of gar meat into it, McTimmons announced he had a plan. He wanted to steal more horses and take them to Louisiana again to sell. Bill immediately recalled bashing the brains out of the Mexican, much like he'd scattered the brains of the fish three hours before. McTimmons said he wanted to raid north Louisiana and relieve them of their best horseflesh. His plan was to take quality over quantity and to use the power of the Word of God to draw the crowds. He said he wanted to take the last name of Moody, a powerful name in religious revival circles, and travel to small, out-of-the-way communities to hold a service. At night, while the faithful prayed and sang hymns

McTimmons would be leading, Bill and Harmon would pretend to steal McTimmons's, or Moody's, horse. The congregation would be either moved to give or purchase McTimmons a new horse so he could continue and travel and spread the Word. McTimmons said he and the recently deceased Doty's twin brother, Thomas, had run the same ruse in central Alabama about fifteen years prior. The difference was, Thomas had a preaching background and fine singing voice, so McTimmons did the false theft of the horse during the service. McTimmons said he'd want to practice up on some Bible passages and wanted to also memorize at least four or five popular hymns to lead the singing.

Of course, as first lieutenant, McTimmons only suggested operations. Harmon would be the one to decide whether it was worthy of the effort and worth the risk. As he finished his fish and potatoes, Harmon blessed the stolen horse and traveling pastor scam but added that if they were going out and leaving the safety of their hideout, he wanted to do more. He wanted to steal another half dozen slaves in central Tennessee, take them to Natchez, and resell them to the Fork in the Road Slave Market. Bill and McTimmons agreed to doing both deeds. Harmon said his plan was to first call a clan meeting outside of Mobile and check on the loyalty of his men, if there were any left. If there were, he'd ask if they needed a job to refill their purses. The clan was the priority. After that job, they could raid Tennessee, sell the slaves, and go to Natchez. It has been over a year and a half since the Doty incident, but also since Harmon had sent three clansmen to get on as night-watchmen in Mobile. It was time to reap the fruits of his planning.

CHAPTER EIGHT

Well-Laid Plans

The three outlaws needed to get the word out; Bill would ride south to put a meeting notice on the Spanish Trail and Three Notch Road. McTimmons would ride east into Alabama and post on The Federal Road. Harmon would go north and west to notify clan travelers on The Natchez Trace and General Jackson Military Road. Their rides would produce a semi-circle of notifications, from New Orleans to Jackson to Mobile. It produced the results. When the three rode up to the clan meeting house, there were thirteen horses, eight clan members, and five prospective new members. Harmon and McTimmons interviewed the candidates and then sent them off to await a verdict. Harmon knew better to discuss any clan business in front of non-members. Immediately after that, a middle-aged clan member by the name of Sellridge announced no one had seen D. J. Doty since the last clan meeting. Another member named Ryan said he had a place near Doty's and confirmed he'd never made it back home after the last time they were all here.

Harmon, McTimmons, and Bill stayed cool and displayed no emotion nor said any words. Finally, member Ryan spoke again, saying D. J. was very much like his twin, Thomas—was known to be a notorious hothead and fond of picking a fight. Ryan said more than likely D. J. picked a fight with the wrong man somewhere between here and his homestead, likely Biloxi. Ryan added that Thomas had met his demise five years earlier in a pistol duel under the oaks in New Orleans' City Park. The topic was dropped and never resurfaced.

Harmon announced it was time to rob Mobile again. The three night watchmen would again assist. They would use the newspaper to determine the most lucrative targets and make their getaway via a sloop on the Dog

River. This time, instead of heading east and then into Georgia, the sloop would sail to New Orleans. Once there, the goods would be off-loaded onto a small packet boat heading to Memphis, as Harmon was impressed by the wealth of the citizenry there. He'd take a ninety-day note, if necessary, but preferred gold and silver coins, as he surmised the people of Memphis had plenty of coins. The room erupted with cheers and huzzahs as Harmon finished speaking. This is what the men wanted to hear as they had all profited well from the first raid on Mobile. He added that the prospects of new members would further divide the pie, that there would be a delay before any new men joined, and all agreed. He said he would start preparations, put notices on the major roads of when and where to meet next, and the meeting adjourned.

Ten days later, the three were again out on their assigned roads posting their cryptic message of the details to begin the Mobile raid. Seven days after that, the members met at the headquarters on the first night of a new moon. Harmon verbally gave the orders of who would work together as teams, and which stores and businesses each team would steal. All pillaging would be completed by 2:30 a.m. at which time the wagons would head south to the dock on the Dog River to load up their wares on their New Orleans-bound ship.

The great second fleecing of the city of Mobile was underway, June 19, 1840. Once more, as before, Bill Campbell spoke glowingly of Harmon's methodical and precise method of robbery.

Everyone followed orders. The three night watchman in the clan immobilized the one that was not and that got things moving. Like before, one clansman rowed to Blakeley Island and set fire to multiple hay fields as a distraction. One new wrinkle had the men secure damp burlap bags around the horses' hooves to decrease the noise on the cobblestone and brick streets. The men had instructions on which stores held the best and most expensive goods and concentrated their efforts there. Harmon had specifically told them to find as many watches and clocks as possible. He'd recalled the words of the flatboat man, McSween, that he wished he'd carried more of them, as those items were in big demand and selling for phenomenal prices these days.

However, there was one incident that did not go so smoothly. After the robberies were complete and the men and their wagons headed west on Church Street, Bill spied one of the clan's watchmen in a heated wrestling match with another watchman, also in the same uniform. Carrying a torch, Bill jumped down from the wagon and could see that one watchman was not a clan member. The clan member was using most of his strength to keep the mouth shut of the real watchman and was being pummeled. Bill acted fast, pulled his knife, and plunged it hilt-deep into the watchman's neck from the rear. The act severed his spinal cord and he instantly collapsed without making a sound. Bill and the clan watchman tossed the body in the wagon bed and continued west to rendezvous at the corral to pick up their horses. An hour later, McTimmons approached Bill and told him to have the watchman's body ready to sink into the Dog River upon arriving at the sloop.

Bill knew what those instructions entailed. He would have to disembowel the man and fill his hollow body cavity with weighted items to force the man's corpse to the bottom of the river, at least until the alligators, fish, and crabs had destroyed it beyond all recognition. The wagon train arrived at the dock and Bill knew what had to be done. He rolled the corpse down a small incline onto a mud flat next to the river. He removed the blouse and cropped tunic of the man and shoved them into his pant legs. Hesitating, he contemplated asking McTimmons to come and take over, but McTimmons was busy organizing a train of hands to off-load and then to load. No, he had no one to substitute. Closing his eyes, he penetrated the chest just below the sternum and pulled down hard toward the waistline. Next, he made a horizontal cut halfway from his vertical one. He shoved the knife inside; his forearm was halfway covered up by the man's body. He moved the knife in a big circle, cutting as he stirred. Sometimes, the organs resisted being cut and he had to stand over the man to get a better angle on cutting. His knife hand severed something, the intestines he guessed, as then arose a foul stench of feces into his face and nostrils. He continued to cut until he believed he'd done enough damage. Now, with two hands, he plunged into the job and began grabbing and pulling the slick and slippery organs out of the body. Many times, as he was just about to remove one, it would slip and fall back inside the man. Adapting, he used one hand to expose the organ while skewering it with the knife point and tossing it into the river. The fish and crabs would do the disposal work. Next, he looked around for rocks, shells, waterlogged wood, and large clumps of clay. The putrid smells were increasing, but he knew he had to finish. Stuffing the man as full as he possibly could, Bill then walked out into the river as far as possible, shoved the body toward the middle, and watched as it disappeared underwater. Bill grabbed fresh mud, rubbed it into his fingers, rinsed his hands, and then found a grassy spot to dry them, hoping the blood and guts would be gone by the time the sun came up and he could see them. He stumbled off away from everyone and, behind a clump of bushes, wretched his stomach contents up and out until there was nothing left to vomit.

Sailing off the coast of Mississippi was a joy to Bill, with the seabirds, fresh wind, dolphins playing, and sandy offshore islands, shimmering like mirages floating on green water. Past all that, things got edgy. Enoch Perkins was a good friend of D. J. Doty and a sounding board for Doty's ideas of overthrowing Harmon and McTimmons back then. When Harmon announced that they were only allowed to work transporting the stolen Mobile inventory to the small steamboat they were taking to Memphis, Enoch Perkins rejected the plan. He stated New Orleans was plenty far enough away to begin selling. Harmon countered that only a fool would steal in Mobile and, two days later, begin selling in New Orleans. There were probably a dozen ships a day making the Mobile-New Orleans route, and people talk, especially when there's big news like a major robbery. If that wasn't enough, Harmon said both cities had newspapers, and the exchange of them between travelers was something he was sure happened. He added that Rule Two included strict adherence to the leader's instructions.

Perkins countered that Harmon was too busy, either out pulling his own private heists or hiding out to avoid detection. Perkins said Harmon should either lead the clan daily or get out of the way for someone, like himself, that could give that needed attention to the clan. He said he was renouncing the Harmon clan and taking three others with him. All they wanted was one wagon load of goods and there'd be no trouble.

Harmon said he needed a minute to decide whether he should allow this and called Bill and McTimmons to go with him, alone, to the stern. Two minutes later, Bill and McTimmons went back to the bow where Perkins and his three comrades were sitting. They told Perkins that Harmon wanted to see him alone, at the stern, to work out a compromise. Bill and McTimmons accompanied Perkins as he walked back but stopped midship and let him go alone. As soon as he made it to Harmon, Bill and McTimmons wheeled back around to face the bow and put their hands on their pistol grips. Harmon, offering a handshake to the arriving Perkins, took his hand and jerked it with all his might, pulling him to the rail, where he used his other hand to grasp Perkins's waist sash, lifted, and pushed Enoch Perkins overboard, six miles from the nearest strip of dry land. Perkins's three confederates made a brief move, but the sight of four already drawn pistols stopped them in their tracks. Staring hard at the spot Perkins entered the water, Harmon never saw Perkins's head break the surface. Only after that did Harmon give the three would-be traitors a choice: either state their loyalty to Harmon and the Rules or get off the boat here and now. They all made the right choice, and Bill was glad there would be no more inter-clan killings for now. The boat's crew was well-aware that their passengers were outlaw gang members, members who paid double the going rate for the crew's silence, and made no interference.

Once in Memphis, they found the same fellow the three outlaws had used a couple of years earlier to move the goods from the docks to the weekly market. After two weeks, their inventory of stolen goods was completely gone. The boatman, McSween, had been correct; watches and clocks were in big demand and sold briskly, for top dollar. After deducting expenses, Bill and the other clan members made $1800 a piece, while McTimmons took a $2000 cut as Lieutenant and Harmon took $2250 as the leader. They were all very pleased and celebrated at a waterfront saloon where Harmon instructed the six to split into three groups on their return trip to south Mississippi, Alabama, and Louisiana. He instructed them to all lay out for a minimum of nine months. There would be a clan meeting called at that time. He did not tell the other three of his plans, as the fewer that knew, the better. The next morning, Harmon stayed behind at his hotel with Bill and McTimmons. They had learned the best cotton in Tennessee was produced in Carroll, Gibson, and Gibson counties, which in turn meant the largest plantations and number of slaves. Harmon gave instructions to await his arrival in Huntingdon, in Carroll County, and seek out William Roberts, also known as Bit Nose Bill. He was a first cousin to one of the gang's benefactor chieftains, knew the type of trade Harmon plied and could be trusted. Bill bought a horse and McTimmons found a mule team and covered wagon. After a five-day ride, the first two completed their journey. Two days later, Harmon found them, having taken up residence in Bit Nose Bill's barn. After picking Bit Nose's brain for information on plantation locations, the places of slave congregation on Sundays, and the local law, the three took out from Huntingdon, heading south and east. Harmon's instructions were again to find females and males, preferably in their upper teens, and to avoid any gigantic, hulking, muscular beasts like Timothy.

The first two couldn't find any unaccompanied slaves that weren't in the presence of whites or in numbers much too large for them to approach. On day three, a Sunday (typically the slaves's day off for worship and social gatherings among themselves and with slaves from nearby plantations), they finally saw what they wanted. There were three teenage girls and one teenage buck off alone, enjoying a big bush of honeysuckle and another line of bushes loaded with blackberries. Harmon decided this was it, no more waiting and wandering as strangers in a strange land, not willing to chance the Underground Railroad angle. The three outlaws simply approached, pulled their pistols, and forced all four into the wagon. Bill sat among them and held his pistol aimed at the teenagers, threatening that if anyone spoke so much as a whisper, death would be upon them in a flash. McTimmons gave them some hardtack and a canteen of water, of which he'd previously warned

Harmon and Bill not to drink. Once more, McTimmons resorted to his laudanum supply to subdue his quarry and render them asleep, or at least extremely groggy, and therefore harmless.

After they passed through a small village called Poplar Corner, McTimmons had Bill assist him in building a fire to heat the iron poker. Harmon and Bill carried each slave over near the fire. All four were like rag dolls, deeply asleep from the opioid drug. By the light of a torch and the campfire, McTimmons began his cutting work. They worked out a system: McTimmons cut the tongue tip off, Bill cauterized the wound, and as the searing heat of poker would knock the effects of the laudanum out of them, Harmon would quickly walk the slave back to the wagon and shackle them to the interior. All four cried and screamed, a muffled yell, as the pain set in, but to no avail. There wasn't another soul around for five miles in either direction.

The next morning, they set off in a southerly direction for Natchez. The previous day, Bill had recorded each of the slaves's first names. The male was Moses, one female was Trudy, another was Sally, and the last was Thomasina. Bill would use that information to create false bills of sale to produce to the manager of the Fork in the Road Slave Auction house in Natchez, Mississippi.

Harmon's travel plan was to continue south through Jackson, Tennessee, into Bolivar, Tennessee, and then to Holly Springs in North Mississippi. From there they would veer west and use the series of roads that ran parallel to the Mississippi River to find Natchez. It was a good choice; other than Vicksburg, there were no towns of any consequential size on the route. To avoid problems like they'd had with Weegie and Timothy, they kept these four slaves in a mild drug stupor the entire trip. Harmon said when they got within a few miles of Natchez, they'd go into hiding and let the slaves regain their strength and stamina before going into the slave auction. His plan, as did most of his, worked, and there were no incidents. The bills of sale looked perfectly authentic and the slaves were back in good health when they were sold. Their sale brought in $2600 to the three outlaws, plus another $50 for the mules and wagon.

Their current location of Natchez positioned them perfectly. McTimmons was able to find a parson suit for sale and a good size canvas tent. They then took the ferry across into Louisiana. Harmon had picked up a newspaper, the *Natchez Weekly Courier,* and in it was a small advertisement for horses placed by a Mr. Marigny and Mr. Tayloe, who co-owned the racetrack in New Orleans. The ad mentioned it was not for racehorses but good sturdy riders, to assist in the operations at the track. Harmon told McTimmons and Bill that New Orleans was their destination after the traveling preacher had done his good work. As was his usual method, Harmon took the trio out to their furthest reaches to begin his stealing and worked his way back toward home. Russellville, almost on the Arkansas line, would be their first camp meeting. Bill was pleased the operation was to be underway, McTimmons's constant singing of hymns while on the road was driving him batty.

After assisting in raising the tent, Harmon and Bill stayed back. Bill had used his artistic hand to make flyers, announcing Reverend Moody's arrival and intent to preach the gospel at one hour after sunset. McTimmons, as Moody, made a big deal about his pride-and-joy horse before he began his sermons and psalms, and showed him off to the men in attendance. One and a half hours later, the reverend called an end to the proceedings, making sure he was at the only exit of the tent as he did so. He stepped outside and immediately yelled a horse thief had hit the meeting. Most of the men jumped aboard their mount and quickly rode about. They eventually returned and saw the reverend already beginning the job of dropping his tent to pack. One of the men said it would make the people of Russellville look bad to other towns that a traveling preacher was forced to walk, carrying a heavy load, because of their town's behavior. The preacher must be compensated for his loss. Two of the men had a brisk little argument of which one would donate a horse to Reverend Moody. They worked it out and within an hour he was presented with a fine spotted saddle horse and $28 in coins from the other man.

The three outlaws continued their ruse southward through Monroe, Columbia, and Marksville, before Harmon decided they were too close to New Orleans to continue the routine. All in all, they had run the scam nine times and had six good horses to show for the effort, as well as $205 in sympathy money. Harmon decided it would be better to have the local clan member, Mr. Benny, transact the sale to the owners of the Eclipse racetrack—to lessen the possible connection of a traveling preacher with six horses, plus the horse he rode in on to call the camp meeting. It took about half of the week for a satisfactory price to be agreed upon, with the average sold at $110. Harmon gave Benny $25 for his effort after a stop by their bank to deposit their total, approximately $3700 profit a piece from the Mobile raid, the Tennessee slaves, and the preacher's horse scam. It was time to find a few fallen women in the "Swamp" area of New Orleans, between South Robertson and South Liberty streets, and a spot of whiskey to celebrate, before heading home to South Mississippi.

CHAPTER NINE

Lost Control

"Hello deputy," Sheriff Smith said upon entering the jailhouse. "Uhh…and how is our prisoner?"

I shot Campbell a look and glanced back at the sheriff as he took his coat off and hung it up. I was correct in what I was thinking.

"Sheriff Smith, a question," Campbell began. "How go the carpenters? Will they finish today?"

"Well, as you know, the judge didn't put a date on it, just said the day after the scaffold was ready. But to answer your question, no they won't finish today. All these little rain showers run them off and they go back to their shop and get involved in something else. They may finish tomorrow if they get a full dry day but can't say for sure. Why? Are you in a hurry?" he said and laughed a little at his own words.

"No, no hurry," Campbell responded, and then added, "They can take as long as they want. If it was up to me, they'd never finish. However, there is a question I'd like to put to you. I've asked your deputies, both this one here and the night shift one, if I might have a few drams of whiskey to ease the burdens of my mind. What say you, kind sir?"

Sheriff Smith paced the room in silence and turned his back to Campbell. "A drink? You want a drink. I see. You know someone of lesser principles, in this situation, might offer a deal. I'd give you a bottle and you'd give me information. You know there's word about in these parts you've buried a virtual treasure in gold coins."

Neither man spoke, and I was spellbound at the notion that the good sheriff would result in shady dealings with a common criminal. I wanted to say something, but didn't know what, so just watched the play unfold.

GALLOWS RECKONING

"Well now, I'd have to agree there on one point," Campbell said with a sly smile as he moved up and grabbed the cell bars with both hands. "Someone of lesser principles might want more than a bottle for a fortune in gold. Someone might want to go further and might even say go as far as their freedom, might they?"

"You can stop with your wishful thinking right there," the sheriff said, approaching the cell. "'Lesser principles' was the key phrase. However, we've got men of high moral character here. Both of my deputies come from outstanding stock. Deputy Daniels's father was a State Supreme Court judge. You've probably noticed he's studying for the bar right now, and he'll be a good lawyer someday. Deputy Bacot here was a man of the cloth before joining me in law enforcement, as was I. No, there'll be no deals, but if you want a little taste of the spirits, really, at this point, I see no harm. Deputy, you can give Campbell a cup of rum with his noon day meal, and I'll tell Daniels the same after his supper."

I looked at Campbell. He'd won a small victory but didn't seem all that pleased. For a moment, I believed he actually thought Sheriff Smith would trade his freedom for gold. I knew better. Sheriff Smith would never consider trading favor with anyone, much less the notorious William Campbell. The sheriff just wanted Campbell to know what type of men were being forced to live next to him, and that these three men were living life as God intended, not as he'd lived his. It was more subtle than my lecturing him earlier, and I knew Campbell was of the intellect to understand that so he took no great pleasure in the relaxing of the No-Drinking Rule.

The sheriff took care of some official business in silence at his desk for a few minutes, including reading the letter from the governor, hand-delivered by Sgt. Bailey, before announcing he had to ride out on the Augusta Road to see a man named Edward Pollard, who had sent word into town that a chicken thief had been raiding his flock. As he walked out of the jail, he turned to me and made sure Campbell heard him, "Deputy Bacot, you be sure and not cheat our guest of his noon day rum. Fill his cup to the brim of spilling. Good day, all. Oh, and Campbell, I just read a letter from the governor and, sorry for your sake, he says there will not be any commuting. He ain't gonna stop the hanging."

Campbell stared at the door after it slammed. Then, he produced a half-smoked cigar and lit it as he moved to his chair. "That news is of no surprise. The people hate me. The governor's got to please them for the next election, so no surprise there. You ready to write some more?" he said to me.

I nodded and took my place, pencil in hand, half-amazed at how cool Campbell was with the news, how his last hope of turning a death sentence into life in prison could be so easily absorbed into acceptance. It hit me. He'd dealt in death since his teen years. His blood is ice cold when it comes to matters of death.

He picked up his story after they'd returned from New Orleans after selling horses. All three went back to the main hideout of the old Choctaw village. Harmon had told the other gang members to stay low for nine months, and Bill assumed they'd all do the same, but they didn't. Bill should have gathered supplies because they had not prepared for a nine-month respite from civilization, more like one month. Lo and behold, what did they find upon arriving at the old Choctaw settlement, but one old Choctaw. He had to be 65 and his eyes were cloudy. They didn't even know he was there until he came out of one of the lodges and just walked right up to McTimmons, who was frying bacon over the fire. He had a pronounced limp. Later, he explained his captors had snipped the tendon behind his right knee, rendering running impossible, and even a brisk walk an extremely painful experience.

The Indian spoke English well and explained why he was there. This was his ancestral home, he'd just escaped slavery in Florida, and came back to be with his tribe. Where was his tribe? Harmon explained the tribe had contracted smallpox fifteen years prior and their numbers were severely decimated. Then, the Indian Removal Act had shipped the remainder out West about five years ago. The Indian said his name was Manitema, that he'd joined Chief Pushmatha's army of Choctaw warriors and General Andrew Jackson to make war upon the Creeks in their 1813 Uprising. He was wounded and captured by the Creeks in battle, taken east past Pensacola, and sold as a slave to the Seminoles, who in turn sold him to their cohorts. For almost thirty years, he'd toiled as a servant of a band of renegade Spaniards who'd joined forces with the Seminoles to fight the Americans, not so much for political reasons as for reasons of robbery. Manitema said that last week he'd stowed away on a ship heading for Mobile, slipped ashore in the night, and trekked up the river to the old village, hoping to see his brothers and sisters. When he asked if he should be leaving at first light, Harmon told him not to, that the three whites would be moving soon, and he could reclaim his old home. McTimmons gave him some bacon and hardtack and the old Indian smiled, before retreating to his little log house.

Harmon announced he had some scouting to do over north of the Bay of St. Louis, and McTimmons chimed in that he was going to Bradish Allen's home north of Pearlington, was intending to find a new place to live and did not plan on returning here. Bill said he watched as both of his allies retreated from the camp with shovels and came back with heavily laden leather pouches. He surmised this was their local stash of coins. When the three were all back together, in a low voice so Manitema would not overhear, Harmon said for Bill to come to Handsboro in one week, that the two of them would go upriver, climb the cypress, and move their stash closer to the Pearl River, which separated the lower tip of Mississippi from Louisiana, which would be closer to their new hideout.

Campbell then paused in telling his life story as the jailhouse door swung open.

"Hope I'm not interrupting," said a voice. It was Micah Bailey, the state executioner, back again. "I forgot to get some information earlier."

Careful not to get too close to the cell, he asked me for William W. Campbell's height, weight and age. I looked at Campbell to see if he would rather answer but got a view of his back. I supplied Bailey with my best estimate on each question. Then he asked me, not Campbell, Campbell's religious affiliation and who the state should contact and put in charge of the condemned body. I looked at both men but said nothing.

"Just put Protestant down on the form, Mr. Executioner. And for the other, I don't know. Maybe somebody will show and let you know, but I doubt it. My family has all moved to Texas because of getting harassed on a-count of me," Campbell offered in an angry tone. He waited half of a minute, and in a more regular tone, spoke again. "Just place me deep enough in a hole to keep the hogs off me and mark my grave, is all I ask. Just in case someone in my family does come by someday."

Bailey and Campbell's gaze both came up and they locked eyes. "Now, Mr. Executioner, I have a question for you. If this has to happen, I want it done quick, and I want it done right. I don't want to be left choked for fifteen minutes at the end of a rope. So, here's my question for you. How many times have you hung a man, and did they go off smartly, or did you slowly strangle some poor fool along the way?"

Bailey stepped back a bit and looked at me, as if he was wondering whether to answer or not. I nodded and gave my silent approval. "Well, Mr. Campbell, I will say you will not be my first execution and there have been no problems with the physics, and well, this isn't the best word, but execution fits, there haven't been any issues."

"You only half answered me. How many?" Bill demanded.

Again, Bailey paused and looked my way, and once more I gave him a nod. "You'll be my second hanging, but…but I was trained by a man who had done at least three dozen, and he not only gave me verbal instructions, but written ones also, and with calculations, depending on the man's height and weight."

"Oh, he wrote down some directions, that makes me feel a lot better," Campbell spat sarcastically and even threw in a quick laugh. "Deputy, I think I'm gonna need that rum the sheriff allowed me about right now. In fact, when I relay that I'm basically a practice run for the high and mighty state executioner, I feel good the sheriff will indulge me in a whole bottle of rum, instead of a cup. You only get the one chance to kill me...do it right!"

With that Sgt. Bailey left in a huff and slammed the door. Campbell was well pleased and shot me a big grin, which I did not return. Then, to my surprise as well as Campbell's, Sgt. Bailey came back inside. He stood at the door and gently shut it, and in a calm and collected tone, spoke. "Condemned men die five deaths. The first, when they're apprehended for their unsavory deed. The second, when the jury declares them guilty, then when the verdict on appeal is upheld, and then again when the governor refuses to commute the sentence, and finally when the gallows's door drops, and the rope does its job. I *will* kill you right, sir." He spun about on his boot heels and left, leaving Campbell speechless, and me as well.

We took a break from my writing and his talking for about half an hour. I perused my Bible and stopped at Romans, 8:13. It read: "if you live according to the flesh, you will die, but if by the Spirit you put to death the misdeeds of the body, you will live." It seemed to hold meaning for me. I pondered if Campbell would agree and so read it aloud. "It sounded like you were troubled that all your family had left Mississippi," I added after the Bible quote. It elicited no response from him, or so I thought at first.

Campbell rolled over on his small bed and faced me. "Genesis. 16:12. 'He will be a wild donkey of a man, his hand will be against everyone, and everyone's hand will be against him, and he will live to the east of all his brothers.'"

He took a big drag on his cigar, blew the smoke my way, and smiled.

My little offering was not helpful. Who was I trying to help, me or him? No, Campbell did not want sympathy, or religion, or a shoulder to cry on. He was a hard man. He would die a hard man. I put the Bible away and mentally told myself it was pointless to try and save Campbell's soul. He didn't have one, obviously, or if he did, he lost it twenty-plus years ago.

With a smug and satisfied look on his face, Campbell started back on his tale.

He said he asked Harmon if he could ride with him because he didn't want to be left alone in the middle of nowhere with an Indian. Harmon said he understood, and yes, to pack up as they were leaving for good. Unsure of quite what to make of Manitema, the trio left two hours before sunrise the next day, to be sure he didn't tag along, and rode their horses hard and fast for the first twenty minutes.

Midway through the second day of their journey, McTimmons stayed due west on the course, but Harmon and Bill veered south, toward the Biloxi River and their hidden treasure high in a cypress tree. By mid-morning the next day, they were again in the little village of Nugent, not far from their hidden cache. This was the only road in these parts, and even though Harmon was uneasy showing his face twice in the same place within three months, there was no choice. Harmon told Bill to hang back, let him ride through alone, and to follow a half hour later. They both made it through without incident. Five hours later, they were at the spot, recognizable by the three giant cypress trees grouped on the opposite shore. They cleared off a little area to toss their sleeping blankets, built a fire, and ended their day. They would cross the river and retrieve their horde of coins in the morning.

Negotiating the trees and climbing the one was no easier the second time, and once again, Bill almost fell twice. Later, it would cross his mind. What if he had fallen and broken his back? Would Harmon have taken him back to civilization to let him recuperate and return to health? Or would he have left him there at the base of the cypress, among the trees, to eventually die of starvation, or worse, be a meal for a panther or a bear? Harmon would have Bill's $3000 if he died, so it had to be a temptation. These were wasteful thoughts. He had not been injured. Harmon did not desert him, so why torture his mind? Harmon had given him the opportunity to become a wealthy man. No one else had done that. Fools work from dawn to dusk, seven days a week, for minimal gain. Bill was no fool, anything but, and at this point in his life, just wanted to be a rich man at a young age.

Campbell's life's tale was interrupted as the jailhouse door burst open.

"Help! We need help! I was just out on the Augusta Road and saw a man laid out on the road face down. My name is Edward Pollard. I sent word for Sheriff Smith and when he didn't show this morning, I rode in to see if he'd heard I needed him. That's when I discovered the sheriff laid out."

"I'm Deputy Bacot. The sheriff is laid out in the road?"

"Yes and...I think he's dead. I hate to break it to you so, but I checked. It didn't appear he was breathing at all. I think his neck was broke, and if I had to guess, maybe he got throwed from his horse. Come quick. Maybe I'm wrong. I hope I'm wrong."

I stood up, pushed my pencil and paper aside, and began quickly moving toward the door before it hit me. This could be a sham. Pollard could be in Campbell's gang and this could be a ploy to draw me away from the prisoner, to spring him loose. With that thought, I opened my desk drawer and holstered my pistol. "I need your help Pollard. Go down to Widow Batson's Boarding House and find Deputy Daniels. He's likely asleep, but rouse him, and have him come see me. Hurry man, hurry!"

In less than five minutes, Pollard and the deputy were back. I instructed Pollard to go four buildings south of the jail, raise Dr. Boudreaux, accompany him to the spot where Sheriff Smith was, and to take a wagon in case the sheriff needed to be carried. Deputy Daniels was to ride out fast and do whatever he could until the doctor arrived. After they were gone, I gave my attention to Campbell, to see if he appeared to be upset that I did not leave the jail. From appearances, he did not seem to be either happy or sad about the possibility of the sheriff's possible death.

It wasn't easy to sit with Campbell. I wanted to go to the aid of my friend and mentor. Campbell seemed to sense the same and stretched out for a nap. I paced the floor and said silent prayers for Sheriff Smith. Time seemed to drag. I wish I knew how far out on Augusta Road Sheriff Smith was. Was he close to town? Was he way down the road?

Finally, the door opened, and it was Deputy Daniels. I immediately saw his red eyes and long face and knew what he was about to say before his mouth moved. "He's gone Larry. The sheriff's gone to his reward. I hate it. Hate it."

"Oh, dear God. This can't be. Oh no!" I replied.

"Doc Boudreaux tends to agree with Mr. Pollard. He thinks something spooked his horse, he lost control, and Ajax threw him, and he must have landed wrong and broke his neck," Daniels added as he moved over to Sheriff

Smith's desk and sat down. "I did my best to look around, you know, seeing if there were footprints or horse tracks around the sheriff. Only saw the ones from Pollard and his horse. We had just enough rain late yesterday to wash all the others away. Plus, Ajax was there, just grazing off to the side, maybe twenty-five yards away from the sheriff. Oh, and I couldn't even be 50 percent sure, but there might've been the outline of a snake's trail in the dust, too. It was very light, so I don't know, but it could've been what spooked Ajax."

I felt a welling up of tears and the urge to let them out, but I knew there wasn't time for that now. I had to find the sheriff's wife and tell her the sad news. Poor Sheriff Smith, gone much too soon. Poor Mrs. Smith, poor Ella Smith, was a widow now.

CHAPTER TEN

Do Things Really Happen for A Reason?

Batson was terribly quiet for the two days following the sudden death of Sheriff Smith. On the job side, I was named acting-sheriff of Perrine County, until the election could be held in six months. Daniels didn't want it. He was going to be a lawyer in the long run, and besides, I not only had seniority on him, but the town council and County Commissioner both held a quick meeting and decreed I was the replacement. Technically they told me it was a $5 a month raise, but really it was a bigger badge, a bigger desk, and more responsibility. It would also mean I'd read out the death sentence at Campbell's hanging, whenever that would be. The carpenters told me it wouldn't be respectful for them to be loudly hammering, with the sheriff's passing and the somber mood of the town. They'd finish after his funeral day after tomorrow.

In the meantime, the sheriff's office was a three-man job, so I visited Roy Moody who lived just outside of town with his son and daughter-in-law on their hog and goat farm. Roy was the sheriff before Junius Smith and had retired. He wasn't an invalid by any means but had a bad hip and didn't get around too good for a man of sixty-seven. However, if he would agree to come on as a deputy, I could use him to watch things, hold down the office when I was out on a call, and just be around to handle simple and mundane chores in my absence. Moody's son was actually keener on the idea than the old man and convinced him to at least try it for one month.

Campbell seemed terribly quiet during all the turmoil of the sheriff's passing, me replacing him, and bringing Moody on board. The outlaw spent most of the day Smith died, and the day after, sleeping. There was so much to be done on both days, I'd forgotten his mid-day meal and only served him breakfast. Daniels did remember to feed him at night. Campbell never complained on those days, but on the third day, he reminded me he was allowed a cup of rum or whiskey at noon. I complied, but kept it on the sly, not knowing what Moody would say. I fed Campbell leftovers from breakfast and gave him his rum. Then I changed into my best suit and waited for the new widow, Mrs. Smith, to drop by. I'd asked Daniels to request her presence, as I wanted to again tell her how sorry I was and explain how even though I wanted to attend, I must miss the sheriff's funeral service because of the nature of our prisoner and the possibility of his clan trying to break him out and set him free.

Ella Smith dropped by, clad in black and her face behind a veil. I could immediately see her reaction when she saw me behind the sheriff's desk instead of her Junius. I had found a little notebook the late sheriff kept in his bottom middle drawer and passed it on to her. I had no idea what was in it, but it was personalized in gold leaf. It drew a smile from her, and she said Junius could write a decent poem now and then, usually about the beauty of nature, and this was a gift from her on their first anniversary. I gave her my condolences and explained the reason for my absence, and being the wife of a lawman, she understood and left for the church.

After she left, I changed back into my regular clothes and noticed Campbell was up from his nap. The church bell rang out two peals. I looked out the main window of the jail and saw a crowd of people all dressed in black heading to the Batson First Methodist. Campbell turned around and looked out from his cell window at the same scene. When they had passed, he spoke to me. "What did you all do to the sheriff's horse? The animal was responsible, or so I heard Deputy Daniels say so."

"I took the liberty of selling him to Roy Moody's son. He'll keep him out of town, so Widow Smith won't have to see the animal. I gave her the money."

"I hope you gave Moody a bill of sale. You know how I feel about those. His horse was named Ajax. Ajax was a brave warrior in Greek Mythology. I always named my horse the same name: Surrey. That was Richard the

Third's horse's name from the Shakespeare play. You know? 'My horse, my horse, my kingdom for a horse?'"

I didn't want to get into it with Campbell, so I gave him a brief nod and then asked him if he wanted to take his story back up where we stopped, in the morning two days ago. He stretched, yawned, and said he did. I retrieved my paper and pencil, moved back to my old deputy desk, sat down, and waited on him to begin.

The outlaw said Harmon and he took the money from the cypress tree and followed the road south, where he knew of a little-used path that would route them due west toward the village of Pearlington, where McTimmons was located. The path was an old Indian trail, but since their removal it had become terribly overgrown, so the going was slow. It did offer one advantage; it hid them so well that a sow and her piglets didn't see them approaching and Harmon's new rifle took her down with a clean head shot. Campbell said he watched with envy as Harmon took his knife and expertly butchered the hog entirely to make pigs feet, pig ears, pork chops, steaks, and even bacon. Campbell did a superb job of cooking for their evening meal.

I lost interest in Campbell's story. I was thinking that Sheriff Smith would be lowered down into his grave about now and it saddened me. What of his wife, Ella? What would happen to her? If she stayed here in Batson, what would she do for money? Would she move to Biloxi and live with her sister? She was much younger than the late sheriff. Would she stay a widow for the remainder of her life? That could be a long time. Yes, the late sheriff's coffin was being lowered into his grave, dust to dust. I, too, had seen coffins lowered into the grave. The coffin of my wife and two small children, when the Yellow Fever gripped them. Dust to dust for my family, too.

It was at that point I noticed the silence both in and outside of the jailhouse. Campbell had ceased talking when he saw I wasn't writing. There were no sounds of boots scuffling along the wooden sidewalks of Batson or the jingle jangle of metal as the horses and wagons made their way up and down the dirt street. There was no conversation of the people normally moving about town. It was a fitting moment of silence for their departed sheriff.

I rose, moved back to the sheriff's desk, and then opened the drawer. Inside were two tin cups and a bottle of rye whiskey. I removed the cups and poured each roughly half full. I moved closer to the cell, ordered Campbell to move back under the window, and placed one cup about a foot from the bars. I then moved back to the deputy desk with my own cup.

"Take it, Bill. We're gonna toast the memory of a good man, Sheriff Junius Smith, may he rest in peace," I said in a stern and steady voice.

"Here, here," Bill responded as he took his cup, clapped it gently against the iron bars, just enough to make a clinking noise, and sat down in his slat chair. We both sipped the rye in silence. We were in a situation we'd never been, nor had ever thought to be in.

I contemplated changing the mood by telling him about my family and how happy we were before the Yellow Fever, but then thought again. Maybe I could tell him of my childhood in rural Simpson County, outside of Westville? Those were happy times, too. I thought some more and decided against it. Those were private reminiscences of mine, not to be shared with a callous killer like Bill Campbell. He should talk. Afterall, he likely had less than forty-eight hours left before being hurled into oblivion by the hangman, forever silenced. "Okay, keep going. You were telling me that you and Harmon were moving your hideout from the western border of the state, by the Alabama line, to over near the Louisiana line, right?"

The story picked up, with the two finding McTimmons in the little town of Pearlington. The three decided it was time to adjust their ways. First, a trip to their bank in New Orleans to withdraw all their money. Both McTimmons and Harmon admitted they had a nice stockpile of better than $30,000. Bill said he'd accumulated around $7200. They would pool their funds and travel deep into the Catahoula Swamp, north of the Bay of St. Louis, and hide their treasure. Each would have a ledger of the exact amount of each man's cache, and each would have a map, written in the clan secret code, to locate the stash, hopefully years down the road. Harmon said he was both tired and wary of traveling, so no more long trips to the likes of Cincinnati, central Georgia, or East Texas. McTimmons agreed, he was also wary of the road, and desired to find a good woman to comfort him in his remaining years. Harmon remarked it was time to leave the clan as its leader. Bill remained silent. He understood why they might feel that way, but he was still young and adventurous, and not even one-third of the way to his $30,000 goal.

Heading a few miles east from Pearlington, the three outlaws traversed up the Jourdan River which was wild and only populated by a sporadic homestead, but still was not their goal. Harmon wanted to go deep into the surrounding swamp, way back and far from any nosy traveler. They traveled by canoe against the current. Harmon verbally made the other two notice how after the Jourdan started north, after about three miles, it took a hard left to the west and stayed westerly for ten miles before again shooting up north. At this point would be landmark number one. They beached their canoe on a white sandbar and studied the land. To the east was a vast plain of nothing but alligator trails and bulrush grass. Far off in the distance, maybe a full mile or more, was a tree line of mimosa trees and swamp Magnolias. This was too important and too much money to mark anything with even a clan symbol. No, this would be done by dead reckoning of marking off and counting the number of steps from a huge dead cypress trunk just inland from the little beach. It would be landmark number two. Harmon noted that among the mimosa and swamp Magnolias was a small copse of trees, closer to them than the rest, but still nearly a mile away. That would be landmark number three. Out of place was a slight hill in the northern distance, with a dozen yellow pine trees; landmark four. Each man selected a target from number two, three, and four and walked to the corresponding destination. From there at a given signal each would walk toward the center of the imaginary triangle, counting his steps as he went. The triangulation meet up was perfect, there was nothing at all in any direction for 700 yards except thick marsh grass stems three feet high. Bill dug a hole four feet deep and McTimmons placed an old wine cask in it while Harmon covered the hole with fill dirt, dead reeds, and grass, and then proceeded to have them walk out in a single file as he did his best to erase their footsteps. And like that, the gold and silver coins, with a value over $68,500 were hidden deep in Catahoula Swamp—a hellhole filled with mosquitos, snakes, and gators, of which no one wanted any part of, and known only to three men on the face of the earth. While Harmon was clear he wanted none of the clan's mystic alphabet used around the treasure trove, he did agree it was best to use it for the maps.

McTimmons set about making himself appear to be a respectable citizen of Pearlington, Mississippi. He bought an old barn that was in disuse and converted it into a livery stable. He did know about horses, and he wasn't trying to get rich from the endeavor, he just wanted to make enough money to survive on and not dip into his $30,000 stash. After he finished the barn, he had a small house built behind it, about 500 square feet, plus an outbuilding for a kitchen and outhouse. Harmon moved to the little town of Jourdan Community, about ten miles northeast of Pearlington. The main industry there was charcoal, something he was well-versed in. He found a stylish raised cottage of five rooms and purchased it for $650. Bill could no longer live with Harmon, as the latter had made it clear he was in pursuit of a wife, so wishing to stay close to the Catahoula Swamp and his money, bought a small home in the tiny village of Pearl City, about five miles south of Pearlington. Bill set up a barrel production operation, like the others, not trying to get rich, just survive. After all, it was a skill he'd learned from his parents as a boy, and Pearlington had a sawmill, so lumber for his craft was nearby.

After all three were settled in, Harmon announced they must ride out and post a call of a clan meeting next month to announce his and McTimmons resignations and that he was recommending Bill Campbell as the next leader. Bill said he was surprised by the recommendation; he figured someone older would likely take the lead, but Harmon said Bill would be the best fit. Bill, he said, had brains, brawn, talent, the fortitude to lead an outlaw band, and the fire in his belly to gain wealth, which was very important. They put the word out, and five weeks later found themselves riding east toward the ghost town village of the failed grape and olive oil settlers from forty years prior.

GALLOWS RECKONING

Counting themselves, there were seventeen clan members in attendance. There was some attempt to talk Harmon out of retiring but he would not have that. He made it very clear he was done and put his hand on his pistol butt for emphasis. Another man, J.J. Hopkins, was nominated for clan leader, and a vote was taken, eight apiece for Hopkins and Campbell. Harmon would cast the deciding vote and Bill was elected. The next order of business was the meeting of Bill Campbell and the county chieftains. The county chieftains were distributed through central and South Mississippi, one to each county. Each one was a man of wealth, political power, and influence. They helped the clan when a member fell into a bad legal situation, in exchange for an annual tribute of $250 apiece from the general fund of the clan's books. After all, Harmon, in all his years of crime, had only done jail time once, and for kidnapping. Harmon told the group that without the assistance of the county chieftains, he'd have been tried, convicted, and hung before his twentieth birthday. He pointed around the meeting room to another seven members who likewise wouldn't be breathing the air of freedom today, if not for the arrangement with the twenty-eight powerful men in place. This was all new to the five new members of the clan. For the sake of secrecy, only the leader knew who the chieftains were. Harmon would take Bill out for the introductions over the next three months. The meeting adjourned and after Bill, McTimmons, and Harmon were away from the meeting house and back on the main road, Harmon gave Bill the advice that his life and job as leader would be a lot safer if he killed J. J. Hopkins.

I broke into his tale there. "So, Hopkins is going to be murder number five? Am I keeping count correctly?"

"Would have been, but some sailor in a Biloxi bar took him out for me. They caught him with a pair of aces and kings up his sleeve and blasted him, so he was out of the way, but I had nothing to do with his death," Campbell said with a satisfied smile. "Yeah, sometimes things happen for a reason, I guess. Hopkins wasn't meant to lead the clan or set up a coup d'état to overthrow me, so you could say it wasn't in the *cards*."

CHAPTER ELEVEN

To Each Their Own

Harmon and Bill set out for Mobile and visited the bank where the clan's money was kept. Bill was added to the account, and they withdrew $7300, of which only $300 was their traveling expense money. Bill had known nothing of the twenty-eight men that worked the justice system for the clan all throughout central and South Mississippi. A man could say what they want about Harmon, but the man could sure keep a secret. As he did when out on a raid, they would travel to the farthest distance from base and work their way back. First stop would be Clarke County and the town of Quitman. Bill was introduced to a Mr. Bob Troutt, who, according to Harmon, was a rich lawyer and one-time state senator who held sway over the sheriff due to some long-ago election-rigging favor. The situation of Harmon stepping aside and Bill arising as head of the clan was explained over dinner in a fantastic mansion owned by Mr. Troutt.

The next morning, they rode west into Jasper County and the thriving burg of Paulding. Harmon and Bill went into the building that housed *The Eastern Clarion* newspaper and met the owner, editor, and publisher, Mr. Samuel R. Adamlee. In a back office, Harmon made the introductions and paid the $250 tribute. Later, when back on the road, Harmon told Bill that Adamlee had information on half the county, and it wasn't the type of information they would want to read in the newspaper, so he carried a lot of clout. They continued, going to each of the twenty-eight counties, paying their tribute, and announcing Harmon had handed the reins to Bill. It turned out that in Monticello and Woodville, their surreptitious contacts there had been called to either Heaven or Hell. These two stops lengthened the time of the ride, as Harmon was forced to find suitable replacements, which he did. In Woodville, it was another newspaper owner, and in Monticello, and a judge named Runnels. The entire trip took nearly three months and both men were dog-tired at its conclusion, but it had to be done. Harmon had done an excellent estimate of the amount of money it would take for the trip, and they returned with about $15 left over.

With the trip complete, they stopped in Pearlington to visit McTimmons, who invited them to his wedding in approximately four months, when the circuit preacher would be by. Clan member Bradish Allen's middle daughter had said yes to marriage. Congratulations were abundant as Bill and Harmon were introduced to the bride-to-be. McTimmons seemed very happy and satisfied with his new station in life as a livery stable owner and soon to be husband. All three men went deep into their cups that night and Bill and Harmon stayed over, not leaving until around noon the following day. However, before they all retired for bed, Bill made sure to buy a supply of laudanum from McTimmons for some future use. Away from McTimmons' place, Harmon announced he was heading to Miss Joseph's brothel in Biloxi for a few days, but that he'd see Bill in four months at the wedding.

Meanwhile, back home in Pearl City, Bill was in for a surprise. Two of his three older brothers, Phillip and Simon, were waiting for his arrival. After an update on their father, mother, and Bill's younger brother John, they both announced their days as hog farmers and makers of turpentine and pitch were over. They desired money, and they wanted it now. They yearned to be like Bill and be rich men at a young age. They had no idea there was an outlaw clan operating in the southern third of Mississippi, as Bill revealed to them, and stated they needed to join. Equally flabbergasted were the brothers when Bill told them he was the clan's leader. He told his brothers he'd rest for two weeks, then call a gang meeting and have his brothers initiated into the Beaver Creek Clan of outlaws.

The time passed, and Bill and his brothers showed up at the clan meeting house. He'd called the meeting time for sunset but waited an hour past to begin, to see if there were stragglers. There weren't. Of the seventeen present at the last meeting, only six showed. That was not unexpected to Bill; Harmon had predicted it. He'd suggested to Bill that if the membership fell off, each existing member should have six months to bring in a minimum of one new clan member. Bill was then pressed by the current members about what kind of raid he had in mind, saying Mobile was out, at least for four to five years, but Baton Rouge was a possibility, and he was going to ride over in the near future and spend a couple of days to check it out as a possible worthy target.

Once back home and with his brothers tagging along, Bill made ready for a trip to Baton Rouge and down to New Orleans to meet former clan member Mr. Benny. The three Campbell's hired Bradish Allen and his boat to take them west, through Lake Pontchartrain, Lake Maurepas, up the Amite River, to disembark at the village of Marietta with their horses and a short fifteen-mile ride to Baton Rouge. They found a room at a crude little hotel on Floridana Street and slept the rest of the day away, feeling they'd have more freedom to explore after dark. Just before midnight, Bill led them down the stairs and out of the back of the building. After just a few minutes, he immediately assessed that Baton Rouge did not employ night watchmen. That told him that he couldn't use the insider ruse and that the merchants were not affluent enough, or didn't care enough, to hire watchmen to protect their stores. The nighttime walk did not teach him too much. The next morning, after a hearty breakfast, Bill found a copy of the *Democratic Advocate* newspaper, published in Baton Rouge. His disappointment was sealed as the paper carried very few advertisements hawking goods and wares. It was mostly a political debate paper and market news for farmers. With no reason to stay longer, the three pointed their horses south and started off for New Orleans.

Their journey took an ominous turn just outside the small village of Bringiers, about two-thirds of the way down to New Orleans. Right on the side of the road were the decapitated heads of three men that all appeared to be around the age of twenty, stuck on the end of a six-foot pole, for display. Their faces were a greenish color and huge strips of skin were missing from their cheeks and forehead where the crows and vultures had landed and taken a meal, revealing streaks of white bone beneath. All three dead men stunk, were covered in flies, and it wasn't pleasant, but Bill wanted to read the posted written notice nailed to the pole supporting the middle head. It stated they were highwaymen who were guilty of robbing a group of pilgrims heading to a religious meeting near the town of Bringiers. A local posse was rounded up and upon finding the men with possessions of the pilgrims, held a quick trial, hung the men from the tree behind these very posts, and then cut their heads off. It was a simple and brutal example that the local people did not think twice about dispensing justice, even if it could be labeled vigilante justice.

The scene made a definite impression on Phillip and Simon. For them, in their collective minds, robbery was an easy thing to do. One sticks a pistol in a man's face, takes his purse, and rides away at high speed. For Bill, it was sloppy work. Harmon and McTimmons had taught him that you don't leave witnesses if you rob someone. Dead men tell no tales, of course, and that was how it was done. These amateurs with their heads on a pike either didn't know better or didn't want to get their hands *that* dirty. Bill saw it as a teachable moment and verbalized the same, but the brothers hadn't been exposed to the same lessons Bill had learned at the heel of Harmon and McTimmons, and the rotting flesh falling from the heads of three robbers was enough deterrent.

Phillip and Simon began to mull over a harried desire to return to Pearl City, to Bill's home. If the locals were willing to take their anger out on these robbers, surely, they'd have no reason to do any less to the Campbell brothers if they should be caught committing a crime. The two lagged behind Bill so as to have a private conversation. After a couple of minutes, they rode up to join him and announced this area was too dangerous and they wanted to get away. They weren't afraid, they proudly said, but were just being prudent. Bill reined up his horse and looked his brothers directly in the eye.

Bill inhaled, held it, and expelled a long stream of cigar smoke directly at them. He thought about how things have flipped in the relationship between him and his older brothers. Once, they were his leaders and mentors, but the situation had flipped, and recognizing such it was time to assert himself. Not as brother kin, but as clan leader.

Bill pushed his overcoat to the side and leaned back in the saddle as he plainly placed his hand upon his pistol grip and spoke in a calm, but firm, voice. "This business I'm in is all about risk and reward, so we need to find out, right here and now, where you two stand on that issue. Is this riskier than making pitch? Well, hell yeah, it is, but the reward is five hundred times better, too. Are you risking your life leading a herd of sheep to market? Probably not. Are you risking your life when you shove a pistol up in a man's face and demand all his money, everything he owns in the world? And you know he probably ain't real keen on handing it over and might be reaching for his own gun to stop you? Yes, again it's a big risk. But if you deliver those dozen sheep, you might pocket $3 after father takes his owner's share, but this man you're a-holding up could have his whole life's savings on him, maybe $1000 in gold coin on his person. So, you see? That's the decision, your decision. Did I make that clear to you, Simon? Phillip?"

Simon and Phillip both stood up in their stirrups and twisted their respective necks and backs to stretch their tense muscles. They weren't used to being talked to like this by anyone, much less their kid brother. Neither knew what the other would answer. What if Simon said it wasn't worth the risk? What if Phillip said it was worth the risk? None of the three said a word for over a solid minute. This was their in-or-out moment, it had nothing to do with family ties or siblings rank, and they all knew that fact. Bill purposefully removed his hand from the pistol and emphatically closed his coat, an inference that his say in the matter was over and it was now up to Simon and Phillip. They could fall in behind his horse or wheel about and head back toward South Mississippi and their parents' homestead. Bill trotted his horse south, toward New Orleans, and after a short delay, his brothers followed.

Bill was glad they were riding behind him and had decided to stay loyal to him, but he was not fully satisfied. The fact they even had such thoughts of running away because of three decapitated heads on pikes bothered him.

GALLOWS RECKONING

When he was starting out, he never wavered when given a job, no matter the danger or unpleasantness. He did what was required of him, but Simon and Phillip, would they? Before he got into a real fix where there were real men with knives or guns, he should test the mettle of his brothers in something—maybe not quite as fatal—to see if they had the means not to crab[10] it.

They arrived in New Orleans and found Mr. Benny at the Absinthe House tavern on Bourbon Street. Bill delivered his request along with a few dollars. He wanted Benny to find sugar or cotton plantations west of New Orleans that needed slaves. Not completely divulging his plan, Bill was going to run a stolen slave scam, in reverse of the last one. His scheme would be to raid west central Alabama and off-load the acquired slaves in south central Louisiana, but he wanted to know exactly where to go with his dark human cargo. He didn't want to wander around looking for buyers as that added to the dangers. As soon as his message was delivered to Mr. Benny, Bill gathered his brothers and they rode east, toward home in Pearl City. It was time for a job to replenish his purse and to start one for his brothers.

---

[10] crab it was a nineteenth century term that meant perfection was derailed by an offensive comment

CHAPTER TWELVE

Can The Student Become the Master?

I was quite enthralled by the mannerisms and speech of Bill Campbell when describing his brothers joining the clan and their initial reluctance to participate in what Campbell did. I could see his mind looking for just the right words to dictate as I transcribed them onto paper. Was I a mind reading psychic? No. But I thought I saw him become a consummate professional, the criminal leader. Oh, his chosen source of livelihood was damnable, illegal, and deplorable, but looking beyond what he did, and instead at how he did it, I couldn't help but feel that feeling I'd had before. What could this man, with his mind and inner drive, have accomplished if he hadn't gone astray at such a malleable age of thirteen? Here he was showing forethought, pre-planning where to sell his stolen slaves so his actions would be quick, efficient, and, therefore, safer. This man was a leader. He knew how to raise up those below him, in his own depraved way, and he did it naturally.

"What about something to eat, Deputy Bacot?" Campbell said, snapping me back to the present. "Wouldn't want me starving to death before Mr. Executioner gets to practice his knot-tying skills on me. Oh, not to forget, I've been granted a cup of rum with my meal, as per the wishes of your predecessor, may he rest in peace."

"Okay, Bill, okay. You don't have to remind me every time about your cup of rum. I do have a good memory, all right," I said with a slight tone of disgust. "As soon as Roy Moody comes in from his rounds, we'll get you some food. Well, until he's here, go ahead on with your story."

And so, Campbell picked back up where he was in his tale. He said he employed Bradish Allen and his boat to take them up the Pearl River to Jackson and from there took a stage to Vicksburg. Just as Harmon would have done, they all stayed in separate hotels in Jackson and took separate stage lines to Vicksburg. Simon and Phillip would go together to St. Louis, but have absolutely no interaction while on board, and wait for Bill who was following. Bill was keen on stealing another flatboat loaded with supplies. This would be a good initial break-in for his brothers and after they had sold the supplies, would continue to New Orleans as Mr. Benny would have had ample time to find plantations in need of slaves. Armed with that information, they'd be off to the general area around Tuscaloosa, Alabama to raid, before heading back to Louisiana and selling their stolen slaves.

The three brothers stayed in separate lodgings. Gathering at Lafayette Park after dark, Bill admitted he was going down to the St. Louis docks the next morning. He said he was very surprised to see so many steamboats on the Mississippi, as there had not been nearly as many the last time he was on the river. Finally, on the fourth evening of their St. Louis stay, Bill announced he'd located a keelboat hauling flour, horse fodder and tack, tools, many different types of fabrics, tobacco, wood stains, whitewash, paint, clocks, watches, and whiskey, all of which very much pleased Bill as he knew these to be easily moved and for good money. However, unlike McSween from Cincinnati who operated solo, this was a large keelboat that had an owner and a crew of one already.

They left at dawn the next morning, the owner, Mr. Johansson, barking and yelling profanity-laced orders, especially directed at Simon and Phillip, as they'd never been near a boat of this size and were clueless as to what to do. Bill helped where he could, but his mind was busy plotting. He was not going to waste time and effort docking this behemoth craft at every small village on the Mississippi south of St. Louis, but instead planned to go directly to Memphis and sell his stolen wares there.

By asking about their whereabouts daily, Bill tracked their progress. He wanted to have the owner and his assistant gone, and to modify the boat's appearance before they reached Cairo. So, on night three of their float down the river, Bill passed a bottle of rye among the crew with careful instructions to his brothers to only feign to sip, as it was drugged. Johansson's crewman was a good fiddler, but after drinking his share of the rye, couldn't play his fiddle at all and stretched out on a blanket on deck and went to sleep. He was followed soon thereafter by the owner. It was just as Harmon had done to him when the courthouse needed burning. Having his brothers kill the men would make them equals in the eye of the law and bind them to Bill as never being able to turn on him.

Bill found an axe, just as they had in McSween's craft, and told Simon to smash the skull of the crewman. Phillip would do the same to the captain. From his jail cell, Bill relayed his conversation with his brothers.

"This boat is well-laden, and the wares should easily bring around $3000 at market in Memphis, maybe more."

"We get $1000 apiece?" both Simon and Phillip said simultaneously.

"Talk later. Now they're out cold. Take them to eternity before they wake up and want to fight about why we drugged them. Do it now. Go on."

Phillip had the axe already and handed it over to Simon so he could go first. Simon raised the axe and brought down a heavy thud on the crewman. Brains and blood splattered his face. Simon moved even closer and raised the axe high in case he needed another to the head, but the man neither moved nor made a sound after being struck. Simon handed the axe to Phillip and Bill gave him a slight nudge toward the enclosed shed midship, where the living quarters were and where the boat owner had gone to sleep. Simon and Bill watched from the doorway. Phillip hesitated, then raised the axe and held it high. He continued to hold it there until Simon and Bill heard muffled sobbing and crying. They both told Phillip to hit him, but he didn't. The talking noises aroused Johansson, a big man and easily the largest and most physical of any of the men aboard.

"What is this?" the owner said, just as Bill plunged the knife into the man's neck, right where it joined his chest. The man sat up in bed, gasped a loud sucking sound, and his eyes were as big as saucers.

"Hit him Phillip!" ordered Bill in a guttural yell, "Hit him! Kill him!"

Phillip let the axe drop and it struck the owner on the side of his head with a glancing non-fatal blow. The man swung about on his bunk, as if to rise. He pulled the knife from his own throat and reversed its blade to menace the Campbell boys who all backed off and retreated out of the door, onto the back deck. A large steamboat just happened to be passing close by, its band loudly playing a jaunty song. Johansson staggered toward Bill, who was closest and had pulled his pistol, but he was reluctant to fire with the steamboat and witnessing passengers so near. The Campbell's kept moving around with the owner in a slow step-by-step pursuit. The wake of the steamboat hit the flatboat and everyone staggered from the powerful slap of water. Only the owner fell, and Bill moved quickly with the slack end of a tie up line and wrapped it around the man's throat. He placed his feet up against the man's torso, leaned back, pushed with his feet, and pulled back on the rope with all his might. Shortly thereafter, all movement ceased, Simon approached Johansson, and soon pronounced him dead.

Bill was disgusted with Phillip, but this was not the time to blast his brother's lack of nerve. Instead, he ordered Phillip to move about the boat and gather any small unused anchor, bits of metal, or iron and to tightly secure them to the bodies for a permanent sinking. While Phillip was off and about, Bill rifled through the men's clothes, looking for personal items and money. Simon began tying rope around each man's neck, waist, and ankles as Phillip began bringing in a bevy of iron rods he'd found in a barrel up front. Bill watched each body being carefully tied to the iron before pronouncing it done, saying they could be pushed over the side later. With that out of the way, he instructed Phillip to get some full color, like green or blue, paint, and a brush and begin painting the exterior of the living quarters, which were currently a faded, dull, dirty-white color. Still disgusted with Phillip, Bill moved around to the bow and opened a barrel of whiskey, into which he dipped a tin cup and took a long sip.

"Simon, untie us and shove us off. We'll drop these bodies off in the middle of the river. Then you get a torch and position yourself on the bow to watch for snags. I want to float downstream and put some distance between us and this spot. Hop to," Bill instructed as he took the tiller and felt the current grab the boat and push her south. "Phillip, hurry along with that painting. After that, I want our smokestack shortened, and I want two extra windows cut in the living quarters. I saw a barrel full of saws on the front deck. Oh, and find the name of the boat on the stern and paint over it in black. Light some more torches, we're working through the night. We'll pull over to the bank at dawn and catch some sleep then." Bill took on the responsibility of dumping the bodies and watched carefully as the two corpses sank.

Later, after they had pulled to the muddy shore and tied up, Phillip started off for a bunk, but Bill stopped him in his tracks. Bill told him he was on watch and to keep his eyes open while Simon and he slept. Bill also mentioned that Phillip would been docked $250 of his share of the profits, should there be any, after the fiasco of not putting the owner of the boat down and endangering not only the success of the trip, but their lives, too. Phillip dropped his head, then shrank up to the bow and sat down next to the whiskey barrel. Bill, seeing his choice of seats, warned him he could drink one cup and that was all. Simon watched and listened to his younger brother during it all and was in awe of how in command Bill was of the situation. Simon greatly admired the take-charge attitude his little brother possessed.

Trying to make amends, Phillip cooked the midday meal right after they shoved off to continue south to Memphis. The air was thick on the deck of the boat, and each ate in silence. Bill remained at the tiller and, from time to time, took out his copy of *Hamlet* he'd purchased on his last New Orleans visit, reading a few pages. About an hour after the meal, Phillip approached and said he was sorry for his actions, especially for not killing the boat owner with the axe. He promised it would never happen again. Bill still wasn't over how close they'd come to disaster. It was then he knew it wasn't just about the trip or the money. No, he wanted to show up at McTimmons's wedding, pull Harmon aside, and show him at least $7,500, reaped from a flatboat raid and a stolen slave sale that he, only he, had planned, orchestrated, and successfully conducted as leader of a group of clan members. *That* would be true satisfaction.

Turning his attention to his apologetic brother, Bill spoke firmly again. "Damn right it won't happen again. You either run with me or you're a liability. If you become a liability, so help me God, I will cut you off, and see if you can swim home. In a situation like we had, he who hesitates is lost. You saw what I did to that big fellow Johansson last night. You hesitated and he near 'bout turned the table on us. I didn't hesitate and I did him in. That's how it is, and that's how it has to be. Got me? Now it's over and we shall never speak of it again."

Both Simon and Phillip gave Bill a wide berth the rest of the afternoon, hoping his anger would finally subside. It did, and around dusk Bill asked Phillip to distribute a handful of venison jerky, bread, and a cup of whiskey to all. It appeared, true to his earlier word, Bill had gotten over his brother's error and lack of will. The large keelboat was extremely unwieldy and, with two novices aboard, more than a few times did the powerful river slam them into the bank when she took a sharp turn in the meandering giant. Luckily for all, the boat was well-made and very sturdy, and it mostly just injured their pride.

Within a few days, the three managed to improve their boating skills enough to successfully approach the docks in Memphis. Bill managed to throw a line around a mooring piling as he waited for two other keelboats to complete their maneuvering and untie to leave. Before they could do so, a pair of small skiffs rowed out to Bill's craft. A heightened degree of concern, but not panic, shot into his brain. Both skiffs had four men, two rowing and two armed with shotguns at the ready. Did this have anything to do with the theft of this vessel and the murders of the crew? Under his breath, he ordered Simon and Phillip to go inside, arm themselves, and come back out, hiding their weapons. They followed orders and, at that moment, the rowers stopped their forward movement and began a stationary sculling.

The man in the bow of the nearest skiff yelled out that the dock and the town were closed to any incoming travelers either by land or water. Bill asked why and heard there was a Typhus outbreak. People were free to leave Memphis, but not to enter. He added that the City Health Department said this was the rule, in effect for the next three weeks. He said tying up across the river in Arkansas was an option, if he wished to wait three weeks. Bill said he understood, and the two skiffs turned back toward the dock. Bill instructed Simon to man the steering oar and Phillip to grab the sweep or gouger. Bill let loose the mooring piling and the current took them away from Memphis. Doing nothing while tied up to a tree on the Arkansas shore was not something they could afford or do. They would have to stop at the small villages on the Arkansas and Mississippi shores and begin selling quickly. To complete the bad news, a strong thunderstorm moved in from the west and thoroughly soaked the Campbell brothers.

Past Memphis, the Father of Waters got tricky. A series of five small islands cluttered the main channel and obscured any traffic coming up from the south. After the first three islands, a small steamer packet passed much too close off the fourth island, sending the keelboat rocking and causing them to lose two barrels of flour. They saw their first sign of life on the Arkansas side, at a small community named Blues Point. Bill asked the old man fishing on the muddy bank what they called this place. The old man told him it was named after a freed Jamaican Negro slave, Billy Blue, whose benefactor advanced him a loan to buy a ferry to run across to Mississippi and the village of Commerce. Angling for more than fish, the old man told Bill that for $5 he would ride his mule about the locals, telling them a well-laden keelboat had docked and was willing to deal. Bill negotiated the price to $2, with a promise of $4 more if he drew a decent crowd. They ended up staying two full days and sold about $150 worth of goods.

Next, they keeled across to Commerce and again stayed two days, but as many had taken the ferry over to Blues Point to buy earlier, they only sold $70. However, the locals told the Campbell's to continue downstream to the county seat, Peyton, a much more affluent town. Bill found out the word affluent means different things to different people. Peyton did have a decent dock, warehouses near the river for storing cotton, and somewhat of a downtown area, but he found out that at this time of year, once the heat set in, the real affluent ones left town. Those who could afford it would escape the Mississippi heat and either visit the Northeast or even Europe. The Campbell's were disappointed in their two-day haul of only $350. These locals told them to be sure and stop at Helena, Arkansas, as it was truly an affluent town.

Finally, the words of the locals seem to hold true. Helena was a bustling riverport, serving southern and central Arkansas as their main hub for shipping cotton down to New Orleans' markets. The good-sized crowds came in and their sales topped $1000. At the end of their last day, Bill noted a scruffy looking character with a large scar across his cheek, as if he'd been hit by a saber, come aboard and look over the merchandise, but didn't buy anything. They pulled in their gangway and Phillip started cooking their evening meal. Bill was uneasy. There was something about how the man with the scar paid more attention to the crew than the wares. It would have been impossible to miss, to a keen and watchful eye of a robber, how much money had been transferred from the people of Helena to the Campbell's in the last two days, and that might be too much of a temptation for some men to resist.

Bill insisted they eat hurriedly and allowed no whiskey rations. He told his brothers to be sure their weapons were loaded and at the ready. He instructed Simon to light torches for the bow and stand watch, as he planned on slipping downstream into a less congested part of the river. They sculled out toward the main current just in time, as Bill noted a band of six men rode up to the dock in great haste. He could hear them talking and yelling among themselves and could only deduce that was the scarred man and his gang of thieves, arriving too late. Bill felt good about his intuition and would relish telling his old mentor, Harmon, about their exploits in Helena.

The boat floated southward, and they made decent sales at Bolivar and Princeton in Mississippi, and Columbia and Providence in Louisiana. Bill took inventory and announced they were done stopping at the towns along the shore. They had taken in $2775 and had enough food stores still on board to complete the trip down to New Orleans, where they would find out what news Mr. Benny could share.

CHAPTER THIRTEEN

Brothers And Brothers-In-Law

Bill decided to sell the keelboat in Baton Rouge, as there were around 3,000 inhabitants there versus the 100,000 in New Orleans, meaning that was just that much less of a chance of someone figuring out the boat really belonged to Mr. Johansson from St. Louis. No one bid on it as an intact item, so he sold it off as piecemeal lumber and saw it go for $60. They had docked at night, and Bill had Phillip immediately jump ashore to go find a room in a hotel, so there only looked like two men aboard. They traveled separately over the next four days, via different steamer lines, the short jaunt down to New Orleans. While rafting down the Mississippi, they looked the part of boatmen of everyday crude cotton shirts and pants, but upon arriving in New Orleans, a haberdashery visit was necessary. They wanted to be seen as businessmen, wearing frock coats, woolen trousers, cotton shirts, silk vests, attached collars, and cravats. Bill had instructed his brothers to go separately and buy their nice clothes at Gore Brothers on Royal Street. They were to meet at the Dueling Oak in City Park on Saturday morning at 10:00 to coordinate their next move. Then, Bill had his brothers wait in a tavern across from the park as he went to see his insider contact, Mr. Benny.

Mr. Benny lived in the Second Municipality area of New Orleans, on Camp Street. Benny had a real side job, not like chopping firewood or making charcoal. He was a bookkeeper for a myriad of New Orleans businesses, mostly on Canal Street. Bill went alone to his small but tasteful brick townhome. Mr. Benny answered the door and led him into the main parlor, where they sat across from each other in brocaded chairs. Benny started off by congratulating Bill on rising to head of the clan and Bill acknowledged. Then, as Bill looked over Mr. Benny's head, he saw a vision of loveliness enter the room from the door. It was a gorgeous young lady, probably seventeen-years old or so. Bill, remembering the manners his mother taught, rose to his feet. Benny twisted his head around to see what was going on and explained that she was his niece, Violet Kimmons, and that she was attending the St. Simeon's Select School for Girls for the new semester, here in New Orleans.

Bill immediately thought she was fizzing[11]. She had a silver tray, silver pot, and three teacups with her. Benny caught on and asked for all to sit down to a respite of tea. Bill was caught off guard. He was not used to being in polite society anymore. He knew how but was very rusty. He was glad he'd visited the haberdashery and arrived presentable. If not, the girl likely would have steered clear and not joined them. After she had poured all a cup of tea, Violet chose to sit on the small loveseat next to her uncle. Bill had to mentally remind himself that staring was bad manners, but it was hard not to do so. Violet sat quietly as Benny did most of the talking, or rather, asking. He inquired about how many members their club had in membership now, then about what Harmon and McTimmons were doing, to which Bill answered as ambiguously as possible, saying they had both purchased homes and settled, without mentioning the location or what they'd settled from.

Benny took leave from them for a while and Bill's mind raced. He didn't want to seem like an uninteresting dunce but couldn't quite find the right topic to bring up, so she did instead. They discussed how Benny knew Bill would be arriving sometime this month to pick up information about local plantations. Bill nodded a yes, confirming that he was doing just that. He remained silent without a clue what she would say next. Violet said that her uncle revealed to her that Bill was both a slave trader and a valuable piece to the southern state's economy. He tried to hide the surprise on his face, as that was probably the last thing he would have guessed she'd say. However, it did make some sense. A sweet, innocent thing like her could not possibly dream that men, like himself, tricked slaves into believing they were going

---

[11] fizzing was the nineteenth century equivalent of stunning

North on the Underground Railroad, only to then betray them by transporting them hundreds of miles away to be resold to a different plantation. Violet said she had no dealings whatsoever with Bill's line of work, but it must be a demanding job, traveling and gathering slaves for the auctions.

Going along with the lie, Bill said yes, it was a job that took great efforts not only in traveling long distances, but handling the slaves, who were always looking to escape, and some would, and could, become violent to reach that goal. However, he stated, they are not like the Yankees up north, a people of shopkeepers, teachers, factory workers, and other vocations of the indoors. Southerners are outside in God's fresh air, growing cotton, tobacco, flour, meat, and sugar, and managing the fields that put food on the table, improving everyone's life. He could tell from the look on Violet's face that he's said some things that she agreed with and liked to hear.

Mr. Benny returned to the room with a pencil and paper that he handed over to Bill. He told Bill he had the names and towns of Louisiana plantations in the area that were short-handed and needed more slaves. Benny listed Pleasant View in Oscar, Arlington in Washington, Belle Grove in White Castle, Eldorado in Livonia, and Frozard in Grand Couteau. Bill looked up as he finished writing and caught Violet staring at him. He blushed a bit, and moved his line of sight to her uncle as he laid down the pencil and stuck the paper in his coat. He had $25 to give Benny for his services but didn't want to hand it over in front of Violet.

Then Benny threw in that Violet and her family, his sister and brother-in-law, lived in Opelousas, basically just down the road from Arlington, the plantation in Washington. Bill immediately wondered why he'd said that. Was he trying to play matchmaker? Was he alluding that Bill should call on Violet after he delivered his stolen slaves to Arlington? Violet obviously picked up on it, too, and excused herself from the room. Benny and Bill rose, and Bill took the opening to hand Benny over the money for getting him the information he requested, then began walking toward the front door. Bill asked that Benny say goodbye to Violet for him and to tell her that, though he had business to attend to, he enjoyed meeting her.

GALLOWS RECKONING

The Campbell brothers met again at City Park and, together, they took the short walk to find a horse to buy. Bill knew exactly where to go, the Eclipse Track where he, Harmon, and McTimmons had sold horses after their preacher's stolen horse ruse. Once there, Bill described to the man they had dealt with before, Mr. Duplechain, that they needed three horses. He explained that they could be older and nearer to death than birth because this was about price. It turned out there were plenty like that, about to head off to their last auction, and in no time, the Campbell brothers were mounted.

Phillip and Simon were surprised Bill wasn't leading them eastward out of town but instead down to the Swamp, where the nymphs of the pave worked. Like his mentor, Bill wanted to indulge in the pleasures of the flesh, so the three brothers spent a few hours drinking and carousing. The house of ill-repute Bill chose was not fancy, but as he'd learned from an earlier visit, employed the youngest women of their selected line of work. The Madam not only sold flesh, but other goods a strait-laced apothecary might have access to but would not sell openly. After Bill had finished his fun upstairs, he had the Madam sell him some laudanum, a small vial of chloroform, a pair of fake eyeglasses, and a bottle of hair dye. Once all the transactions were complete, the trio headed east toward home—still a little drunk, spent, and all three with a satisfied grin across their face.

Once back at his place, Bill divvied up the money from the Mississippi River haul. After expenses of hotels, clothes, food, and horses, Simon gained $800, Bill took $1225, and, true to his word, Bill gave Phillip $550. He suggested they each take $125 for their Alabama journey. It likely wouldn't run that high, but it was always better to take 50 percent more than necessary as a safety net. Besides, if you did need it, there it was, and if you didn't, replace it in your stash when you return. Another resourceful lesson learned from Harmon. Bill had Phillip take their horses up the road to Pearlington, to McTimmons's stables. They would be traveling all the way to Tuscaloosa via water. They would sail from Shieldsboro, a few miles east of Pearl City, across the Mississippi Sound and up Mobile Bay where they would then find passage on a river paddle wheeler. They'd begin up the Mobile River, then to the Tombigbee River, and finally up the Black Warrior, all the way to Tuscaloosa. Once there, they'd acquire two horses, two mules, and a wagon with some type of covering, in which the slaves would ride and stay hidden.

Once more leaning on lessons he'd learned, Bill had altered his look. He was now clean-shaven, and his brown hair was dyed blond. He'd also left his casual straw hat at home for a broad-brimmed felt variety. After hanging around the docks at Shieldsboro all the first day, Bill and his brothers caught a break when a freighter sailing vessel, coming from New Orleans to Mobile, needed an emergency stop in Shieldsboro. One of the crew was in terrible abdominal pain and needed a doctor. Bill took the opportunity to inquire if three paying passengers could make the rest of the journey with them and received a yes.

Bill enjoyed watching his brothers, and they, just as he had, enjoyed their first trip on the salt water, taking in the sights of the dolphins playing at the bow and the noisy gulls following along. The green-tinted waters of the Sound contrasted with the brown waters of the slow-moving bayou and streams of South Mississippi the brothers were used to. The bright white sand of the offshore islands was also a sight unseen to the brothers, but after only an hour or so of enjoyment, a line of squalls met the ship and forced the Campbell's below deck.

After disembarking, they headed into downtown Mobile with Bill leading the way, Simon and Phillip following behind a good twenty yards or so. He was looking for the Coxworth & Bryan Company that ran most riverboats in Alabama. He found them at the corner of Water and Government Streets. By dealing with a major player, Bill was able to secure tickets all the way to Tuscaloosa on the three different steamers they would need to make the entire journey, and even have a printed copy of each boat's arrival and departure schedule. As usual, Bill had instituted a No Acknowledgment policy between the brothers on the steamboat. They were to act like they were total strangers all through the trip.

The steamer was smaller than those in use on the Mississippi, but Mobile River had nowhere near the power of that river, either. At Fort Stoddert

GALLOWS RECKONING

Landing, the steamer docked, and all the passengers transferred to a slightly larger steam paddle wheeler. Shortly after continuing the journey, the vessel pushed upward until the river split and became the Alabama River heading northeast, and the Tombigbee continuing due north. Approaching midday the following morning, the steamer put in for a stop at Jackson, Alabama to take on wood, cargo, and more passengers. Bill went to the dockside rail and took in the goings on. Jackson appeared to be a very prosperous port town, obviously one made rich from the transport of cotton bales from the interior downriver to Mobile, the northeastern US markets, and England.

As did many of these vessels, they carried and played a steam calliope on her top deck. The signal for all ashore to come aboard was when the music stopped. Bill enjoyed a cigar and a rye as he watched the commotion, when suddenly a fine carriage, pulled by four of the finest Morgan horses he'd ever seen, came roaring up to the gangway. Two men exited the cab, while two well-dressed slaves off-loaded their luggage. Bill's interest was piqued. One man was barely that, probably seventeen, maybe eighteen years of age, but nevertheless fashionably dressed. He was followed by a doddering older man, again well-dressed, but pushing seventy-five if a day. Bill was determined to find out more about these two and their situation.

Not moving too fast, Bill worked his way around the boat inquiring as to the identity of the distinguished older gentleman who'd come aboard at Jackson. The first mate told Bill he knew them as they traveled the river a half dozen times a year, between Jackson and Tuscaloosa. The elder was Eli Collier, the younger was his grandson, Perry Hawn. Mr. Collier was extremely wealthy and owned four cotton plantations between Jackson and Tuscaloosa, but his biggest reason for travel was that he was half-owner of the horse racetrack, also in Tuscaloosa. He added that Mr. Collier was a sharp-minded businessman, even at his age, but the grandson was arrogant, flaunted the family wealth, not as smart, and tended to lose big at the nightly casino aboard the ship, mainly due to excessive drinking. Bill thanked the first mate and took off for his stateroom. He had an idea.

Three years ago, while traveling near here with Harmon and McTimmons, Bill had studied with interest the promissory note that Mrs. James had given them for $1000 for the sale of Timothy, Weegie and L.T. He'd had the image seared into his brain, he looked at it so often. As he lay down in his bed, the idea came to him: he would forge a promissory note, tell Perry Hawn he was in financial difficulties and couldn't wait for the maturity, and thus would sell the note, heavily discounted off its face value, in exchange for money here and now. He reached into his traveling bags and found ink, paper, a cottonwood block, gaugers, and his new steel pen he'd picked up in New Orleans.

While they were in St. Louis, before meeting Johansson, Bill noted the finest bank building in town was under the name of Boatman's Savings Institution. He'd use them as an issuer for the note payable. He had decided on using a St. Louis bank for two reasons: forging a New Orleans banknote might cause local trouble and he could always say he'd purchased the horses in St. Louis. It took him all day, but he carved out a tiny steamboat on the wood block and, with ink, made an impression in the top left corner. In his finest hand, he began by dating the note three weeks prior and then added the amount of $5000, also written out in words. Next were the terms, of ninety days payable at 3% fixed interest. The note was secured by six racehorses known as the April lot C, 1842. Sold by holder: Jimeas Williams of Biloxi, Mississippi. To debtor: Andre Duplechain, Manager of Eclipse Racetrack of New Orleans. Holder in due course: Boatman's Savings Institution of 500 Olive Street, St. Louis, Missouri.

Bill was pleased with the outcome of his efforts; it looked every bit authentic as any note payable he'd ever seen. The next step was to get Perry Hawn away from his grandfather and ply him with a bottle of whiskey. That was no easy task as the old gentleman kept a tight rein on the kid. He began roaming the steamer, up and down the main parlor, relentlessly waiting for Perry Hawn to show alone, but he never did that entire second day traveling up the Tombigbee. Again, Bill found the first mate and inquired their location, to which he learned they were approximately twenty-five miles south of their next scheduled stop, Demopolis.

Then, just a few minutes later, on the eastern bank of the shore, came a tremendously loud booming noise. All looked over and were surprised to see a huge white smoke plume drifting away from the mouth of a war cannon. What was this? The steamer slowed down, unsure if it was under fire or not. A soldier upon a horse rode right to the water's edge and, with his sword raised high, began yelling at the steamer to stop. Behind him, two more soldiers on horseback also yelled for the steamer to stop, and even further back, four dozen men stood in a line with rifles shouldered at arms. The boat pilot nudged the steamer as close to the shore as the water depth would allow, two Negro deckhands pushed the gangway out, and it reached the muddy shore. The lead soldier dismounted, came aboard, and was met by the captain in the wheelhouse.

All eyes were on the wheelhouse when the well-dressed soldier and boat captain emerged, taking up stations to address the crowd gathered on the bow. The captain introduced the soldier as Major Frisby Siddon, head of the Alabama Militia in Marengo County. The Creek Indian nation was on the warpath. The terms of the Treaty of Cusseta had been violated and bands of hostile Creeks were raiding isolated farms and small villages, killing men and kidnapping women and children, before burning homesteads and crops. The major had been alerted by friendly Creeks that a war party of nearly one hundred braves was moving west toward the town of Linden. An attack was imminent. The major reached into his breast pocket, produced a paper, and read. It stated by order of the Alabama Governor, Benjamin Fitzpatrick, all able-bodied men between the ages of sixteen and forty-five were formally inducted into the militia for a minimum of one month, or until the major deems the emergency quelled, whichever comes first. All the white men aboard the steamer, except those employed by the ship, were now conscripted and had one hour to make ready for a ten-mile march.

Bill headed to his stateroom and changed out of his good clothes into his every day. He took upon the confusion to approach his brothers separately and told them to comply, as causing an issue would only bring upon their heads the last thing they needed, attention. He added to carry all the food, pistols and ammunition they could and stay out of the way of harm, if possible, to let someone else be the deceased hero.

The men on the steamer joined the other men ashore. All in all, the major had added twenty-two men to his ranks. A wagon pulled up and a soldier began handing out muskets, shot, and powder. They were told to form two lines, and off they marched toward Linden with a handful of friendly Creek Indians leading the way. As they marched, a sergeant worked his way among the conscripted, taking names, ages, and home addresses for the company records. After walking about two hours, they stopped for a break and Bill took the effort to seek out Perry Hawn, who was lounging under a mimosa tree. Bill introduced himself as Jimeas Williams of Biloxi and Hawn returned the formality. He let Hawn do the talking as he tried to gather information on what approach to try on him. Hawn immediately began to complain of their circumstance, being forced into the militia with no regard for what matters of financial importance they may have had waiting, or how this might cost them from making money by being conscripted. Bill sympathized, said it was uncalled for that gentleman be taken away. If the state wanted men, let them choose men of low station, where a week's time meant nothing financially. When they were told to form up again and march, Bill made sure he was beside Hawn, to continue to gain his trust.

After an hour more of marching, they arrived in Linden, a small place consisting of one main street traversing north and south and a shorter one traversing east and west. There were probably a dozen commercial buildings and fifty residences. It appeared that a courthouse was under construction at the far end of town. All the young women and ladies turned out to greet them with tea, coffee, cakes, and other sweet confections. After our greeting, the major had us move to a grassy open field just beyond the outskirts to have a rest. Bill found a spot by Perry, who had chosen to lay down a good fifteen yards away from the next person. Perry continued his bemoaning of the situation the governor had put him in and told Bill his family would see that there would be retribution in-kind toward the governor. Bill knew he'd made the right choice by listening to the teenager's arrogant boast. After a while, the major approached and called the men in close. He explained they were now a part of what was being called the Second Creek War. The Creek Nation, known as the Lower Creeks, had left their lands provided by treaty with the United States and were resisting being removed to the west. The federal government in Washington was aware, and US Regulars were boarding trains from outposts all around the Mid-South to form up and march into Alabama, to quell this rebellion. How long that might take was anyone's guess, the major said. He added that the volunteers would be spared picket duty tonight and the regular militia would handle that task. Also, bacon, hardtack, and an ear of corn each would be supplied via the company's cooks, but that the regular militia would eat first.

Those revelations touched another nerve with Hawn and more complaints flew. Bill listened, nodded, and emphatically agreed that sleeping out in the open didn't appeal to him either. Bill suggested after all the nightly activity subsided, Hawn and he should steal away and, at the very least, find a nice dry barn and soft hay on which to sleep. Hawn liked the idea and readily agreed. Later, a quarter moon rose above the tree line and Bill said it was time. He and Hawn brazenly walked right past two sleepy sentries toward Linden's main area and in no time found a dark barn with the door wide open. As they settled in, Bill set his trap. He started off by claiming Hawn was not the only one this conscription was going to cost money. There was a cotton broker in Columbus, Mississippi, known for buying notes payable at a discount of face value. That was where Bill was headed before this interruption. Bill mentioned how he had a $5000 promissory note and that this broker had said, by mail, he would buy before maturity for $3500. However, he had to present the note by the week after this one. That would not be happening. Hawn was interested as he sat up on his pile of hay and asked what type of note payable it was. Bill replied it was for six racehorses he'd sold to the Eclipse Track in New Orleans and a Mr. Duplechain. Hawn sprang up. He knew Mr. Duplechain! He knew him well, or his family and grandfather did. Duplechain owed Bill $5000, but he'd rather invest in a land speculation venture in Jackson, Mississippi over where the railroad depot, roundhouse, and workers quarters would be built. Bill stated he had inside knowledge from a slightly sleazy politician and had to move fast. He needed to sell the note but knew that would only be possible if he took a sizable discount and it had to be in gold and silver coin. The possibility of buying land valuable to the railroad would not last long. In secret, a company was already formed to build a line from Vicksburg to Jackson, and Bill wanted in on the ground floor.

Bill knew what to do next, from the lessons learned from Harmon. The next person that talks would lose, so he shut up. After a few moments, Hawn spoke, and said he possibly could help. He just happened to be in the racehorse business himself, had money handy that he was planning on using to buy three horses, but if he could get six for the same price, that would help him out. It would also help Bill, who needed money fast. Hawn started at $1700 for the note. Bill countered at $3000, and after a little more dickering, they met at $2200 and shook hands. Bill agreed to sign over consignment of the note to Hawn when they got back aboard the steamer, and Hawn agreed to hand over the money likewise.

All during his travels with Harmon, Bill had somehow learned to have an internal wake up mechanism for an hour before dawn. He did so, roused Hawn, and they snuck back into camp with no one the wiser. The men, volunteers, and conscripted began making their morning fires before dawn, in hopes of more bacon, bread, and coffee and they were not disappointed. A lieutenant in the militia then addressed them after the sun was up, said the friendly Creek scouts had been out all night looking for the advancing hostiles and should be back in camp soon. It turned out to not be soon at all. It was well after the sun was directly overhead that the first two scouts returned, their horses completely spent. The men watched in rapt interest as the officers spoke through the interpreter to the scouts.

All of a sudden, the major called all around him and announced the affair was over. Militia from Barboursville, in Wilcox County, and Cahaba, from

GALLOWS RECKONING

Dallas County, had successfully attacked the advancing Creeks from both the north and the south and killed more than half of their number, the other half retreating eastward. The combined militia only had four killed and seventeen wounded. Militia from Lowndes and Butler County had heard the battle and joined in the pursuit. The scouts said there were probably better than 300 men now pursuing forty Indians. It was just a matter of time before riders on fast horses got ahead of the retreating redskins and surrounded them. The threat was over, and the conscriptions were too. The regular militia and the conscripted both let out a mighty "Huzzah! Huzzah!"

Funny how word can get around. The major sent word for Hawn to ride a horse back to the riverboat; the Creek scout could walk. Bill could only shake his head. Evidently the major had political aspirations in the future, was planting some seeds of the good will of favoritism in the ground right now.

CHAPTER FOURTEEN

Reward and Risk

By late afternoon, they were back aboard the steamer, none the worse for wear except for a little shoe leather. They were treated like heroes by the other passengers and the captain had the main parlor converted for a massive feast for the returning volunteers. The wine flowed in copious amounts, but Bill kept his wits about him enough to wrangle Hawn off toward his lavish stateroom to exchange the money for the promissory note. Bill signed the back of the note naming Perry Hawn of Jackson, Alabama as recipient of the funds. They shook hands, and before Bill could even drop a hint not to mention the transaction to his grandfather, Hawn let it slip that his business was private and no one else needed to know, especially his grandfather, what had just transpired. Bill nodded and gave the young man a slight bow and bid him good night.

When the sun came up the next morning, the steamer was docked in Demopolis. The Negro deckhands were knocking on doors, waking all and saying it was time to disembark and board the other steamer in port if they were continuing up the Black Warrior to Tuscaloosa. Bill exited his cabin just as Phillip was walking down the passageway toward the bow. Other than brief eye contact, there was no acknowledgment.

The encounter took him back to how Harmon and McTimmons interacted a couple of years ago. Harmon believed any money taken in by the clan, or portions of the clan, was community property. When it was time to divide the money they had taken in during McTimmons' ruse as a preacher, Harmon suspected McTimmons of holding out. He confronted him, right in front of Bill, with his hand an inch away from his dagger handle. McTimmons had been passing the hat while inside the tent, preaching and leading hymns, but did not intend on sharing those gains. Harmon, with no visual proof, figured it out and told McTimmons to share, but that since he did the preaching, he should have 20 percent more than Bill and himself. It seemed equitable to McTimmons, and he emptied his small purse out, kicking in another $200. So, Bill's fake promissory note was somewhat similar. He'd share with Phillip and Simon but give them $300 each and keep $1600 himself.

The first mate on board had been a big help, but Bill needed a little more. He did not want to go all the way to Tuscaloosa. Bill approached the first mate later that day and, after some small talk, said he needed a favor. If it was possible, he'd like to disembark short of the destination. As he did, he pulled out a $10 gold coin and laid on the bar in front of the first mate, who deftly swept it up and said there would be no problem. The captain liked to be refreshed when the steamer docked at a port of any decent size and would always retire to his cabin for a nap prior to docking. So, the first mate would be at the helm the last two hours of the journey. He agreed to slow the boat down at a place called Foster's Ferry. There, Bill could just step off the gunwale onto the broad, open ferry boat. So the plan was set for the following day in late afternoon. Walking around the boat, he found ample opportunity to bring his two brothers up to speed on the plan at Foster's Ferry.

Just like the first mate had promised, the next afternoon, while most everyone aboard retreated into the main parlor for tea, coffee, or a libation drink when the bar opened, the Campbell's slyly departed with no one even noticing. Mr. Foster not only operated a ferry, but an inn as well. He advised the brothers that if they wanted a bed tonight, they better claim one, and pay now, as there was always a run on them just after dark. His wife would also cook supper and breakfast all for the bargain price of $4 per head. Simon complained, saying he'd got the same deal north of the Back Bay of Biloxi a few weeks ago, for $1.50. Mr. Foster nodded, smiled, took a long drag off his pipe, and said Simon might find a cheaper bed in either Scottville, twelve miles to the east, in Carthage, eleven miles south, or in Tuscaloosa, a dozen miles north. Take it or leave it, is how he ended. Foster had made his point and for $12 the brothers were able to share a bed and at least not sleep on the cold, hard, wooden floor.

After breakfast the next morning the brothers began their quest for horses and a wagon. Foster told them to go north and that halfway to Tuscaloosa, there was a man that could accommodate their needs. As they walked, Bill had Simon and Phillip practice breaking their southern drawl to try to sound more like a northerner. They'd be using the Underground Railroad ruse that had worked so well in the past.

The trio did not want to approach Tuscaloosa too close, as Tuscaloosa meant more eyes, more ears, more mouths, and more chances of something jarring a person's memory and then - trouble. So, once they found their mounts, they came back to Foster's Ferry and paid to be transported to the west side of the river. Bill's target was Greene County as he'd heard of fabulously wealthy men and plantations in the area. After less than a day's ride south, they were in Greene County. Simon and Phillip mostly kept quiet and let Bill lead. He set up a hiding spot between the plantation of Ephraim Banks and the widow Elizabeth Webb's plantations, well outside the town of Erie, and waited for slaves unaccompanied by whites to walk or ride by. Foster had given Bill the information that those two plantations owned the most slaves in the county.

Two old cotton-top males were the first to walk by, but they were well past their prime usefulness and more likely a drain on the profits of the farm than contributors. Bill let them pass. Later, Bill's sharp eyes saw a group of six slaves coming their way, but still nearly a mile down the road. He instantly instructed Phillip to stoke up their small campfire and start a batch of hoecakes. Upon closer review, it was a mixture of slaves that approached; a male in his thirties, a female in her upper twenties, two preteen boys, one girl barely into her teens, and a cotton-top female that lagged behind.

It was Saturday, and Bill had learned from Harmon that most plantations generally started to slow down the slaves's work in that afternoon in anticipation of their Sunday off. The slaves were a happy group, the females all singing a spiritual song as they walked their way down the dusty, hot road sandwiched between two massive fields of one-feet-high cotton plants. Before they reached the brothers's position, they paused and let the old woman catch up. When they reached the brothers, even with the large row of bushes the brothers hid behind, Bill came forward, stopped them, and inquired if anyone was hungry or thirsty. A hearty "yes, sir" was spoken by all.

Phillip came forth with a skillet full of hoecakes and offered them to the slaves, all while doing his best to add a nasal-quality inflection to his voice. Then Bill recognized the old lady. It was the same one who had escaped during the fight between Harmon and Timothy, the hulking slave. They had never bothered to learn her name, even after McTimmons shaved her head. If she recognized Bill, she'd sound an alarm and ruin the trap. Afraid that might happen, Bill disappeared from the gathering to the other side of the wagon and put on his fake eyeglasses. What to do? The others appeared perfect and, more than likely, were a family unit and those are highly desired by the plantation owners. He couldn't afford to miss out. There were three females of child-bearing years, a handsome and strong buck, and likely two more bucks just a couple of years shy of full physical maturity. Here was a jackpot of maybe $7500 or more.

This old woman had messed up his plans before. Not this time. Bill's plan was direct, but he had to have confidence that his disguise would work. He had to move fast, as Simon and Phillip were on the verge of losing them. They had not even mentioned the Underground Railroad yet. He zeroed in on the old woman. If she had not been in a dress, it would have been difficult to discern her sex. McTimmons's razor had cut so that very little of her hair had grown back. In a Eureka moment, Bill's heart and spirit rose. One of the preteen boys was leading the old woman by her hand so she would not step into the campfire or on Simon, who was seated nearby. The woman was very much blind!

The old lead-the-slaves-up-North-to-freedom speech worked, and soon all were in the wagon and passing around a canteen laced with laudanum. With this haul, there was no need to dally, and Bill quickly headed the troupe off to the southeast, toward Livingston. Knowing the overseer would likely not find out until Monday that six slaves were missing, Bill intended to get as far away from Greene County as possible. And then the rain started.

Three days after procuring the slave family, Bill's entourage was stuck just past Livingston, at the Sucarnoochee River, which was running fast and high. The small wooden bridge was washed away; they were stuck. Harmon's lessons were to never show your face twice in any one place too quickly, but Bill had no choice. He had to backtrack through Livingston and take the road due south, toward Moscow, Alabama. He and Phillip tied their horses behind the wagon and traveled inside the wagon, hoping to look like a different troupe that had passed through hours before. Luck was on their side, as they were able to ride through Livingston without being noticed due to the rain falling so hard that one could not see ten feet in front of their nose.

A day later they were near Marion, Mississippi and continuing southeast. Bill was familiar with these roads and places, having been on his introduction tour as clan leader, earlier with Harmon. Their trek went through Quitman, Paulding, Ellisville, Columbia, and Liberty. While Bill slept in the wagon, Simon and Phillip failed to turn south toward Port Hudson, Louisiana. Instead, by continuing west, they ended up in Woodville, where they were up against the Mississippi River. Here Bill realized the mistake. There was no bridge, of course, and no ferry, so Bill had them set up camp, well-hidden five miles outside of Whitesville, while he located Mr. Magee, the county's leading citizen, newspaper owner, major cotton planter, and a clan Chieftain.

Bill's first idea was to stop the journey here and have Magee buy the slaves. That would have been easy and safe, but Magee was in sell-off mode, saying he was going from three plantations to one, and if anyone was interested in buying a profitable newspaper, he'd be willing to deal. His wife had recently died, and he was seeing a much younger woman, a woman very interested in traveling and seeing the world. Magee was very much trying to comply with her wishes.

Magee sent his brother-in-law, Keith Elgee, to be the guide for the Campbell's. He would lead them from Whitesville to Ft. Adams, once an important military bastion set high on a bluff overlooking the Mississippi. The fickle river had changed course, leaving Ft. Adams landlocked and no longer of military value. From Ft. Adams, a road led south toward the Red River Landing Ferry, where they could cross into Louisiana in a secluded spot. Once they had found the road, Elgee turned back, but not before Bill gave him $5 for his trouble.

The next spot of civilization was Marksville, Louisiana, a three-day ride from the river, per Elgee. Thirty-six hours into their westward ride, the Campbell band and their slave captives could not have been any further sequestered from interaction with other humans if they had been marooned on a desert isle. Then it happened.

On a lonely stretch of a small, thin section of road, four armed horsemen suddenly came riding straight at the Campbell's. Bill wheeled his horse around to see about fleeing, but three more men on horses, brandishing shotguns, had cut off the line of retreat. They all wore masks and big broad hats that cast deep shadows on their faces. One man from the group at the rear came riding up-close, grabbed the wagon reins from Simon and forced them to stop. Bill, who had pulled his pistol, now holstered it back in place. The lead bandit felt obligated to introduce himself as the right hand of the Reverend Devil, John Murrell, but that his name was Virgil Stewart.

Bill had heard plenty about Murrell, known as the Great Western Land Pirate. McTimmons had an acquaintance who'd rode with him and told vivid tales of the atrocities Murrell committed against victims after robbing them. One night around the fire in the old deserted Indian village, McTimmons stated Murrell not only would rob and kill, but strip them of their dignity to boot. Murrell was sick in the head, as they say, not content to shoot or stab a man to death, but rather liked to cruelly torture them and took immense pleasure in doing so. Virgil Stewart he had not heard of, but if he spoke the truth as being close to Murrell, Bill knew big trouble was upon them.

Bill was kicking himself. He should have had Simon and Phillip on lookout, with shotguns ready. He should have been riding out front, at half of a mile, scouting for trouble. This mess was his fault. The robbers ordered everyone out of the wagon and off their horses. They ransacked the wagon first, somewhat disappointed to only find foodstuff, some ammunition, and one copy of *Hamlet*. That brought a huge roar of laughter to those who knew what it was.

The slaves were ordered back into the wagon and the two horses were confiscated. Then, four of the robbers came after the Campbell's personally. The three brothers were ordered to throw down their pistols and shotguns and they had no choice but to comply. Simon and Phillip had not had the time to learn one of the tricks of the trade for travelers, as did Bill. The robbers rifled through Simon and Phillip's attire, finding leather pouches of coins in their shirt pockets, pants pockets, and stuffed into their boots. It was almost the same for Bill except he had a hollow belt in which he'd stuffed as many gold coins as it would hold. He also, likewise, had a hollow hatband and boot heels for hiding more coins. They did not discover his belt, boots, or hat.

Bill decided to see if Virgil Stewart could be talked to. Bill mentioned that they were members of the Beaver Creek Clan. It made no impression, so he went personal. He asked Virgil if he knew James Harmon or Norby McTimmons. Stewart did not say anything, so Bill volunteered that he'd ridden with them for the last four years. He asked Virgil if he'd heard of the two Great Raids on Mobile? That made him pay attention. Bill said Harmon had planned them and that he had participated in both. The only acknowledgment was a slight smile and approving nod from Stewart, who then moved away a few feet. Then Bill, feeling his freedom of speech was about to be squelched, asked one more question. Did Virgil know Keith Elgee? Although there was no verbal reply, he completely froze for a moment, and his sly grin told Bill all he needed to know.

What would the right hand of the Reverend Devil do next? Bill knew what he would do; he would eliminate all witnesses, except, of course, the slaves. As soon as the robbers retreated a few feet, and as everyone leaned in to hear what Virgil Stewart had to say, Bill yelled "run for it!" and took off directly into the thick brush to the north side of the road. Three seconds later, he heard a cacophonous roar of shotgun fire and the zipping noise of pellets flying past. Bill turned and saw Simon was close behind and that Phillip was laying in the road.

He could not stop or even slow down. Escape. Escape. Escape was all he could do. He could hear his brother Simon tearing through the vines, creepers, and bushes behind him, and the loud cursing of Virgil Stewart ordering his men to kill them. Bill and Simon ran for a solid half hour as fast as they could go, all the while being ripped apart from the myriad of thorny bushes in their path. Finally, Bill announced it was time to stop running and instead find some place to hide and wait out their pursuer's patience. Simon was crying. Phillip appeared to have been shot point-blank, with two shotguns, and was surely dead. Bill told his brother they could grieve later, but right now, they must find safety. That's when Bill noticed Simon's right ear was hanging by a few thin sinews. A partial blast from one of the shotguns had ripped his ear right off. Bill took a handkerchief from under his hat and told Simon to press it hard up against where his right ear used to be, shocking Simon, as he had no idea he'd been hit. Bill told his brother to grab a leafy stick and erase their footprints in the soil, that they were going up a tree. Simon did as he was told and followed Bill as he scrambled up a gigantic Southern Magnolia until the trunk narrowed and could not support their weight. They were seventy feet above the ground and the thick, nearly-solid cover of green leaves hid them well. Within ten minutes, five of the robbers walked by underneath them, and then fifteen minutes later headed out of the woods and back to the road, none the wiser that their prey had given them the slip.

Bill and Simon stayed in the tree until mid-morning the next day. Warily, they retraced their steps back to where the robbers had overpowered them and shot Phillip. Expecting to see their brother all bloodied and pale, Bill tried to console Simon just before they reached the spot. To both their surprise, there was no corpse to see. Phillip's tattered and mangled straw hat was in the road, as well as a couple of their sleeping blankets, thrown aside in the wagon search.

Bill deduced they'd dragged Phillip off and dumped him somewhere even the scavengers would have trouble finding him. Standing around wasn't doing any good and there was no longer any reason to head west to the plantations, so without discussion, Bill began walking east and Simon followed. His brother's ear was a concern. McTimmons talked a lot about the curative properties of dandelion weeds. Bill saw a mess of them, picked some, and crushed the stems and flowers together. With a handful of clean gray clay as a binding agent, he pressed the poultice to his brother's head and tied it off with a bandanna. McTimmons claimed this was a Chickasaw Indian remedy. Both Simon and Bill hoped it would work.

Three days later, they reached the Red River Landing Ferry, but did not want to use Bill's scant remaining money to cross. Bill said they would wait until after he saw the operator extinguish his lanterns for the night, then borrow the ferry for a cross-river trip. It was not the easiest of tasks as a ferryman usually possessed massive arm, back, and leg muscles, but they eventually crossed. Bill would use dead reckoning to find St. Francisville. If he did, he knew traveling due east would lead them to Franklinton, where they could steal a boat, float down the Bogue Chitto River, eventually join the Pearl River and make it home at last.

CHAPTER FIFTEEN

The Clan is Lost

I set aside my pencil and paper, as Bill Campbell was distracted. The carpenters had started back at their work of building his gallows and he looked concerned. "Well, I was wondering?" he said, as he went over to the cell's exterior window and peered out to his left.

I struggled to say anything, before inspecting how far along they were toward finishing their job. He knew he would hang at noon the day following the completion of the hanging scaffold. I had given up trying to salvage the soul of Bill Campbell, in fact, I knew he'd just mock me again if I tried. Little had I suspected Roy Moody to come in and intervene.

Roy entered the jail house, went straight to the deputy desk, removed his pistol, and then approached Campbell. "Not too close, Roy," I cautioned, which made Campbell turnabout and come close to the cell door.

"Mr. Campbell, my name is Roy Moody. I just want to tell you it ain't too late to repent and I'd like to guide you and help."

"Why? Besides, I'm not interested," Campbell replied coldly.

"But after the...after the...you know, your words won't be able to reach the ears of the Lord. It'll be too late," Moody tried again.

Campbell pulled himself up higher on the cell bars and clenched his teeth, "I said I ain't interested! Got it, old man?"

Roy was at a loss for words. Later, he told me that he had spent a lot of time, had studied the Bible and had marked specific quotes and passages to read to Campbell in his last few hours, hoping to comfort him.

He retreated to his desk, sat down, and just stared at Campbell. I mentioned I hadn't eaten, so if he'd watch the prisoner, I'd go out. Watching as I passed by Campbell, I saw the outlaw lay down on his cot and pull his blanket over his head to signal to all he was not available for conversation.

I walked to the hotel's restaurant and ordered greens with onions, cornbread, and a pork chop. I could feel the eyes of the others looking at me. They were probably judging me for not making an appearance at Sheriff Smith's funeral service. They didn't understand, and I wasn't about to explain my work duties to a bunch of civilians. About halfway through my dinner, who should come strolling in but Roy Moody. I dropped my fork and waved him over. "What the hell are you doing here, Roy?" I said angrily, but still at a normal tone.

He stated that he'd ordered pie with his dinner, but they forgot to bring it to him when he was in here earlier. I glared at him, and he tried to calm me, saying Campbell was asleep. Infuriated, I sprang from my chair and hustled out the door, rushing the fifty yards to the jail. I caught Campbell with his right arm stretched as far out of the bars as he could shove them, flicking his suspenders at the exposed pistol Roy had left on the desk, where I usually sat and wrote. I immediately retrieved the gun and pushed it into the top drawer. With that, Campbell pulled his suspenders back inside the cell and sheepishly grinned at me. We just stared at each other for over a minute.

That did it. This was my career at stake. I'd be fired if Campbell escaped, and if he shot anyone on his way out, heck, they might prosecute me for criminal behavior. I vowed then and there, I would collect my daily belongings and move into the jail until after the hanging. Bill Campbell had my future in his hands, and I was not going to allow him to torch me.

Two minutes later, Roy came back with a slice of pie in hand. He told me to go finish eating and he'd watch the prisoner. With a look of major disgust, I shook my head and told Roy to go get my meal and bring it here. I gave him a quarter dollar, as I had not paid for the meal at the time of my leaving. Roy looked at Campbell, who was all smiles. It dawned on me Roy could be a major liability, so I must think for him as well as myself.

The jailhouse door slowly opened, and a shaft of bright light came in, masking the person inside the doorway. "Deputy? Deputy Bacot?"

"Yes, ma'am," I knew it was Ella Smith without seeing her.

GALLOWS RECKONING

"I hope I'm not interrupting, but I ran across this and thought maybe the office would like it back. It was Junius's back before I knew him, back when he was a county deputy," she explained as she retrieved a tin star from her purse and came forward, toward me at the sheriff's desk.

"How nice. Thank you, Mrs. Smith. Yes, I guess when he won the sheriff's office he didn't have any use for his old badge. As a matter of fact, now that Roy Moody is on as ancillary deputy, and we didn't have a badge for him, well thanks to you, now we do. Look Roy," I said, as I picked up the star and showed it to him.

With a mouthful of pie, it was all he could do to acknowledge with a head nod and smile. I offered Mrs. Smith a cup of coffee. I didn't know if she was wanting the company of people or not but thought it best to ask anyway. However, she declined and with a goodbye, was gone.

"What kind of pie you got there, Moody?" Campbell asked.

"Egg custard. Mrs. Conway in the kitchen said she made it this morning," he replied.

"Deputy, oh sorry, sheriff, Sheriff Bacot do you think I might get a piece of pie?" Campbell asked sincerely. "Tried to demote, you didn't I? Still getting used to it is all."

I smiled at his faux paus. He was so very different from other outlaws I'd had brushes with and completely different from the one other murderer I had spent time around about three years ago. "Sure, Bill, we'll get you a piece of pie. Roy, run over to the hotel after you finish up and charge it to the county jail's bill. Oh, and wear your new badge, too. And after that, walk the afternoon rounds for me. I'll sit with Campbell. And don't forget to bring me the rest of my pork chop and greens, first."

In about five minutes, Roy returned with my partial lunch and Campbell's pie and then left. Cautious as usual, I put the pie and plate about two feet from the cell door, on the floor. Campbell knelt and retrieved it but was stymied by the width of the bars and could not bring the plate inside. He protested, but I told him after that stunt with the suspenders, it had to be this way. He could maneuver his hand and the fork to feed himself through the bars, and he knew it, too. I let him eat and then asked if he was ready to continue telling me his life's tale.

Campbell started back into his story where he arrived back at his house in Pearl City with his one-eared brother, Simon. The first matter of importance was to get word to their parents that Phillip was dead, and worse, that they didn't have a body to bring home and bury. Mother would be doubly devastated, and father would heap so much anger and wrath upon Bill. Simon, not so much. Bill figured that if he would be riding to Jackson County he should call a clan meeting, since he'd be less than a day's ride to the meeting house.

The reunion with his parents was as bad as he'd imagined. Bill tried to rationalize it somewhat by saying these were ruthless highwaymen, of the infamous Murrell Gang, that had murdered Phillip. It was bad luck to have stumbled upon them and it could have happened to anyone. Neither Isaac nor Mary would hear it. They were furious about why Phillip was out in the middle of nowhere with Bill and Simon, and no, it couldn't have happened anywhere or to just anyone. If Phillip was here, making pitch or tending a flock of sheep, he wouldn't have had a run-in with factions of the Murrell Gang. Bill knew they were correct and quit trying to argue his point. He got on his horse and left. About fifteen minutes later, Simon caught up with him on the road toward Mobile. Bill was glad to have his brother by his side; at least he'd have one ally at the clan meeting tomorrow night. Five minutes after Simon's arrival, another horse could be heard coming up from behind them. Always wary, the brothers pulled off to the side and hid behind a wall of giant wild azaleas. The fast rider went whizzing by without seeing them, but Bill and Simon recognized the rider. It was their younger brother, John. They took off after him.

Bill was surprised at John's message. He was expecting more reproach from his parents, but it was more of the opposite. John wanted to join his brothers, taking Phillip's spot. A wide smile crossed Bill's face and taking the cue, Simon smiled as well. Bill agreed and was glad. Even though he was a little short of two years younger than Bill, he was half a foot taller and fifty pounds heavier. He'd be good muscle, and his happy-go-lucky attitude was welcome. Bill immediately slipped his hand into his saddlebag and gave John an old single-shot pistol he still carried. John beamed with pride and let out a joyous yell. Poor Phillip, Bill thought, he was never cut out for this lifestyle, but John, he just might be okay.

The three brothers camped by the banks of Beaver Creek that night, leaving them less than two miles from the clan meeting house. Bill went out hunting before sunup and, with his rifle, bagged a small yearling doe and a turkey. He would take the meat to the clan house and begin the cleaning process prior to cooking, so all arriving would be able to enjoy the feast. Bill tore off the turkey's long beard and presented it to John, telling him that since he couldn't yet grow a beard, this could substitute, and was a present for his hatband. Both Simon and John laughed heartily.

Being the first ones at the meeting house, Bill used the time to get things set up as he wished. First, he brought in his rifle and spare pistol and placed them under a blanket behind the chair where he would sit. Next, he arranged all the seats, two old church pews and seven rickety chairs, all in one grouping to hopefully prevent a division, not only physically, but philosophically. He instructed Simon and John to take the two seats nearest him when the meeting started in case something happened and he needed their help.

Just before dusk, a few riders began showing up. Bill met them outside and instructed them to try the venison and turkey. He had portioned out the deer meat into sections and had them split between two separate fire pits. For the turkey, he had segmented the legs, neck, back, wings, thighs, and breast and was frying them over a fire in a huge iron skillet they had found inside the meeting house. Bill had brought along a few pounds of bacon and fried a portion of it with the turkey to add flavor. Someone produced a bottle of whiskey, and it began making the rounds of the men gathered around, adding a slight party atmosphere to the gathering. The good mood lasted about an hour after sunset until George Welker and his followers showed up.

George Welker was likely the most senior member of the clan now, with McTimmons's retirement. He was probably in his upper forties and had been in the club since it was founded. Bill never had much interaction with him but remembered the meeting where everyone chose a side. Welker had followed Doty and Enoch Perkins who were against Harmon. Welker had nine men ride up with him, outnumbering the Campbell's and four others There was no guarantee those four would even side with Bill, should this meeting turn confrontational.

Once the meat was eaten and the men went inside, Bill called the meeting to order and immediately presented his brother, John, as a new recruit, providing he passed Initiation. It was at that point that George Welker stood up. He moved to the back wall of the room and was immediately followed by nine others. Welker addressed the brothers, saying it was a waste of time to discuss new members coming into the Beaver Creek Clan. He said they should vote now on dissolving the clan, naming the reason as lack of leadership and interest in the overall well-being and prosperity of the clan. Mentioning Bill and Harmon by name, he claimed that most members pay money into the clan's coffers to buy off the Chieftains, but the clan did so little in the way of major heists, it was a waste. There was a hearty "hear, hear!" from the nine men standing beside him.

Bill was taken aback. He thought Welker might try and use his majority vote to push some scheme through, not dissolve the clan. He thought about Harmon and what he would do. Harmon would likely call Welker outside for a private conversation and then slit his throat. Bill rejected that idea and instead, offered a compromise. Bill said the clan should stay together, and that if Welker had an idea of a heist, to voice it. He added that the Chieftains were worth every dollar they paid them. Just as Harmon had done in the past, Bill reminded the group that likely one-half of the clan members, at one time or another, had been spared an arrest, a conviction, or a jail sentence thanks to the Chieftains.

Welker then suggested the two votes be combined into one. A vote to quit paying the chieftains was also a vote to dissolve the clan. This hit a nerve with Bill. Welker said he knew the clan carried an account at the State Bank of Alabama, and if the clan dissolved, then the money should be withdrawn and equally distributed to any clan members in good-standing as of today. Again, a rousing "hear, hear!" reverberated through the meeting house.

Before Bill could even raise the issue, Welker announced Harmon and McTimmons were not in good-standing and would not receive a share. Bill intervened, saying Harmon had probably put most of the money in the account years ago, and should therefore be entitled to his cut. Once more, Welker suggested a vote to dissolve would also confirm Harmon and McTimmons were not in good-standing and a smattering of "hear, hear!" could be heard.

One of the nine men with Welker yelled out to call a vote. Bill tried to protest, but his voice was drowned out. Welker yelled out, "all in favor of dissolve, say aye."

The entire room, save the Campbell brothers, said aye.

The room quickly emptied after the vote, except for Bill and Welker. A staring contest ensued for a minute, until Welker broke eye contact and suggested he and Bill leave at this moment for Mobile, to be at the bank when they opened in the morning. All the clan members were planning to stay around the meeting house until Welker and Bill returned from Mobile with the money. Bill tried to get Simon to ride with them, but Welker nixed that idea and backed it up with a show of force from his minions. No, Bill and Welker would go to the bank alone.

About halfway into their fifteen-mile ride to Mobile, Welker asked Bill to rein up, he had something to ask, and it was important. Bill instinctively placed his hand on his pistol grip, but kept it hidden inside his coat. Welker said he had an idea. The clan members had no clue as to the amount of money in the bank, so why not give them one-third of the money, to be divided between them all. He'd take one-third and Bill could pocket the last third.

The concept of *honor among thieves* flashed through Bill's thoughts and he unconsciously gave a half-snort-half-laugh. Here's George Welker, venerable clan member, wanting to disband the group and stick it to them as he goes out the door. Ha! Bill told himself to think before he responded to Welker's corrupted idea. If he said no, Welker might try to kill him and take all the money. If he said yes, the secret might later get out, and he might be hunted down by the other thirteen clan members in retribution. Bill didn't want that hanging over his head for the rest of his life. The best option was to remove Welker from the equation.

Bill had his horse's left flank move closer to Welker's horse's right flank. "That's a really terrible idea, George," Bill calmly said to him. With those words, he drew his revolver pistol and shot Welker two times in the torso, knocking him off the saddle. Bill dismounted quickly and drew his knife. He was ready, should it be needed.

Welker was not dead, but it would only be a matter of time. Time Bill did not have, so he adroitly jabbed the knife twice into Welker's throat, once on the left side and once on the right, and then quickly stood back from the now-spurting fountain of deep red liquid shooting from the arteries of Welker. In less than fifteen seconds, it was all over. Bill took Welker's pistol and placed it in his own saddlebag, then rifled through Welker's clothes, finding two small leather purses of coins; one held about ten dollars, the other about two hundred. Knowing his ways, Bill then checked Welker for a hollow belt, heels, and hatband, but all proved to be of the normal variety.

Wanting to continue to Mobile and transact his banking business, Bill took Welker's body and his saddle about fifty yards into the woods and stripped the body, in an effort to let the creatures of the forest do what they do. Bill then set Welker's horse free. He saddled up and rode hard to downtown Mobile.

Bill dismounted on Royal Street and before entering the bank, he made his way to a general store and stood before a large mirror. He wanted to be sure none of Welker's blood had splashed him. He was clean, so he went five doors down to the State Bank. It was somewhat crowded, but after a twenty minute wait the cashier came to him. He presented his bank book and said his name was Benjamin Luckney of Mississippi, Harmon's alias. He filled out the necessary paperwork and made it clear he wanted his deposit redeemed in coins. Ten minutes later, the cashier came back with a leather bag and poured the contents on his desk as Bill watched. He counted out $942. Bill's first thought was that maybe Welker was right, the clan's money stream had been ignored, but nevertheless, he bundled up the money and again rode hard back to the meeting house.

Fearing a confrontation with Welker's supporters, as they would certainly question why Welker was not present, Bill had to think. He took $150 out of the bag; $50 for him and the same for Simon and John. Once he had tied his horse to a tree about ten yards shy of the meeting house, Bill spied Simon and John both lying under an oak, relaxing. He quickly made his way to them and told them to mount up. As suspected, upon entering the house, he was questioned about where Welker was, to which he replied that Welker was overcome by the call of nature and was squatting in the woods not twenty-five yards from them. He then produced the paperwork signed by the cashier and the bank president, verifying the account balance of $942. He pulled out the bank bag of coins and let it fall to the floor, then apologized, saying that was all there was. A huge discussion started up, and half the men went for the bag, its contents spilling on the floor and causing more chaos. Bill slipped out the door unnoticed, mounted up, and he and his brothers took off at full speed, never again to see the clan's meeting house.

CHAPTER SIXTEEN

Time Marches On

Campbell seemed anxious. The carpenters were hammering less and less now. They were getting close, as was Campbell's impending execution. He had roughly twenty hours left on earth. I knew it. He knew it. I was also aware, if there was going to be any attempts by his friends or family to spring him free, it would likely happen tonight. I would be here with Deputy Daniels and Roy Moody, but that might not be enough. Should I bring in some trustworthy men and add them to the staff? Possibly. It couldn't hurt to be cautious. I started thinking of who I would ask to assist and even wrote down their names. After hard thought, I realized bringing in too many people could defeat the purpose. Two guards in front of the jailhouse, and two behind it, would suffice. Deputy Daniels could take the rear, with one volunteer, and Roy Moody could handle setting up on the sidewalk outside the front, with another volunteer. The town sported two army veterans: Harvey Harris had fought in the Mexican War and was known as a crack shot; Pete McGinnis had done US Cavalry duty in Texas against the Commanches and would be a good addition. When Roy got back, I'd send him to ask Harvey and Pete for their assistance and for them to sneak in a nice afternoon nap, because they'd be awake all night.

I had another important chore to complete. I had to get the rest of Bill Campbell's life story on paper before his time was up. Campbell was, again, at the window, straining to look to his left and see what stage of completion the gallows were at. All of the sudden, Campbell backed away from the window, rushed to his chair, and lit a new cigar. When the door to the jailhouse opened, I could see what caused his rush. Micah Bailey entered the room, avoided gazing toward the prisoner, and made a beeline for me at the sheriff's desk.

GALLOWS RECKONING

"Afternoon dep...I mean Sheriff Bacot," Bailey said as he removed his hat. "I was just speaking with the carpenters, and they say they'll be done within the hour. I must say, they went all out on their effort. Most gallows are simple steps, a platform, a crossbeam for the rope, and supports. These fellows really overbuilt, in my opinion, unless they were told to build one to last for the next fifty years. Y'all must plan on keeping me busy for the next few decades. Anyway, when they're out of the way, I'll do my rope rigging and run a test with a sandbag to make sure everything is like it should be."

Bailey extended his hand. I shook it and told him we'd be having a gathering of lawmen here at the jailhouse all night tonight, and he was welcome to drop by and chew the fat, if he was so inclined. He said thanks and that he'd likely drop by after supper, to which I insisted he come eat with us at 6:30 sharp. Bailey accepted the invite and left, once again intentionally diverting his eyes away from Campbell.

Just as I was digging out my pad and pencil, Gideon Gray, one of the carpenters, came into the jailhouse. Gray told me that aside from sanding and greasing around the trapdoor, they were done. He wanted to know if they could they get paid now, before the bank closed. I told him the work had to be inspected, but I couldn't leave the prisoner alone. Gray said he'd watch Campbell, but I told him the prisoner must be guarded by a member of the law. I said if Roy or Deputy Daniels was to come in, I would go make not only my inspection, but the state executioner would, as well. If all that was possible, I had no trouble paying them the $8.50 each that Sheriff Smith had promised them. With that he left. satisfied.

I waited to see who would come through the door next. Campbell picked up on the same feeling, stood up, and watched the entrance with me. After a couple of minutes, we looked at each other and then took our spots for his talking and my writing. Campbell placed a half-smoked cigar between his teeth and went to light up, but discovered he had no more matches. I knew Sheriff Smith smoked on occasion so I went back to his former desk, found a small metal box full of Loco Foco matches, and tossed them through the bars to Campbell.

"Much obliged, sheriff," he replied as he lit up. "Lemme see, where'd I leave off?"

Looking down at my pad I quickly scanned the final paragraph, saw the man named Welker, and decided to ask Campbell how he felt about murdering Welker. He gave me a shoulder shrug, inhaled slowly, and exhaled a copious blue stream of smoke in my direction.

He went into detail, saying he knew an outlaw's nature well, and the only reason Welker had not killed him when they were first alone, was he was waiting until they had cleaned out the clan's money in the bank. Once that had transpired, the next time they were alone, Welker would kill him.

I was again transfixed by the outlaw's brain power. I'd have never made that deduction. My mind doesn't work that way. But Campbell's mind instinctively told him his life was at risk as soon as he was worth killing. I made an exclamation point in the margin of the paper and drew an arrow pointing to the last few sentences.

Campbell continued.

No, Welker had to be eliminated. This was a good opportunity. If it wasn't today over the money in the bank, it would surely be later, over something else. He and Welker were too much alike to get along, so one killing the other was bound to happen. The man who hesitates generally loses, and Welker lost. Killing Welker was business; he didn't hate the man, or have any grudge or vendetta against him, it was just something that had to be done. He and his brothers rode their horses as far as Biloxi, and considered riding all night to Pearl City, but a howling storm, complete with hailstones, forced them to shelter in Biloxi at the Shady Oaks Hotel until morning.

Once back in his home, Bill told Simon he was anxious to pull a heist. The paltry $50 haul for riding to Mobile and dispatching Welker along the way had upset him. Also, it still stuck in his craw that he'd been robbed of a fine family of slaves by Murrell's man, Virgil Stewart, and missed a hefty pay day. The goal of becoming a rich man at a young age seemed to have taken a detour, and he was ready to get back on course. First, there was the matter of McTimmons's wedding, which was more of a delay in Bill's opinion, but after that, he was ready to make some money. In the meantime, he would rusticate, wait for the wedding, and write a letter to Mr. Benny in New Orleans.

Bill had an idea to pull off a kidnapping. Where were the rich people? New Orleans. Would it be possible to find someone rich—someone just *visiting* New Orleans—not from there and with connections that might end up involving the law? Mr. Benny would be his eyes and ears to find just that kind of person. Using the clan's mystic alphabet, Bill wrote to New Orleans and requested Mr. Benny identify someone to kidnap that met Bill's criteria.

In the meantime, there was a social event he had to attend. McTimmons wedding to Bradish Allen's daughter's was quite the lavish affair. There was wine everywhere, with shrimp, oysters, and crab on ice to feast on. McTimmons seemed happy, as did the bride, but the biggest of all the smiles was on Allen's face. He had six daughters, and this was the first to marry off and ease the financial burden on his house. After the ceremony, Bill sought out Harmon, who was sipping on a bottle of wine while seated on a loveseat that had been brought outdoors and nestled under a huge water oak. He wasn't alone, but with Bradish Allen's second oldest daughter, Fanny, who was all of fourteen years old, while Harmon was likely pushing forty. However, in Bill's opinion, Fanny didn't look fourteen, but had the look of a real woman of closer to twenty. Harmon immediately requested Bill bring McTimmons to him so the three of them could take a walk and discuss a business proposition.

McTimmons was more than happy to get away from his new wife. McTimmons told Bill she had made him swear not to drink alcohol on their wedding day, so he needed to get away and have a dram or ten. Once the three outlaws were alone, they walked Allen's driveway for privacy. Bradish Allen had approached both Harmon and McTimmons with a money-making scheme. And money-making it truly was. Allen had been on his legitimate job of ferrying people up and down the Pearl River, between here and Jackson, and a stranger took him aside. Allen said the stranger was old and nearly decrepit, but still had his mind about him. The stranger wanted to sell his metal ingots, chemicals, tools, and stamped dyes used to produce counterfeit gold coins. Allen said the old man would even give instructional lessons for a while, until they mastered the art. However, the old man wanted $3000 for all his equipment, and Allen said he could only raise a quarter of that. Allen wanted to bring in McTimmons, Harmon, and Bill as equal partners on the investment. McTimmons said he wished his livery stable was doing better business and that he was in. Harmon said he wanted to see samples of the old counterfeiter's work. If it passed his eyeball test, he'd join. Bill said no. He had a scheme cooking now, and after that, was planning on a raid of Alabama plantations for slaves to sell in central Louisiana. He had too much going on at the present, but he might buy in later. Done with their walk, the three were not surprised to see Bradish Allen awaiting their return. Harmon took him aside and gave him the outcome. Allen then took Harmon, alone, down to his boat on the river, to meet the old man and see his workmanship. McTimmons finished off a half-gone bottle of whiskey and returned to his bride inside the house. Bill took his cue to leave and mounted up back for Pearl City.

Bill laid out with his brothers in Pearl City and told them all he'd learned. If you have some money, you need to appear to have a means of support. He suggested that Simon take up selling firewood, and that John hideout while posing as a fisherman on the Pearl. Bill said he would continue to make charcoal and the occasional barrel. Bill loaned John the money so he could buy a fishing boat, on the promise John would pay him back within six months. With their false occupations set, they set about creating their false scenarios. Later in the month, Bill received a letter back from Mr. Benny. Again, in the clan's secret code, it said he knew of someone that would be worthwhile for Bill to kidnap.

The next day, Bill saddled up and rode to New Orleans alone. He found Mr. Benny at his home on Camp Street. As he walked up the front sidewalk, he wondered if Violet Kimmons would be visiting while she was in school. Bill knew he looked completely different from that first meeting with Violet. He had kept up the ruse of being a blond with his dye kit, and he'd started growing a beard just before McTimmons's wedding—it was in full glory a month later. He'd bought a fancy silk top hat upon his arrival in the city this morning and was eager to show it off.

Alas, Bill was crestfallen to learn Violet had gone home for a four-week school vacation. However, Benny had good news. He explained that he was a weekly regular at a poque game every Thursday night, upstairs at Two Jacks Public House on Decatur Street. A few months ago, when the new school year began, a flashy, young medical student at the Medical College of Louisiana began playing with Benny's group. He was the son of a friend of a friend. His name was Lane Kent. He was from Alexandria, where his father, McKeegan Kent, was a successful cotton planter and steamboat and racetrack owner. Lane had grown up around gambling and, after his graduation from the College of Charleston, decided on a career in medicine. Lane was the only son of a multi-millionaire father who would gladly pay the ransom for his kidnapped male offspring.

Together in the parlor, Bill and Benny discussed the operation. Benny had already scouted out Kent's route home after the card game. Kent lived in a townhouse on St. Ann Street and his route took him through Jackson Square. In the square were ample amounts of large, overgrown clumps of azalea bushes and trees, perfect for hiding in to spring a midnight trap on an unsuspecting rider. Benny told Bill he would go to the north-facing window of the poque room at 10 p.m. and light two matches consecutively for his cigar as a signal that Kent attended the game that evening. The games started at eight and ended at midnight. Benny told Bill that young Mr. Kent was an outlandish dresser, wearing bright-colored blouses and pants and a huge, oversized Mexican sombrero for his headgear. Bill was operating alone and would use his supply of chloroform to incapacitate Kent, bind and gag him, and hide him in a hogshead barrel, in a rented delivery wagon. Benny had also arranged to hire a small merchant sailboat owned by a Captain Blaylock, who was the kind of man who, if paid the right amount, would ask no questions about the cargo. John and Simon would meet him at the dock in

Pearl City and complete the delivery. Then, Benny would ride to Alexandria and hire someone to deliver the ransom note to Mr. Kent.

Bill ruminated over the amount of the ransom. Lane Kent had a lot of value and Mr. Kent was very wealthy. Still, there was a touchy aspect. He had to ask for enough to make all this effort worthwhile, but if the amount went to an outrageous number, Mr. Kent would call in experts in law enforcement. Bill wanted an amount to satisfy his work, but not touch off Mr. Kent's ire. He wanted Mr. Kent to see the amount, make a rational business decision it must be paid, and then for it to all be over. Bill settled on $5000.

They didn't have to wait long after the plan was settled. Thursday night was only forty-eight hours away. Benny signaled during the card game that Lane Kent was present. Bill, in disguise, set up to ambush his prey amid a low, thick fog. Just after the church bells finished their midnight ring at St. Louis Cathedral, Bill saw a lone rider, unmistakable in his yellow coat and sombrero hat. Stepping into his path, Bill grabbed the man's reins with one hand and wrenched them free, while pulling his pistol on the man with the other. He ordered Kent down and behind the bushes before getting behind him and gagging his mouth and nose with chloroform. Kent's struggling ceased and he collapsed in a heap within a few seconds. Bill quickly tied his hands and feet and gagged his prisoner. Kent was about five feet six and one hundred and ten pounds; he slipped into the hogshead barrel without incident. Bill easily guided his horse and cart down to the docks and met his sailboat at the pier, as was discussed yesterday. The boat had a captain and crew of two middle-aged Negroes. A nice, steady, westerly breeze enabled the captain to set up a nice beam reach, and they were out of the river and into the Gulf just after daybreak. At this pace, Bill would be tied up in Pearl City by early evening, when there was little to no activity or prying eyes. Kent was off-loaded and Bill paid the boat captain his $75.

All was going as planned. Mr. Benny would be off this same morning, for the four-day journey to Alexandria with the ransom demand. Now it was time to sit and wait. Bill instructed John and Simon to keep up normal appearances. Lane Kent would be chained and kept in his gag in the back bedroom. He was given bread and water and a bucket to relieve himself, nothing else. The next ten days would be a long, but important, wait. Finally, on day thirteen, a message arrived from Mr. Benny. The same boat captain Bill had used two weeks before, Blaylock, delivered the letter. The ransom would be paid at place called Grand Island, a small, elevated sandbar at the mouth of Lake Borgne. Bill was to land on the east end of the island, Mr. Kent's representatives would land on the west. A meeting would take place in the middle of the island at noon next Friday, for the exchange, where Lane Kent would be released and the ransom paid. Bill made arrangements for Captain Blaylock to transport him out to the island next Friday.

The day came. Before sunrise, Bill and his brothers had moved Lane Kent, now back inside the hogshead barrel, to the sailboat. His brothers, both armed with long guns, would row out to Grand Island as soon as possible. It began.

Grand Island was only six miles off the coast, and halfway there, Bill could see another, larger sailboat anchored just off the western edge. As they drew closer, Bill could make out the forms of five men: three with long guns, one Negro, and one dressed in a fine suit and hat, all already on the beach. The captain tightened up his sails to make better time and Bill moved to the bow to see better. Was the captain going to make a course adjustment for the east end of the island? They were only a half mile away and the boat was still heading for the center. Bill had gone over the instructions with him when they left the dock. Had he forgotten? Captain Blaylock then did the unthinkable. He steered the boat even more off course and was heading straight for the west end of the beach. Bill was livid and screamed for him to adjust his direction, but he just smiled as his Negro deckhand came up on deck and aimed two single-shot pistols directly at Bill. Bill froze, unsure what was happening. The captain hailed to the men on shore as he pulled his centerboard up and beached his boat. They were immediately swarmed by the men from Mr. Kent's group, guns up and ready. The Negro in their midst held back, but Bill recognized him as Blaylock's other deckhand. What was he doing here? Bill cast a look back toward land. He could barely make out his brothers, likely almost two miles away. Lane Kent was quickly released from his barrel and the man holding a shotgun nearest Bill used to butt end to crack Bill's head, knocking him unconscious.

When he awoke two hours later with a terrible headache and huge knot on his head, Bill was in the Hancock County jail in Bay St. Louis. The amiable jailer filled him in on the details. During their initial sail over, Lane Kent had slipped out of his gag, conversed with Blaylock through the air hole, and then somehow cut a deal. The men Bill thought were with Mr. Kent were actually lawmen from the neighboring Harrison County. Captain Blaylock had sent his deckhand to Alexandria who contacted Mr. Kent and, together, they devised a rescue plan and set it in motion, for a $500 fee. Lane Kent was in decent shape, a few pounds lighter due to his meager diet, but no harm was done. The man in the fine suit on the island was the father, millionaire Mr. McKeegan Kent. The jailer had no idea that Bill's brothers, while they were supposed to participate, saw the problem and fled back to Pearl City.

Bill was arraigned and charged with kidnapping under Mississippi law. Three months later, a trial was held in Bay St. Louis, where he was found guilty and sentenced to four years at the state penitentiary in Jackson, better known as the Walls. Of all his wrongdoings, this was his first mistake of which he would pay a price.

Bill's inherent good nature rubbed off on the guards, and while he was not treated well, he was also not beaten or starved like the other miscreants were. Simon hired an attorney, and he was able to have Bill's sentence reduced in half. On the day he was released from prison, he'd expected Simon, John, or maybe even Harmon to greet him and provide him transportation, but there was no one at the gate, save for an old blind man asking for a handout. Unsure what to do, Bill walked down Lamar Street, then took a left on Amite. There, standing on the corner, in front of two loaded wagons and a string of mules, also packed to full capacity, were his parents, Isaac and Mary.

GALLOWS RECKONING

His mother called out to him using his childhood nickname. She came forward and hugged him deeply. Isaac stayed back. She said this was a biblical moment, as in Corinthians, 5:17: "Therefore if anyone is in Christ, the new creation has come. The old is gone, the new is here."

"Do you remember that? Do you? We, your father and I, are making a new creation. We sold the homestead and we're moving to Texas. We want you to make a new beginning, too. Leave that world of sin behind and come with us. We're going to raise cattle and hogs. We'll be needing good hands to work. We'll portion off a part of the farm as yours, and yours alone. Come with us, Billy, please, for my sake and yours. You can find a nice girl and marry and raise a family," his mother pleaded.

Finally, Isaac spoke, echoing his wife's words and asking Bill to come to Texas.

Bill wanted to say something, but he went blank. He was touched that his parents had detoured from their westward journey to come and take their son to Texas with them. They still loved him, even after all the bad things he was sure they had heard about his life, even despite Bill's part in involving Phillip and costing him his life. Finally, his thoughts gathered.

If he'd pulled off the sale of the slave family from Alabama, if the clan's bank account had held substantially more and been worthy of stealing, and if his kidnapping scheme gone off as planned…well, yes, combined with the money buried in Catahoula Swamp, he'd be close enough to call it quits. Those were all wishful thoughts. No, Texas was not in his foreseeable future, and for two reasons: first, his three latest ventures had ended in catastrophes, and he didn't like the feeling of failure; and second, he was not a rich man at a young age…yet.

He told them of his decision to return to South Mississippi and asked where in Texas they were settling. His father said he'd purchased land outside of Preston Bend, in the Northeast quarter of the 28th state. Bill hated to ask, but he was penniless, so his father gave him $60 to get home. His mother began crying and Bill gave her one last hug before walking on down Amite Street, looking to buy a horse.

DOUG WHITE

150

CHAPTER SEVENTEEN

Cascading Catastrophes

Bill's new horse wasn't much to look at but was a spirited filly with a fast-paced trot. He made it to his house in only five days. No one was at his house and, from the looks of things, neither of his brothers had been there in at least a month. It took a few minutes but, looking near his bed, he saw a note. It was scribbled in a shaky hand which Bill recognized as Simon's handwriting. It stated that he and John had joined up with two former clan members, O. Reed and Z. Williams, on a journey deep into Florida to steal a herd of horses and run them back up to northern Louisiana. Bill was immediately worried. He knew Reed and Williams; both were more muscle than brains. Simon and John were unseasoned in the ways of crime. They could steal, sure, but doing it right, where you leave no clues for the law, is another thing. He wished he knew their departure date. Maybe Harmon knew?

Bill made the short ride up to Jourdan Community and Harmon's home. He was greeted at the door by Bradish Allen's second youngest daughter, Fanny. She wasn't fourteen anymore, Bill thought, as he looked at her and noticed a bulge in her mid-section. She was pregnant and evidently not for the first time, as just then, a baby cried from one of the back rooms. She invited him in and, as she retreated toward the cries of the baby, mentioned that James was in the back getting water from the well. Bill continued down the long central corridor until he reached the backdoor, which was already open. He heard the squeak of a metal cylinder going round and round as Harmon hauled up a bucket of fresh water. They met on the back porch and Harmon yelled into the house that the water was ready for the baby's bath. They shook hands and stared into each other's faces.

They'd both changed. Bill's two-plus-year hiatus in Jackson was the longest time they'd spent apart since Harmon had demanded Bill turn fifteen years old before joining the clan, now fourteen years behind them. Bill's features had hardened; his nose was sharper and his eyes keener, almost just slits in his face. Harmon had numerous wrinkles around his eyes and mouth and what little hair he had left was mostly gray.

Bill teased Harmon about being an old married father, but Harmon assured him that he wasn't all whipped and broken. Harmon was still involved in moving stolen slaves, horses, and cattle, but had devised a system where he didn't have to stray hundreds of miles away from home. Now he just operated as a middleman, transferring goods. Bradish Allen knew a network of men, located in southern and middle Alabama and Louisiana, that would instigate the theft of slaves in either Georgia or Texas and bring them as far as the Mississippi state line. There, Harmon or McTimmons would buy them, greatly discounted of course, and transport them safely upstate from South Mississippi. From there, it was up the Pearl River on Allen's boat to Monticello, where they'd all disembark and go the remaining fifty miles to the Fork in the Road Slave Market in Natchez. They'd make the sale, catch a steamer down to New Orleans, live the high life for a couple of days, catch a transport boat to Shieldsboro, and be back home all in less than two weeks.

Harmon admitted he'd stolen an idea from Bill. Transporting stolen people inside of a hogshead barrel solved many problems. Teenage slave girls, due to their reproductive potential, were now selling higher than big buck field hands, so the new gang specialized in stealing those girls. It just so happens that a pair of them fit nicely into a hogshead barrel.

Once more, like when he was young, Bill had to admire Harmon's thinking. One thing did bother him, though. He'd learned back then not to commit one's crimes locally, but to stray far and wide. Although this was not like robbing one's next-door neighbor, handling stolen goods so near to home made him uneasy. He asked Harmon if he knew any news of his brothers, to which Harmon said yes, but insisted he first come in, sit, and share a drink of the spirits.

GALLOWS RECKONING

Harmon said he'd run into old acquaintances of theirs, Reed and Williams, outside of the courthouse in Mississippi City at a political debate for governor, which always meant a plethora of free whiskey was on hand. Reed told him he'd joined up with John and Simon Campbell for a job in Florida, but on their first day traveling east, who should stop them but Mr. and Mrs. Campbell, bound for Texas to buy land. The parents pleaded for both Simon and John to come along with them. The boys said the only way they'd quit the life and move West was if Bill did so first. Bill now understood his parents 150-mile detour to Jackson.

Harmon continued, telling Bill that the four went almost to Tallahassee to take a herd of stolen horses from the St. Augustine area. Reed, Williams, Simon, and John paid the men and started west. However, more of that same St. Augustine gang was lying in wait for them, just short of the Alabama border. In a running gun battle, the eastern gang regained back about half of the horses, leaving Simon and John's group with about twenty or so. It got worse when an old gang member named Shoemaker recognized the four and wanted hush money. He threatened to alert the well-known local vigilante group, Captain Slick's Men, that stolen horses were being trafficked through the country.

They refused Shoemaker's threat.

It took two days for a band of Slickers, as they were called, to confront them near the old Vine & Olive Colony. Williams and Reed made a getaway, but not the Campbell boys. That was where Reed and Williams's knowledge of the likes of Simon and John Campbell ended. Harmon told Bill to fear not, that he would investigate the matter. He knew there was a good chance Shoemaker would pop up in Biloxi from time to time. He knew many informants there, as well. Perhaps he could even find some that knew of Captain Slick's Men.

Harmon and Bill left that night for Biloxi, and Bill was briefly happier than he'd been in quite some time. It was like old times to ride with Harmon. Bill finally had the opportunity to tell his mentor about his successful commandeering of Johansson's keelboat and the handsome profit it turned.

Once in Biloxi, Harmon led Bill to Howard Avenue, which had a string of saloons, gambling halls, and secret bordellos lining both sides. At the second place they entered, Harmon recognized a local snoop, always in the know of local gossip and rumor. Harmon bought a bottle and seized three glasses. Bill watched him go to work, cleverly playing up that he was in search of information, while at the same time, not appearing desperate to achieve that goal. A little over an hour later, the snitch, enjoying free whiskey and a free cigar, called another man over to their private table. His name was Ladner, and Ladner's brother occasionally rode with Slick's Men. Ladner had no knowledge of the Campbell brothers's whereabouts but asked for twenty-four hours and, if they paid reward money, would meet them at the same place tomorrow night. Bill chimed in he'd be willing to pay $10 for information. Ladner said $20 would be better, and an agreement was finalized.

The following evening, all parties assembled and Ladner produced information. His brother had gone along on a hunt, as Captain Slick's Men called it, for horse thieves trekking through north of Mobile. There were four thieves, but the Slickers only caught two. He did not know the men's names, but their physical descriptions seemed accurate to Bill, and the time frame fit, too. Ladner described what happened: as was customary for the Slickers, Simon and John were both branded on the top of their hands. The right hand was scarred with a letter "H" and the left with a letter "T", which stood for horse thief. They were then tied to a tree and given a dozen lashes across the back with a cruelly modified bullwhip. Their money, horses, boots, guns, food, canteen, and hats were all taken away, and they were left in the wilderness to fend for themselves against bears, wolves, snakes, and panthers. The Slickers called it nature's justice. The exact area they were left was unknown, but it was northwest of Mobile for a full day's ride. He added the two were alive when they were left, but had no idea now, as that was at least eleven days ago, maybe more.

Bill saw his work was cut out for him. Knowing where they were captured and the nearby vast wilderness, Bill thought he had a good chance of locating his lost brothers. They should be somewhere in the vicinity of where he'd hidden alone, back when he'd burned the Jackson County Courthouse sixteen years ago. Bill finished his drink and told Harmon he was ready to go, but Harmon said they should wait and gather their thoughts.

Harmon and Bill eventually rode east, to the small village of Krebs where Harmon's parents lived. They ate well and rested for half a day before beginning their trek north, into the vast wilderness northwest of Mobile. It was Harmon who deduced that if Simon and John were alive, they'd be trying to move west, toward land, and possibly people they knew. Bill agreed and they rode a north-south line, looking for the two missing brothers.

On the fourth day, Harmon announced that he could only search for two more days as he was due to meet a shipment of stolen Louisiana slaves destined for Georgia. On day five, Bill was up early and had started a campfire for breakfast. John saw the smoke rising from about a mile away and came into their camp, explaining that Simon was back in the woods, too weak to walk. Harmon had anticipated this and brought an extra horse with them, so the trio went in, found Simon, and put him on the spare horse. Simon and John were given fresh water, deer meat jerky, and some hardtack. They were both in a pitiful state, but Simon was far worse, dangerously thin and possessing no energy.

Simon's back looked terrible. The bullwhip's damage had festered and there were maggots writhing in some of the deeper wounds. Bill helped Simon down from the horse and took him into the shallows of a little creek. With his bare hands, he cleaned Simon's wounded back and then removed his own blouse for his older brother to wear.

John's problem was his feet. He could not bear to place his full body weight on them due to the pain that brought on. The bottoms of his feet did not have any skin that had not been cut, punctured, or ripped open.

Bill questioned his brothers about the Slickers's numbers. John said there were at least two dozen, all armed with shotguns and revolver pistols. Bill knew it would be foolish to try and exact revenge against that. However, the snitching ex-clan member, Shoemaker, would eventually pay for his disloyal treachery.

Bill brought his brothers back to his house. They both needed medical attention, but sending for a doctor was not an option. Bill got them comfortable and then rode up to Pearlington to ask McTimmons for advice. McTimmons instructed Bill to procure some rabbit tobacco, bits of onion, leaves from a willow, and lots of moss. Those four ingredients would be combined, watered, beaten into a pulp, and then placed directly in or on the wounds of his brothers. After two days, he was to remove the concoction and clean the wounds with clear water, then bandage them in muslin for another three days. Bill did as he was told and both Simon and John healed nicely.

While Bill was housebound nursing his brothers, Harmon, McTimmons, and Bradish Allen finished their first run of bogus coins. Despite vehement objections from Allen, who wanted counterfeit coins of a higher denomination, Harmon's will prevailed, and they produced Liberty Head gold coins of a $2.50 face value. Harmon argued that higher-valued coins would be more difficult for a merchant to make change with and would arouse suspicion. After all, getting the merchant to make legitimate change for the passer was what counterfeiting was really about. Stubborn Allen, outnumbered by Harmon and McTimmons, was extremely unhappy. Allen stated he wasn't used to taking orders, he liked giving them instead, and that with the clan dissolved, the rule to listen to Harmon was no longer in play. Harmon asked that there would be no exchanging of the fake coins within twenty miles of their homes and that they never exchange coins at places of business they frequently visited on the road. Each man took a hundred of the fake coins with them as they split up the spoils of their first run.

McTimmons and Harmon buried their counterfeit near their homes, intent on retrieving and using the next time they traveled away. Allen, on the other hand, stuck about twenty-five coins in his pockets and went around on his daily route. It wasn't even a week into this venture when Allen visited the general store in Hobolochitto, not ten miles from his house. He bought an axe, a tomahawk, and a saw. He gave the store owner three coins for his

$5.50 bill and received $2 of legitimate currency as change. Next, he went to the saloon next door and had two beers for a quarter, paying with his counterfeit coin and pocketing the $2.25 of legitimate change. Next door to that was a barbershop, and Allen used a dollar of their services and received $1.50 back, giving him $5.75, made in just an hour.

The next morning, Allen went to his stable to saddle up for a ride to Biloxi and Mississippi City, intending to pass more counterfeit money. He heard three riders come to his house but stayed back as his third oldest daughter told the riders that he was in the stable. Allen mounted, but not quick enough. It was two deputies from Hancock County and the barber from Hobolochitto, who immediately confirmed that Allen was the man who used the fake money. The barber had noticed the coin date of 1838, and with its nearly new condition, would have to be minted next door in New Orleans, but the identifying "O" was missing. Coins bearing mint marks were relatively new, having just been added to all US coins in 1837, ten years before. There was no mint of origin designated on the coin Allen gave him.

For some reason, the sheriff believed Allen's story that he was an innocent victim of someone else's counterfeit scheme. Allen said he'd received the coins in payment for a few recent services, like taking a man upriver to New Columbia. Pressed hard by the sheriff to reveal the man's name, all Allen could think of was a neighbor in Pearlington, named Jim Charles. The deputies were soon out on the road to arrest this other man, and Allen was released with the stipulation that he not travel. Allen was in a panic, and without Harmon or McTimmons's knowledge, placed the counterfeiting machinery, dyes, ingots, tools, chemicals, and his last seventy-five coins on his boat and dropped them overboard into the Pearl River.

That night, Bradish Allen sat on his front porch, alone with his worried thoughts. Harmon and McTimmons were out of their $1250 investment into the counterfeiting. Then there was the fact that he'd falsely implicated Jim Charles as the criminal. Plus, he'd been ordered not to leave town. What could he do? Allen began to pace, first around his porch and then his yard. Maybe dumping the equipment in the river was a mistake? Maybe trying to get rich quick was a mistake? He cringed at the thought of what might become of his four remaining daughters. With his wife dead and buried, who would take care of them? In a flash, it hit him how willing the sheriff had been to believe his concocted tale. Was this sheriff crooked? Would he take a bribe, or arrest him for even suggesting one? What if he accepted the bribe, but blackmailed him for the rest of his life and bankrupted him? What about the barber? Yes, that was better. Maybe the best route out of this mess was to bribe the barber into dropping the charges. But how? Whatever he had to do, it had to be done in haste, as this trouble was only getting bigger by the day.

Bradish Allen was beside himself, and the more he worried, the more he knew this was beyond his capabilities. He needed a professional. His son-in-law, Harmon, would know what to do. He'd have to be compensated, of course, but that was just the price he'd have to pay. The Charles's were a large family, known for sticking together and going outside the law if they thought the situation warranted it. With his hat in hand, Allen rode over to Jourdan Community and explained the desperate situation he'd foolishly caused. At first, Harmon told Allen it was his own bed, and he would have to lay in it, refusing to help. Allen's daughter, Fanny, begged, pleaded, and cried for Harmon to help her father. After his anger calmed some, it took Harmon less than ten minutes to concoct a plan.

First, Allen had to pay back Harmon and McTimmons. Allen said that he had almost no money, but he offered to sell them his house and land for $1. He was not going to need it anyway. As soon as possible, he was leaving for Texas with his four unmarried daughters. Harmon agreed to the payment.

Next, they had to set the trap for Jim Charles. Harmon's idea was to get Bill Campbell to draw up a fake deed for a property in New Orleans, stating Bradish Allen as the said owner. They would use Mr. Benny's house for the ruse. Allen would give the attractive property on Camp Street to Charles, in exchange for dropping the charges. They'd take Charles to Benny's house, have him look at the property, and convince him it was worth the trade for dropping the charges. They'd bring Charles back to the sheriff of Hancock

County and he would make it clear that there was no cause to pursue Allen for counterfeiting. Then, they'd return Charles to New Orleans to take official possession of the house. Their ally, Mr. Benny, would be sure and have friends over at the same time. Benny and those friends would unwittingly provide cover if law enforcement ever came to verify Allen's story: Charles made it to New Orleans, went to Camp Street to see Allen's friend, but then left alone for the seedy area of town and disappeared without a trace. That happened all the time in New Orleans. Harmon's plan called for Charles to be dispatched on Bradish Allen's boat, in the middle of Lake Pontchartrain, then weighted down and sunk to the bottom. Allen was all in. He had no choice but to be.

Harmon's elaborate plan worked and, like he'd done to Bill Campbell at the courthouse burning, he'd made Allen do the actual killing of Charles, on Allen's boat. The blood on the hands of the one needing favor only strengthens their resolve to forever keep silent on the matter. Allen kept his word and drew up a bill of sale for his property, to sell to McTimmons and Harmon for $1. He loaded up his four daughters, sailed to New Orleans, and caught a steamer for Galveston, Texas.

Bradish Allen was lucky to have escaped. Whether he knew how lucky was debated in Hancock County for years.

The next instance of everything Allen touching turning to horse manure would involve Harmon and McTimmons. No one living in Pearlington was old enough to remember the short-lived Republic of West Florida, established in 1810. No one knew why the choice riverside bluff, where Allen would build his house, was left vacant well after the establishment of the town. A series of disasters, first with Yellow Fever and then back-to-back yearly floods in the 1820s, reduced the population of Pearlington to less than ten adults. Allen arrived and, seeing this prime land of ten acres, simply commandeered it for his house, kitchen, barn, and stable. Time went by and nobody thought anything about what he'd done.

Years prior, the local government of Spaniards had plans to construct a ferry and a ferryman's house there, so no one was allowed to build on it.

However, the United States eventually gained control of western Florida, and the Spanish ceded their rights to the land over to the Americans. With the area being so thinly populated and the government agents being so sparse, there just wasn't a hurry to record the government's deed of the land in the county courthouse. That's when bad timing showed her ugly head.

The government agent had finally submitted his recordings just a week prior to Harmon and McTimmons purchasing the house and land from Allen. When the two went to the courthouse to record their new deed, they were dumbfounded to find out Allen had sold them a pig in a poke. Even though he was the father-in-law of both men, they badly wanted to kill Bradish Allen. Going all the way to Galveston was too much effort, so they decided to quickly sell the land to someone else before it became common knowledge Allen's home was built on government property.

Everyone in South Mississippi knew that if one wished to sell real estate fast, the man to contact was Harley Mays. Mays's place of business was in the Beaver Community, in north central Perrine County. Harmon and McTimmons rode there as fast as possible.

They met with Mays who, surprisingly, told them he had exact knowledge of the place they were offering. He'd ridden to Pearlington many times in the last decade, buying property for next to nothing when most residents fled town. The reason he recalled the place was because a rather drab and unimpressive home had been built on the best piece of Pearl River real estate south of Jackson. He'd buy the land and buildings for $500, to which Harmon countered $1000, and they settled on $700. Harley Mays gave them $300 cash and a $400 note on The Agricultural Bank of Natchez.

Both McTimmons and Harmon knew that once Mays found out that he'd been scammed, he'd come looking for them. Even though they both had wives and young children at home, circumstances demanded they flee. Leaving enough money for their wives to live on for better than half a year, they geared up and rode east, back toward the Alabama state line where they knew myriads of hiding places, including the old, deserted Choctaw village. If their wives needed to contact them, Harmon's father, in the village of

Krebs, was the method. There hadn't been time to go by the Catahoula Swamp and dig up their wine cask of coins, and after leaving money for the wives, they were both in dire straits for money. They rode to Pearl City, and as the injured Campbell brothers were well on their way to recovery, Bill decided to join his old pals.

Hanging around a popular saloon in Biloxi along their easterly travel, Harmon took a quick read through the Mobile-based newspaper. It seemed a Mississippi man, by the name of Davis W. Summers, had been given the job of constructing a double ferry over the Chickasawhay River and a ferryman's house at Leakesville, Mississippi, with a $1225 budget. Harmon recognized the name. A few years back, when making his tribute rounds to the clan chieftains in Greene County, he noted a fine mansion a few miles south of Leakesville. The Chieftain said the owner, a Davis W. Summers, was an architect and builder of public works around south Mississippi and Alabama. The Chieftain went on to say that the time to catch him was when he'd just been given a job, as the county and the state both allow him an advance salary for him to buy materials and hire workers. This newspaper was only three days old. He and McTimmons were dead broke. So, onto Leakesville. Bill went, too.

McTimmons, prepared with his laudanum, and after killing a couple of squirrels and infecting the meat with the drug, was able to silence Mr. Summers's trio of large guard dogs. The night was moonless as the three men crept silently up the drive to the mansion, with their shotguns at the ready. It was an hour or so past midnight, and the house was dark, save a few glowing embers from the main parlor's two fireplaces. The wooden stairs were partially carpeted and helped muffle their boot noises as they made their way upstairs to the bedrooms. Harmon had always marveled at McTimmons's eyes, especially at night, jokingly calling him half-cat for his superb night vision. They went from room to room and, when they were satisfied only the largest, master bedroom was occupied, they returned there and simultaneously lit matches. A middle-aged woman sat up, startled, and screamed. In a flash, Harmon was on top of her, halting her with a pillow to the face. They waited to see or hear if anyone had been alerted by her screams, but after about two minutes, realized she was all alone. They stuffed a small lace handkerchief in her mouth and tied it into place with Harmon's bandanna. Explaining that they did not wish to harm, but only to rob, Harmon demanded to know where the money for the ferry job was hidden. She made no response at all. McTimmons showed her the blade on his knife. Her eyes widened and Harmon removed the gag. She said she didn't know, that it was her husband's area, but he was not here and had gone to Mobile to hire carpenters. Harmon slapped her hard across the cheek and she fell over in bed, but only for a moment. She said they could beat her all they wanted but she couldn't tell them where the money was.

With his anger seething, Harmon pulled back his fist and held it, trying to break her will. He demanded to know where to find the money. She said nothing, so he smacked her jaw and she slumped over onto her left side, falling out of bed, unconscious. Harmon decided they would ransack the house and tear it apart to find the money. Leaving Bill to stand guard over Mrs. Summers, and with McTimmons up in the attic with a whale oil lamp, Harmon began a search of the bedroom's chest of drawers, desks, and armoires. Unsatisfied, they tore the first floor of the house apart, flipping chairs and pulling down draperies. Spent and exhausted, they all collapsed in the main parlor. Their entire heist and internal destruction of the mansion had produced a paltry $19. It was time to leave. Harmon had McTimmons and Bill collect some nearby drapes and table clothes. He stoked the dying fire back up and tossed the fabric coverings in the fireplace, leaving them half hanging out in an effort to set the place ablaze. They rode away to the south, turning occasionally, hoping to see the flames lighting up the night sky, but they never did. Would nothing go their way? The outlaws then fled to hide from the coming vengeance of Harley Mays.

CHAPTER EIGHTEEN

A Gun in Every Hand

I asked Campbell to pause his story, as my hand was experiencing some cramps. He knew where he was in his life's story, and he knew the hour of his death was approaching. I didn't voice it, but the term "deadline" was never more appropriate. Moving to the back of the jail, I stoked the fireplace. Not that it was very cold outside, I just didn't want it to completely die. Checking the clock, I saw we had about two more hours until 6:30, when the extra guards and the state's executioner were to arrive. Campbell never told me exactly where in his life's timeline he was, so, using caution, I returned to the deputy desk and picked up my pencil again. "Alright. I'm ready, if you are?"

Campbell picked up his tin cup and stuck his arm out of the cell bars. "Might I indulge in a spot of rum or rye whiskey? I'm not picky," Campbell said. I nodded in agreement and filled his vessel halfway with some of Sheriff Smith's old bottle of rum. Ever the gracious guest, Campbell thanked me and settled in to recall the next part of his life.

After their unsuccessful robbery of the architect's home, the three men split up. McTimmons went back to an old hideout he'd used before, a small log home in the deserted old Choctaw village. Harmon went to his parents's house in Krebs, to inform them of his whereabouts as he laid out. The last place he'd hid, before finding the old Choctaw village, was on the site of the ruins of old Fort Maurepas, on the east side of Biloxi's Back Bay. Bill was not hiding; he rode northwest. He had a score to settle with Keith Elgee, the man who'd set up his stolen slave caravan with the Murrell Gang's lieutenant, Virgil Stewart.

DOUG WHITE

Bill knew this murder would be different. The other murders at his hands were either for power in the clan or to remove a witness from his crime. Killing Keith Elgee would be for nothing but pure revenge. As he rode west toward Baton Rouge, the inclement weather soured his mood further. A three-day storm kept him soaked, cold, and hungry. He'd purposefully not gone by Pearl City, knowing his brothers would try to join him. It was better that he acted alone. He knew he'd find a meal and a bed on Floridana Street, in Baton Rouge. The weather was clear the next morning, and Bill's horse got him to Woodville just before dark. A cart full of corn, driven by two old darkies, came by on the road south of town. Bill gave them each a counterfeit coin for information on Mr. Keith Elgee's location. They informed him that he nearby, at his house, and to follow them. Ten minutes later, the darkies pointed to a respectable frame house, set back about one hundred yards from the road, before continuing. Bill tied his horse to a tree in the nearby woods and pulled his shotgun from the saddle scabbard, holstering his scattergun. Checking to be sure it was loaded, he snuck from tree to tree, staying on the side porch of the residence. Bill could smell the food and saw, through the open window, the form of Keith Elgee sitting at the head of a large table, alone. There was activity in the house—Bill could hear a woman and several children's voices coming from beyond the dining room. Bill gently pushed the curtain aside and leveled his shotgun on the windowsill. He could have blown Elgee away right then, but he wanted to let Elgee know who he was and why he had his gun pointed at him.

Bill called to Elgee, announced himself by name, said that his double-crossing trick with Murrell had not been completely successful, and let him know that he would pay for it with his life, right now. With that, just as Elgee was standing up to make a run for it, Bill gave him both barrels simultaneously. He saw the bloody result, turned, and ran fast as the screams of Elgee's wife and kids rang through the early evening air. He leaped upon his horse and took off on a full run, south toward St. Francisville. From there, he avoided Baton Rouge, cut due east to go to Franklinton, and rode the Bogue Chitto River southeast into the Pearl River, toward home.

I had to interrupt Campbell, as he'd mentioned this was a different kind of murder. "Bill, you really committed first-degree murder. It was premeditated. You acted, and you took the life of another human. Did that ever occur to you?"

He stood up, stretched his back and arms, and walked to the exterior cell window as he answered, "Like I said, it was different, but only in the reasoning. When you get right down to taking a man's life, you either do or you don't. Your victim doesn't know it until it's too late, generally speaking. Mr. Elgee was sitting in his own house, with his own family, at his own table, and probably the furthest thing from his greedy, stinking mind was that the fellow he set up to get raided by the Murrell Gang was coming for his revenge that night."

Campbell swung around to see if his callousness upset me, but after hearing his tales for that long, it had no effect. "I'm following you. Elgee expected Murrell's lieutenant to kill you, didn't he? That's how Murrell worked. I've heard of him, too. So Elgee put the chance of you coming after him seeking revenge at zero."

"Precisely, Sheriff Bacot, precisely. And...that's what makes it so sweet. You should've seen all the blood drain from Elgee's face when he saw me and that shotgun ten feet away, about to send him into eternity. It was worth the ride all the way there in the rain and slop."

"This Elgee was obviously married and with some youngsters. Did that bother you, Bill?"

"Not in the least. He should have had them in mind when he decided to get into the double-crossing business. It was his fault, not mine."

Feeling very satisfied, Campbell put his rum to his lips and sipped as he moved back to the slat chair to tell me more.

After dispatching Keith Elgee and returning home, Bill was eager to rest and recuperate before gathering his brothers for another venture. His use of hogshead barrels was handy, just as Harmon had said. Just because Bill was laying out at home, it didn't mean all was quiet in the outlaw world.

Harley Mays, on his own, had not been successful in locating McTimmons or Harmon. So, to assist his effort, he unofficially put a price on their heads—verbal only—and passed the word in every saloon and brothel between Mobile and New Orleans that he'd pay for information leading to the discovery of either of their hiding places. For McTimmons, who was holing up at the deserted Choctaw village with the old tribe member, Manitema, it was a simple case of being in the wrong place at the wrong time. The old Choctaw rarely came to town, but took his canoe down to Pascagoula, as he was craving some coffee and sugar. As he waited for the clerk at the town grocery store to come and attend him, he heard two white men he did not know discussing the $50 reward someone had put on Norby McTimmons. Manitema followed them next door to the post office and eavesdropped as they revealed it was Harley Mays in the Beaver Community in Perrine County who'd set the bounty. Manitema forgot all about his coffee and started walking north, toward Mr. Mays.

Four days later, Manitema presented his prize information to Harley Mays, who insisted Manitema come along and act as guide. It was Mays, the old Choctaw, and three young and well-armed employees of Mays. Manitema told them that McTimmons usually drank so much liquor at night that he slept until mid-morning. The group showed up just after dawn, ran into McTimmons's little cabin, and immediately started blasting away with shotguns and pistols. McTimmons probably ended up with twenty or more holes in his body and was dead before he knew what hit him. Mays was pleased with the result, but the swift ending left him unsatisfied. When he found Harmon, he wanted the renegade to know who was doing it and why his life was being snuffed out.

I stopped writing and glanced up at Campbell's face to see if the remembrance of his colleague's death would merit any emotion. "So, McTimmons gets basically ambushed, right?"

GALLOWS RECKONING

"Yep, bunch of scared hens, if you ask me. McTimmons deserved better. He used to talk a lot at night when we were out on the road working. He said he wasn't afraid of dying, didn't relish the idea, mind you, but knew it was inevitable because of the type of life he'd chosen, he wasn't going to die in a soft bed of old age. He just wanted an even chance, he said often. But that scoundrel Mays made sure he didn't. Anyway, that damned Indian...I wanted his hide, I would have my revenge on his red double-crossing skin."

"Continue on, Bill," I asked, and he stuck his cup outside the bars for another drink. I took it and put in half rum half water, a grog mixture, and handed it back. He didn't seem upset with the watered-down version and thanked me.

So, McTimmons was dead. Bill believed that if Harmon had heard the news, he'd have skedaddled somewhere far away, but Harmon was held up so deep in the woods, he never got any information. He was betrayed by an old member of the Beaver Creek Clan. It only happened once, and it was ten years prior, but Shoemaker had accompanied Harmon to visit Harmon's father in Krebs. Later, when Harmon knew more of Shoemaker's slippery skin, he'd regretted it, but it was too late. Shoemaker heard of the bounty on Harmon's head in a Howard Avenue saloon in Biloxi. Not wasting time, he rode over to Krebs and told the elder Harmon's that he had urgent news for their son and needed to know how to relay his message. Mr. Harmon told Shoemaker where he was and, in a flash, he was riding north to alert Harley Mays and collect his reward money.

Mays held off on giving Shoemaker the $50 reward until he saw Harmon with his own eyes. Three days after Shoemaker rode to see Mays, he'd handed over the money. Mays and his three hired hands watched Harmon come out of a lean-to he'd built and start his morning campfire.

Shoemaker did not wait around. As soon as he had the money, he left for Mobile. As Harmon wandered away from his crude little home to gather firewood, to where they assumed his guns were, they pounced. Two ran behind him so he couldn't retreat while Mays and the third hired hand boldly walked straight up to Harmon. Mays shot before he even spoke a word, wounding Harmon in the foot so that he couldn't run and causing a massive amount of pain. Mays had his men place Harmon in front of a gigantic oak tree's trunk. Mays made his little speech of retribution and gave Harmon a chance to say any last words. Bill had heard later in a Biloxi saloon that Harmon told them all to kiss his ass and that he'd see them in hell. Mays and his men executed Harmon via firing squad and left him for the worms, ants, and buzzards.

I paused once again, as this was another major turning point in Campbell's life. "How did that feel? Losing your friend and mentor. Oh, and you said he'd treated you as a kid brother when you were just starting out didn't you?"

"I'll admit it, Larry, hearing word of Harmon's death did upset me for a bit, and then I got angry, but that subsided after another day. The revelation that I was the sole survivor and sole owner of the wine casks in Catahoula Swamp, with nearly $70,000 in gold coins, took the sting off me. Anyway, when I heard about Harmon being dead, I rode to Krebs to see if his folks knew the bad news, which they did. I was surprised by the old man. He offered me $2000 for Harley Mays's scalp and verification of his demise. The money was not really all that tempting, but the idea of revenge for my two friends that had made me what I had wanted for years, to be a rich man at a young age, that did it. Revenge was boiling in me. I'd kill Mays for the rotten deeds he'd done to my friends. My only real friends I ever had," Campbell said, then paused for a moment and took a sip.

He continued, explaining, "Scuttlebutt in the saloons of Biloxi informed me that Mays traveled well-armed and typically with three bodyguards, one of which was his only son. So, I wanted to out gun him. I'd take my brothers, John and Simon, and recruited two old clan members, one by the name of H. Perry, the other S. Woods."

Once more, he paused, and it had me questioning if the recollection of his mentor's murder was revealing a side of him I did not think he possessed.

"So anyway, we rode north to the outskirts of Beaver Community and waited for Mays to ride out. We waited nearly a week in the hot June sun before he and one of his men rode by, heading south. We stayed hidden, well back from the road, and followed at a safe distance. His group turned east on the start of their second day's ride. I knew the area well and he was within an hour's ride of the India community, where there'd be witnesses, so I made my move there in the wilderness. Mays heard us riding up fast and broke from the road, down a skinny little footpath that led to a cabin in the woods. They quickly dismounted and ran inside the cabin. We dismounted and took up positions surrounding it. Perry and John immediately started firing into the dwelling, before I made them stop wasting the ammunition. I yelled out I only wanted Harley Mays and I would fight him alone, if he'd come out alone. He laughed and rejected the offer, called me the biggest liar in Mississippi. The sun was directly overhead and sweat was rolling down my forehead into my eyes. To counter the heat, I removed my coat and rolled up my sleeves. I gathered my troops and relayed my plan to systematically fire at the cabin while Simon rushed the back door and pushed pine straw up next to it and lit it on fire. We'd be ready when they came out of the front. Then it all went to hell."

Campbell, reliving the gun battle, began to quickly recount each bit of information.

"We were popping off a few occasional rounds to hopefully make them keep their cabin doors and windows buttoned up, but I had not counted on there being five more sharpshooting men inside the cabin, and another half dozen in the woods behind the cabin. Mays had set us up. I had to assume it was Woods, because he fled when the first shot was fired. He had evidently told Mays of our ambush, led us straight to this cabin, packed with his men, itching to fight. The doors and window all opened, as did the rifles and shotguns of Mays's men. The six men in the woods began firing and moving from tree to tree in our direction. Simon was trapped on the side porch. We couldn't shoot in that direction for fear of hitting him. The side door opened wider and out stepped Harley Mays, shotgun at the hip. He and Simon fired simultaneously, from point-blank range, each catching a chest full of shot, falling as blood oozed from their shirts. The other men rushed out and came straight for us. Thick white smoke from the burning pine straw billowed over our position. John caught a bullet to the hip and fell. Perry took off into the deep forest, I jumped in my saddle, turned to fire one unaimed volley from my shotgun. I dug my boot heels into my little philly's flanks and she took off. I heard gun report after report fired in my direction, one even taking my hat with it and grazing my scalp, but I made it off and away, relatively unscathed. Mays's men did not follow me. I can only guess it was to treat the wounds of their leader. I rode directly for old man Harmon's place, to tell him there was no scalp but that Harley Mays was pushing up daisies and he could verify in the next edition of the *New Orleans Picayune* or *Mobile Register and Journal*. They hid me, and two weeks later, Mr. Harmon rode into town and found a copy of the Mobile paper with the article about a gun battle involving Bill Campbell's outlaw gang and the brutal, cold, bloodied murder of one of South Mississippi's most outstanding citizens, Harley Mays. He then paid me the other $1000 of the $2000 reward he'd offered for killing Mays."

Campbell rose from his chair and paced his small cell, obviously angered through reliving the tale of his brother being killed by Harley Mays.

"My brother John was captured and taken to the Marion County jail in Columbia. Perry eventually found me, and I paid him his $500 share of killing Mays. I procrastinated writing to my folks in Texas, to tell them that my outlaw ways had cost them another son, Simon. Plus, it was time to cash out, so I rode to the Catahoula Swamp to retrieve the $70,000. The map! In the brutal heat before the gun battle, I'd removed my coat, which always kept the map to the gold's hiding spot. I'd go in anyway and find it from memory if I had to, and then flee South Mississippi. After that, it would be a good time to skedaddle to Texas."

Campbell said he did remarkably well in remembering the triangulations of their spot. "I almost went straight to it, but my heart sank. Right where I was about to dig, there was already a fresh gaping hole in the earth. My map had led someone right to the $70,000. The map was in clan code, which meant someone from the old clan had found his treasure. I was furious, slamming my shovel over and over into the pile of earth that'd been moved aside from the recent digging. The worst thing that could have happened, did. All my efforts, brushes with the law, brushes with death, it was all for naught. Almost eighteen years of operating on the outside of the law, and I had roughly $1200 to show for it all," Campbell said, defeated.

Campbell crumpled down on his cot and said quietly, "Shakespeare's King Lear. Act one. 'Nothing will come of nothing.'"

CHAPTER NINETEEN

A Last Supper of Revenge

It was almost 6:30 and time for the meal. Deputy Daniels and Roy Moody arrived, each carrying a basket of food from the hotel's restaurant. "Time to eat, Bill," I said as I shoved my pencil and paper into the drawer.

"All right Sheriff, if you'll just open the door, I'll take my seat at the head of the table. I'm the guest of honor, no…dishonor, I guess, but I am the reason for this necktie party tomorrow," Campbell said in his gallows humor voice.

"I had Mrs. Conway in the kitchen cook up a little of this and a little of that. We've got three fried chickens, two beef steaks, and about five pork chops. There's green beans, butter beans, onions, cornbread, and tea or coffee to wash it all down," I said, just as Harvey Harris and Pete McGinnis, our additional guards for the night, arrived.

Harvey said he'd already eaten a bit, so he took up the first watch and sat outside the jail. Pete gathered up three pieces of chicken in a napkin and went out the back door, stating he'd have the rear covered. Micah Bailey, the state executioner, was outside. He sent Harvey back in to get me to come out.

"Dep- I mean Sheriff Bacot, sorry. I appreciate the invitation to dine with you gentlemen, but I must decline. I'm just not sure being around Campbell this close to our appointed time tomorrow is best for either of us. Good night," Bailey said sincerely.

"I can respect that, sergeant. I truly can," I replied. He tipped his hat and left, and I returned to eat. Deputy Daniels, in my absence, had made a plate for Campbell of a pork chop, two chicken legs, half a steak, and a mountain of beans.

"Here, deputy, allow me," I said as I moved to the cell door. Showing more bravado than sense, I upheld my key, turned the lock, pushed the door half open, and handed Campbell his plate. He kept his eyes glued to mine, shocked, I think. I closed the door normally and, not in any exaggerated haste, turned the locking key, removed it, and then looked back. Campbell was flabbergasted, unprepared for my bold showing of either trust or power.

There was silence inside the jail, the only sound the metal knives and forks scraping on tin plates. The thought of this being Campbell's last supper was too palpable for any of us to verbally acknowledge. Finally, halfway through the food, Roy Moody said we'd all forgotten to say a blessing before, so he said a short one before the eating commenced again. There was more food than we could eat. Harvey came in briefly, for a chicken back and two wedges of cornbread, and returned to watch the front.

Most everyone except me lit a post-meal cigar. Campbell lit up, laid down on his bunk, and streamed columns of blue smoke skyward, lost in his own private thoughts. All settled in for the digestion period of the evening and it was quiet both in and outside the jailhouse.

Around two hours later, the calm was shattered by two men screaming out in the street near the gallows. I heard footsteps running up the boardwalk toward the jail and my mind immediately considered this might a ruse, the distraction Campbell needed for his escape. I firmly told everyone to ready their weapons and make sure they were loaded.

A boy of about ten came tearing into the room, saying his father and another man were in the street and had knives drawn over a dispute. I sent Deputy Daniels with the boy to defuse the situation and had Roy take a place out front with Harvey. A crowd had gathered, one that didn't want the knife fight to end just because the law showed up, so they roughly handled the deputy and kept him away. Daniels knew what to do. He drew his revolver and fired one shot into the air. The crowd dispersed and the two combatants decided it was time to flee. Daniels quickly returned to the jail and sat out front with Moody and Harvey. He wanted to be sure there was no connection between a jail break attempt and what had just happened.

"Was that for you, Bill? Some of your people are trying one last attempt to spring you before tomorrow?" I asked as it all calmed back down.

"You've been writing so much the last couple of days, but you ain't been listening," he replied, swinging his feet around on the jail floor to face me. "There ain't nobody left but me. My brother, John, was locked away, and the rest were dead or gone to Texas. So, no, that scrape had nothing to do with me. No, Jack Ketch has me cornered, and I ain't getting out alive. Besides, the knife fight just sounds like two bucks chasing the same doe to me, sheriff."

I didn't know whether to agree with his assessment or challenge him, so I said nothing back. Campbell, noticing everyone was outside except for me, asked if I still felt like writing. He said he was near the end, and I paused, a little lump hit my throat. Near the end of his story? Near the end of his life? Both? I guess I'd never allowed myself to think out his story to its logical conclusion. He had. The end of his tale would be in my hands, to describe his going to the gallows, the words being said, the executioner's actions, and the dead body at the end of the hangman's rope. I hadn't realized he was in charge of 99% percent of this story and that I'd do the last 1%.

"Sure, Bill, hand me your cup for a few drams, and I'll ready my paper again, and we can continue."

Campbell stuck his hand and cup out of the bars, saying, "Fill it up please, sheriff. I'm gonna need some help sleeping tonight, I do believe."

Campbell's tale revisited the lament of having nearly $70,000 stolen from him. I noted each time he brought the amount of the loss up, he took a sip of his spirits. I really couldn't blame him. A vast majority would say it was his just-reward to lose his fortune, since they were ill-gotten gains, but scant few might argue it was his money.

Bill Campbell would go to his death never knowing the real story of the theft of his horde of coins. I heard it about a year after the War Between the States ended. It had begun in a Mobile saloon, one day after Campbell and Harley Mays's infamous gunfight outside of India, Mississippi.

One of Mays's hired guns got a little too deep into his cups and was bragging about how he put the first bullet into Simon Campbell. He complained that since Mays got killed, he never saw a dollar for risking his life in the gun battle. Another saloon patron listened, moved closer, and introduced himself as Thomas Shoemaker. The gunman repeated what he'd just previously said, as drunks tend to do, and this time mentioned all he'd gotten was a wool overcoat someone in the Campbell Clan had left as they fled. The coat had one $2.50 piece in one pocket and a paper in another, on which was written some strange foreign alphabet. Shoemaker asked if he could see the paper, to which the drunk said he could not, but if he wanted to buy it for $5, he'd sell it. Shoemaker bought it, left the saloon, read the map, and immediately headed directly for the Catahoula Swamp. That was how that snake-in-the-grass Shoemaker ended up with the fortune.

For Bill's part, he began riding over to Handsboro to find out who had built the two fine homes overlooking Bayou Bernard that he'd seen under construction his last time through town. As might have been expected, each was built by one of the two brothers who established the small town, the Hand brothers. New Yorker's by birth, the brothers moved south to make their fortune in the untapped, old-growth forests of South Mississippi. Their huge logging operation was a massive success, providing capital for them to next build a sawmill and use their water access to ship their lumber around the area. They also opened a foundry and, on a trip to New Orleans, saw the growing infatuation with wrought-iron balconies springing up on the finer homes downtown. They hired some of the wrought-iron craftsmen to their team and found they could manufacture a product of equal value at a cheaper price, while still turning a profit after shipping it over to the Crescent City. All these facts were garnered by Bill Campbell in the surreptitious manner he'd learned from Harmon. One thing Bill noticed on his surveillance trips was that Handsboro did not have a bank. The two Hand brothers likely kept their fortunes in their respective homes. It struck Bill then that he had no one to assist him. McTimmons was dead, Harmon was dead, Simon was dead, Phillip was dead, and John was in jail. How could one man take on a daunting task like robbing the Hand brothers?

He pondered his dilemma. Harmon and McTimmons had both worked alone before joining forces, but the world was a little smaller then, and the law was practically non-existent. Bill had been going to Handsboro in his disguise as a common workman with a beard and glasses under a straw hat. He knew when the time was right, he'd ditch his disguise and appear in town as someone never seen by the locals. One evening, Bill's thoughts turned to one of his favorite subjects, Shakespeare, and a passage from *A Midsummer's Night's Dream* came to mind: "Once I sat upon a promontory, And heard a mermaid on a dolphin's back."

There it was, a diversion. Something that would draw the people, specifically the Hand brothers, out of town, and allow Bill access to their homes. Bill quickly used his artistic hand to begin his ruse. Like many of those who seldom rested under the shelter of a roof, Bill carried some rudimentary knowledge of the local weather. He knew a south wind would typically bring storms off the Gulf, whereas a north wind just the opposite. By waiting for a day with the wind out of the north, he'd be assured the citizens of Handsboro would be more likely to traipse down to the seaside in clear skies. In the meantime, he'd prepare. A week later, he woke three hours before dawn to a fresh breeze coming down from Tennessee. Freshly shorn of his whiskers, he dressed in his best attire and top hat. He rode to the east with a handful of flyers to post on Handsboro's main street, Pass Christian Road, advertising that a real-life mermaid would come ashore, one hour before noon on this very day. The place of her landing would be at the recently completed lighthouse on the Biloxi shore. Her appearance was guaranteed by the great English naturalist, Charles Darwin. A beam of light, visible from the horizon, would draw her to investigate. Bill posted his fliers, including one on the Hand brothers's sawmill and foundry, in the predawn hour, then hid in the woods north of town and waited.

Checking his pocket watch at ten o'clock, the one lifted from a jewelry store during the second Mobile raid, he mounted Surrey, and rode to the edge of the wood line. It was working. Men, women, and children were all filing out of town, heading south to the gulf's waters to see the magical sight.

GALLOWS RECKONING

Stealthily, he rode past the Hand brothers's residences five times in all, before deciding both houses were empty. He had his horse follow a sandy footpath nearby until he was behind the houses. He dismounted and crept toward the nearest house. A large veranda was his first goal, and using the windows, he peered in the home to detect any persons inside. Feeling it was safe, he opened the back door and stepped inside. A floorboard gave a long, creaking sound and a body moved on the other side of the house. Bill heard footsteps coming his way and he quickly darted behind the long, thick curtains that hung down twelve feet. The footsteps made their way into the room he was in, stopped momentarily, then retreated to where they'd originated. Bill's ears told him they were the footsteps of a woman or teenager. Either way, he'd have to either abort his venture or eliminate them as a witness. The image of the empty treasure hole in the Catahoula Swamp made his decision for him. He drew his old rusty knife and crept toward the parlor room at the front of the house. There, with her back to him, was a cotton-top Negro woman sweeping the floor. Bill moved straight to her, her loud humming of a tune helping to muffle his footfalls. With a fast move, he covered her mouth and plunged his dagger deep into the back of her neck. Spying a bedroom to his right, he dragged the lifeless body to the room, shoved her under a large poster bed, and covered her body with blankets from a nearby cedar chest. While in there, he began to rummage through the drawers of the furniture: two armoires, one large chest, and three smaller ones. He pocketed about $50 in coins, a nice woman's diamond ring, a gold necklace, and two pearl necklaces. Across the parlor was another bedroom, in which he found a Hawken rifle, a brand-new Bowie knife, a few gold rings, and about $450 in coins. Feeling time was fleeting, Bill left out the back and crept over to the other Hand house. He made a similar haul—there were no guns or knives, just more rings, necklaces, and coins—and left with a little more than $800 from the second house. His instincts told him it was time to get out, even if he did suspect there was a much bigger haul of coins hidden somewhere. He made his escape. With no small feeling of accomplishment, Bill rode back to Pearl City.

Bill arrived back at his modest home in late afternoon and noticed a horse and buggy tied up to his front porch column. In the shadows of the porch, he could see a woman, holding something. She stepped forward. It was Fanny, Harmon's widow. As she moved, Bill saw a second woman—Fanny's older sister, Janie. McTimmons's widow. Bill noticed Fanny had but one of her children with her. Bill went in and asked the women to follow.

Fanny did most of the talking. They were in trouble. Their father was in Texas and had yet to send any money to them. Their hometowns of Pearlington and Jourdan Community had turned their backs on them, due to their husbands's real identities coming out after their deaths. Fanny's oldest kid had come down with a fever, but the local doctor refused to treat the child and he'd died. Fanny and her sister were near starvation and, as of yesterday, had no money. Unknown bandits had ridden in, threatened them with harm, and stolen their money. They had no place to go and had come to Bill seeking aid.

The four of them—Bill, Janie, Fanny, and the baby—laid out inside Bill's house for two weeks to let the circumstances calm down. Finally, when the food all ran out, Bill was forced to ride to Shieldsboro and restock their groceries. As Bill waited for the clerk to fill his order, he couldn't help overhearing two men talk about an old Choctaw with a gimpy leg. One was telling of how, in Biloxi, the Indian had led Harley Mays to the outlaw Norby McTimmons' hideout and saw him shot to death. Bill seethed in anger. They had been nothing but kind to old Manitema and he had betrayed their trust. Bill would even the score with Manitema. But first, he would exact revenge on Woods, for leading them into Harley Mays's trap, leading to Simon's death and John's capture.

Using the same tactic Shoemaker had used to find Harmon, Bill, having once gone to Woods's family home with him a few years back, paid them a visit. They were some of the first settlers to the Black Creek area, near the Bullis community. The elder Mr. Woods was very impressed with the Hawken rifle Bill carried and freely gave up the information that their son was hiding out with a younger brother, on a secluded sandbar on Black

GALLOWS RECKONING

Creek, four miles downstream of their current location. Mr. Woods, recognizing Bill as an associate of his son, even gave Bill the password to be shouted aloud to designate friend or foe approaching. The word was "springtime," but he had to be careful approaching, because both his sons had just purchased revolving pistols yesterday and mentioned they'd be practicing over the next few days, to hone their skills with a new weapon.

Bill rode Surrey right down Black Creek, which was low at this time of year. When he thought he'd ridden four miles, Bill dismounted and walked. At a bend in the creek, Bill could hear sporadic pistol fire coming from around the bend. They were indeed practicing. luckily shooting away from Bill's approach. Once their shooting ended, both men reloaded and discussed their results. Moving from bush to bush, Bill found a spot in a clearing with an unencumbered view of both Woods brothers. He put the Hawken up to his shoulder, took aim, and waited. As they both began firing, so did Bill, his gunshot cracks intermingling with the pistols. He took out his former associate with a single headshot and then quickly put two in the brother's upper back. The job done, Bill retrieved his horse and continued his ride downstream, away from the scene of his retribution murders. He rode past the two lifeless bodies and calmly muttered, "springtime."

Remembering an old foot trail that McTimmons had shown him, Bill rode toward the Alabama line, to the old hideout he figured Manitema was still using. One day later, Surrey carried Bill into the old Choctaw village. He immediately saw the remnants of a campfire still smoldering, so he knew someone was about. He rode his horse directly up to the old log cabin Manitema had used in the past and heard deep snoring. An empty liquor bottle at his chin, the Indian was sleeping one off and even left a candle burning. In the vague light, Bill could see a disturbing sight. Hanging on the wall above the candle was a long wad of blondish-red hair, exactly McTimmons's color. The Choctaw had taken his friend's scalp! The idea of simply shooting Manitema and ending his life vanished. No, he would pay dearly, and would beg for Bill to kill him and end his suffering.

DOUG WHITE

Growing up in those years just after the Indians outnumbered the whites in South Mississippi, Bill had heard many a tall tale from the old men of the community about how barbarous the natives were. He put the muzzle of the Hawken rifle directly on the top of Manitema's good foot and pulled the trigger, blowing a .50 caliber hole clean through. With the stock, he then rapped Manitema in the chin, knocking him unconscious. He dragged the Indian to a seven-foot-tall post—where they would use ropes to raise up and dress deer for consumption—and tied him up. Next, he gathered moss, limbs, kindling, and dry grass and piled it around the Indian, up to his waist. With his captive secure, he splashed water on his face to awaken him for the trial he was to endure.

Before lighting the fire, Bill took his new Bowie knife and ran an incision around the top of Manitema's head. Then, using the stout post as a fulcrum, Bill placed one foot on the back of the post, grabbed Manitema's long gray locks, and pulled with all his might. With a few well-placed knife cuts, he'd successfully scalped the Indian. Manitema endured the severe pain like a man and made only a couple of muffled sounds. Bill came around the post and held the hair in the Indian's face, driving home the message. Bill then inflicted a dozen minor wounds to the Indian's chest and arms using the Bowie knife, slicing, not stabbing, knowing that they were non-fatal but painful. Still, the old Choctaw stayed stoic. Bill went to his saddle bags, stuffed the scalp in, and retrieved a box of matches. He stared into the eyes of the Indian and then plunged his Bowie up to the hilt in Manitema's stomach area. He lit the fire at Manitema's feet. The old man began to sing in his native tongue—his death song. Bill mounted Surrey and rode by the pyre on his way back home, satisfied that his and his friend's injustices had been avenged.

Once more, as before, when Campbell had described a murder, I paused and asked him to reflect on his mental state afterward. This was a harder, older, and colder Campbell than the one who had first killed the young Mexican *vaquero* and held regrets. This version of Campbell was not unlike the carpenters who'd built his gallows. They were presented with a job, gathered their tools and a plan, and set about completing said plan. Nevertheless, I tried, asking "so you set out to avenge a betrayal by your ex-clan member, Woods, and you take him out along with his younger brother. Any remorse on killing the kid brother?"

"None, just good business. You being in the lawman's life probably know most killings are of the revenge variety, I'd say. Little Woods might have come after me to get after my hide for killing his brother. So it was best to take him out to prevent such a scenario in the future. See?"

He wanted an agreement from me, a justification, but I refused. "How is your cup?"

With that he tilted the bottom up to the ceiling. "Gone. So to answer your question before you even ask, killing the old Choctaw was done in the same frame of mind. Good business. Manitema might come to believe turning in old outlaw acquaintances was a good way to make a buck, so half of me said take him out first, the other half said I owed it to McTimmons."

He extended his cup and I gave him a refill of half water, half rum. "Much obliged, sheriff."

Harvey Harris, meant to be guarding the front, came in the door with an unknown man behind him. I immediately stood up and took out my pistol but did not point it at him. Harvey explained that the visitor was Fred Sullens, a newspaper reporter from Jackson with the *Weekly Mississippian.* Sullens was here to detail the hanging tomorrow. He added that Sullens had been contacted by *Harper's New Monthly Magazine* up in New York, and that he was to telegram his write up for them and be paid handsomely. I told Harvey this wasn't the time for that, to take Sullens away. He did, leaving Sullens with a long face. Before he left, Harvey said he'd been given a letter by the postmaster for Campbell. He handed it to me and left. I read the face of the envelope, first noticing the crude, handwritten name of William Campbell and then the postmark of Mississippi City. I laid it at the base of the jail door and pushed it with my boot into the cell. The outlaw quickly opened it, read it, and folded it in half, before using his cigar to set it on fire in the barren, far corner of his cell.

Campbell gave his cell bars three light taps with his tin cup, as if to acknowledge what I'd done for him. He didn't know it was as much for me as him. Time was short. Campbell needed to finish his tale and I had to record it, without interruptions or distractions. "All right Bill, where were we?"

CHAPTER TWENTY

His Peace, His Way

Bill got back to his house in Pearl City, and the women, to his disappointment, were still there. They still had nowhere to go. Harley Mays's son had evicted their other sisters, demolished the old family home, and, with his inheritance, had begun building a mansion on the site. Although he'd only been gone a week, the three houseguests had gone through a month's worth of food. He told them he'd ride to Shieldsboro in the morning and visit the grocery store once more.

Late that night, when the house was quiet, McTimmons' widow, Janie, crept into his bed and they had relations. When Bill awakened the next morning, he'd felt bad, but he rationalized that Janie was not of the class of female that would mourn in isolation for a full two years, as was customary among the upper crust. Bill's guilt lasted less than five minutes as he was sure McTimmons would understand. The widow was just showing her thanks to Bill for eliminating the sorry soul who ratted out her late husband to Harley Mays.

Fanny, possibly feeling threatened, was not to be outdone. She had relations with Bill that afternoon when Janie went for a walk.

It turned out that Janie and Fanny had not, in fact, eaten a month's worth of food in a week. About half of it was traded for corn whiskey and rum. Both of the Allen sisters indulged heavily and Bill understood why. Their comfortable world had been turned upside down. They were scared and alone, and it was natural to seek a little escape from life's misery.

The two women started their day frying bacon and eggs, each enjoying a cup of rum. After breakfast, they had more and Bill joined their drinking. After two hours of this, Bill decided he would ride to Shieldsboro for more groceries.

He tied up Surrey on Toulme Street and went inside to await the clerk and give his order. Mr. Tripp, the store owner, knew Bill as his alias, Jimeas Williams, and told him the clerk had just left to make a delivery but would be back in half an hour.

To kill the time, Bill wandered next door to a saloon owned by a New Orleans transplant, Mr. Piernas. Bill ordered a beer and found a seat in the back, away from everyone else. The establishment was quite small, with tables for about ten and room at the bar for another dozen. Two sailboats recently docked; in came twenty-five thirsty sailors. Before Bill could even protest, his table was invaded by four sailors, their glasses, and two bottles of whiskey. They ignored each other for the first five minutes, but then a pair of dice appeared, and the sailors began a game of Hazards. Bill watched them play for a bit. One of the sailors offered for Bill to join their game, which he did.

One of the sailors went first and his first throw totaled eight, his main point. The sailors and Bill placed their bets of one dollar. Bill bet the sailor would make his point, while the sailors bet against. The sailor threw a two and six, and Bill, seeing his main point made, reached out to haul in the winnings. At the same moment, one of the sailor's knees rocked the table and the six fell over to a four. Two of the sailors grabbed Bill's arm, claiming he'd lost. Bill explained how they'd all seen the man throw an eight before the table was jostled. One man accused Bill of calling him a cheater, adding that no one does that and lives. Bill released the five coins on the table and smiled as they released his arm. Bill said he'd had enough, would be on his way, and then stood up. All four sailors stood, too.

By choosing the table in the back, Bill's back was to the wall. He was trapped in the corner. The same sailor Bill had suspected of jostling the table said he could leave, but that he needed to empty his pockets first. Bill lost his smile and stared at each man, individually, straight in the eyes. Was this going to be a fight with fists, knives, or guns?

Bill remembered the jacket he was wearing carried about ten of the old $2.50 counterfeit pieces and decided they'd work as a distraction to get him out of the corner. He told them he had $25 on his person and that he'd leave it all on the table, but he wanted to be left free to go if he did so. He pulled out the coins, purposefully dropping half on the floor, and sent them rolling free to aid his escape. It worked on three of the four. The oldest one claimed that if Bill had $25 to give away, he probably had $100. He drew a short knife with a three-inch blade.

Bill drew his Bowie and, quick as lightning, flashed a jabbing stroke at the armed sailor's face, sticking his knife under his left eye, sending blood spewing. The other three sailors rained down fists on Bill, who staggered to get out of the corner, but couldn't. The youngest sailor possessed strength like Bill had never witnessed and wrenched his wrist and elbow so painfully he dropped the Bowie knife. More fists came down, and before Bill realized it, he was on the floor with boots pummeling into his head and torso.

And then everything went black.

When Bill woke up, he was in the Hancock County jail and in a lot of pain. He felt as if he had more than one broken rib as breathing was difficult. His rib was the least of his problems. A deputy told him he'd been charged with disturbing the peace, assault with a deadly weapon, passing counterfeit money, and when the sheriff's rider got back from Handsboro, after showing Mr. Miles Hand his engraved Bowie knife with his name on the guard, he'd likely be charged with larceny, too.

The county deputy was correct on all counts. Even nabbed him for robbing the homes of Miles and Sheldon Hand. How ironic was it that the attorney he hired, W.H. White from Mississippi City, was paid for from the money stolen from the Hand brothers. Mr. White was successful in having the assault charge dropped, as the old accusing sailor was likely 2000 miles from Mississippi, and with Mr. White's courtroom prowess, only the counterfeit and larceny charges stuck. Bill was sentenced to two years for the fake money and three for stealing, to run consecutively. He was once more back on his way to the Walls, the state penitentiary in Jackson.

As in his previous stint, Bill's actions showed the guards he was not any physical or verbal threat, that he was just in to do his time peaceably, without incident, and get out. The only incident was in year two when a rowdy inmate from Vicksburg accused Bill of stealing his tobacco from his cell next door, something Bill denied. The inmate took a swing at Bill and missed. Bill's self-preservation instincts kicked in and he knocked the man out with two fast punches. A nearby guard only saw Bill's fists fly and, as his punishment, he took five lashes with a bullwhip to his bare back and they added one month to his sentence.

Two years and eleven months in, bad luck continued to follow Bill Campbell.

Harley Mays's son, Creagh, was summoned to the Walls to identify a cattle thief who'd hit his farm, but who had been arrested for assault and battery of a Jacksonian. The bad luck? The inmate was Bill's cellmate, and when Creagh Mays came to see the perpetrator, he saw a cattle rustler and the man he believed had shot and killed his father. Of all the Campbell brothers, the two most similar in appearance were Simon and Bill. Creagh said nothing at the time but requested an interview with the prison warden. The younger Mays wanted to have Bill Campbell charged with the murder of Harley Mays. The warden was more than happy to lead Creagh Mays to the correct parties to have his wishes put into action.

That was the beginning of the end. Just twenty-two short days before his release, despite his plan to give up the outlaw life, repent and reunite with his remaining family in Texas, Bill, while still in the state penitentiary, was served a warrant for the murder of Harley Mays. No clan connections or Chieftains could help.

It truly was the State of Mississippi versus William Wallace Campbell, for all the marbles.

Campbell stuck an arm through the bars once again and wagged his empty cup. I rose from my seat and filled it with straight rum, thinking this would knock him out. At least he'd sleep like a man should, even though it was his last night on God's Earth.

The trial and outcome are known. It was Sheriff Smith's idea to secretly hold Campbell in Jackson County, while publicly stating Campbell was still in the Walls, while the death sentence appeal was considered. The reason for the legal sleight of hand was a fierce rumor that had been circulating, claiming that many men, honest and dishonest, wanted to spring Campbell free and force him to lead them to his stash of gold coins. The gossip mill had inflated his treasure's worth to around $200,000 now. Sheriff Smith, ever cautious, saw how such a life-changing amount of money could be very tempting, so he arranged it so that Campbell would only come to Perrine's small and lightly guarded jail before his sentence was carried out.

Campbell drained his cup quickly, then stood up and stretched. "There you have it, Sheriff Bacot. That's my life. Don't think I didn't notice how about every time I spoke of a death in my tale, a murder if you'd rather, you'd stop writing and pose a question to me about that. So, I don't want an incomplete picture for you. I left one out. About ten to twelve years ago, I took out a stranger on the Natchez Trace.

"Harmon, McTimmons, and I had run a successful slave raid and sale and it was time to lay out and rusticate. I was all right for the first month or so, but then some powerful urge overwhelmed me. You know the one I'm talking about, the same one that makes the buck forget his wily nature in November when the doe deer come into heat. Well, I couldn't get that gal in Natchez off my brain, and so resolved to go and lay up with her for a while. You remember me telling you about Little Lost Bet, don't you?

"But back to the Trace. I'd heard the stories, mostly from McTimmons, late at night after his bottle was just about drained. The Natchez Trace was a highwayman's paradise, the keyword being *was*. Once the steamboats became popular and it didn't cost an arm and a leg to book passage on one, the Trace's popularity began to wane. T'weren't much law around when McTimmons was a young man, and none existed out in the wilderness that was the Natchez Trace, so a robber could make a fine living preying off the travelers back then. He said once that a skillful robber could work the Trace for just two weeks or so and live the rest of the year off that haul. So, I was anxious to see Lost Bet but needed funds, so I rode out east of Natchez, to around Rocky Springs, and settled down on a well-hidden little bluff about ten feet over the trail, the floor, of the Trace. I sat quietly and let any group, large or small, go by without action, and finally, late in the afternoon came an older man by himself. Well, I jumped off the bluff in front of his horse, startled it. The beast reared up and threw its rider, making my job easier. I had a stout four-foot hickory stick with me, and I pounded his skull until he stopped any movement. I rifled through his saddlebags and all I found was a bit of hardtack and jerky. I went through his pants and coat pockets, t'weren't nothing but balls of lint to be found. I started to curse him, and then remembered to check his belt, the heels of his boots, and his hatband…and lo and behold, came up with better than $150 on him. He was a crafty old codger. Yep, me and old Lost Bet really cut loose for three days after that bonanza."

I gave Campbell a puzzled look and he stopped talking.

"Bonanza? Mexican word, sort of a new word, actually, I'm told. Picked it up from some fellow prisoner ne'er-do-wells, like me, who'd gone West and tried a little prospecting and mining. Means good fortune or a profitable surprise. Anyway, the old man was dead, but I had to cover my tracks, so I put him back on his horse, led them to a branch of Bayou Pierre, cut him open and filled his body cavity with rocks and mud, and let the bayou hide his corpse. I took McClarey's Path eastward and, two days later, sold his horse in Monticello for $45."

"Can I tell you why I always stopped writing when you talked of taking another human being's life?" I asked Campbell, thinking he'd be interested. He wasn't, and turned his back to me for thinking I'd try to influence him, especially tonight. "Okay, no preaching. So, what was your final tally? How many, Bill, how many did you kill?"

"You mean them that needed killing? How many of those?"

"No. Not looking for reasons. I just want to know a number. What is it?" I replied.

"Don't rightly know myself. Is it important now, to hold a count? I'll see if I can recall them and you make a mark, ready?"

GALLOWS RECKONING

Campbell started pacing his cell as he rattled off names: the Mexican *vaquero*, Doty, the night watchman, Welker, Elgee, Hand's house servant, McSween and Johansson from the river, the Wood brothers, and Manitema. Finally, he reached the end, the story of the Natchez Trace he'd just relayed, and we had a number: twelve. The room went quiet. I said nothing. Campbell neither, for over a couple of minutes, and then he broke the stillness.

"Mighty strange ain't it? I'll be swinging from a rope in what, fourteen hours or so? Hanged for killing Harley Mays. But I didn't kill Mays. My brother did. I'm dying for killing a man I did not kill...I'd *tell you* if I killed him, but I didn't. There's the others we just went over, and I guess I'm really dying for them, ain't I? One might even say it's funny or just plain unlucky! They'll add Mays to my twelve and say I was hanged for killing thirteen men, thirteen the unluckiest of numbers." Campbell looked right at me and laughed. Then he went to his small table next to his cot and blew out his candle. "Night, Larry, thanks for...well, just being a nice fella, and for being right friendly toward me."

Quietly, I said, "you too, Bill." Two words I would have bet my life savings of $142 on, just came from the lips of probably the most notorious outlaw I'd know: a friend? Was I? I suppose I was, in his mind. All the others were dead or living in Texas. Even if they did know him, it would be wise not to let that news go public. Half the people would assume you to be a guilty murderer, too, and the other half would force you to go to Catahoula Swamp and dig for his gold fortune. These were not good times to be even remotely associated with the land pirate known as Bill Campbell.

I snuffed the candle on the deputy's desk and moved to the small cot behind the sheriff's desk. I removed my boots, but then, thinking this would be Campbell's confederates last nocturnal opportunity to spring him, I put my boots back on. On that same line, I knew Campbell had seen that a spare pistol was kept in the top drawer of the deputy's desk, so I moved it over to my desk. I arranged the two pillows on the cot so I could stretch out below the waist but remain in a sitting position, awake and alert. If anything was to happen involving an attempted escape, I would not be caught napping. Sleep could be had later. I shuffled over, poured a cup of coffee to help ward off the urge to drowse, and then made a fresh pot for the others, should they ask for a spot.

The night hours passed quietly. Occasionally, Roy, Micah, Pete, and Harvey would step inside and grab a cup of coffee or water. Campbell slept soundly, I thought. Deputy Daniels joined me inside the jailhouse around dawn. The coffee was disappearing fast and we required another pot. He made the coffee this time. I thought the aroma seemed to rouse Campbell, but he did not rise just yet. He said something garbled, it might have been about breakfast, and fell back asleep.

Daniels sat down to drink his coffee and removed his boots to give his feet a break. I was stiff from my upright position all night. I thought a little short walk would loosen my bones and joints. I noticed the thickness of the air as soon as I stepped outside, or rather, lack of thickness. The humidity was well-off for a normal September day and, like Campbell had mentioned when discussing the weather, a north breeze was felt in Batson this day. Thin white clouds were moving swiftly above in the orange and purple sky of dawn. Unless all these factors were quick to go away, there would be no rain in the forecast of Bill Campbell's last living day on earth. I returned to the jail, spelled Deputy Daniels, and permitted him, if he wished, to go grab a couple of hours rest—I could handle the situation myself. He took me up on the offer and said he'd be back by 9:30 a.m. to help.

My temporary deputy, Harvey Harris, came in. He motioned me with his eyes to follow, and we walked to the back door but did not open it. He told me that newspaperman from Jackson, Sullens, was already outside and requesting—pestering for, actually—an interview with Campbell. I paused and thought about it. I had no experience in this, this hanging of a prisoner. Was it customary for the newspaper to interview the condemned? Was it in poor taste to plaster a man's words in the paper after he was dead? Did the law community or the state owe it to the journalism world? I had no clue, and no one to ask for advice. I decided I'd let Campbell decide for himself.

GALLOWS RECKONING

If Campbell wanted a few minutes with a man from the state's largest newspaper, I'd allow that to happen.

The outlaw was moving under his blanket and let out a mighty yawn. I instructed Harvey to tell Sullens it would be up to the prisoner if he'd allow an interview. He left me to deliver the message. As he moved away, I added to tell Sullens to let Campbell have his morning meal and time to digest in peace, if the answer was a yes. I sat down quietly and removed my Bible from the drawer. I thumbed aimlessly for a moment and then went to John 3:16 and softly read it aloud, "for God so loved the world that He gave his only son, so that everyone who believes in Him may not perish but have eternal life."

Pausing, I looked over the top of the Good Book, at the cell. Campbell was staring directly at me. I froze. He stood up, let his blanket fall where it may, and stretched his arms and back before speaking. "Well, that day has arrived, eh, sheriff. Got a couple or three favors to ask if you don't mind? I'm stealing that line, that Bible quote. John 3:16, if my memory serves me? Stealing is probably not the proper way of putting it, so I'll say borrow. I want to ask you for a pen and paper, as I want to write a letter to my mother. A goodbye letter, I suppose. Anyway, if I put that John 3:16 in there it will help her worries immensely. It's a good quote, won't help me none, but it's still a good quote. Second, if you'd inspect the inside right pocket of my overcoat you've had hanging over behind you, if you'd please retrieve the cigar in there, for my smoking pleasure? It's a real Havana cigar. I took a dozen or so from Mr. Hand's residence and I've really enjoyed smoking them. It's the last one and I'm gonna savor it. The third request is to have some rye whiskey in with my morning coffee. I know you were in the room, up all night last night, and it may have looked like I was sleeping, and I did sleep some, but not very much. I just laid here thinking. I thought too much, really. Life only goes forward. There's a backward in our heads, but it ain't real. Sort of a bad time for me to come to that realization, I guess. Anyway, I'd be much obliged for a little snort in the coffee."

I put my Bible back in the drawer, right next to the rye whiskey, and took the bottle out. I told Campbell I'd oblige him the spiked coffee, the cigar, and the letter materials. I almost opened my mouth again, was about to say how glad I was he'd be writing his mother, that I agreed John 3:16 would be a comfort to her. But I didn't. I knew the man by now. I knew him well. He wanted the world to know he was a tough, rough, hard man, and a man to be feared, even at this hour, so I quietly took him his coffee, paper and pen, and cigar. Instead, I offered him a chance to be interviewed by the biggest paper in the whole state, that the article the man would write was even being sold to a New York City magazine, where thousands and thousands would likely read it.

Campbell perked up. He placed the pen and paper on his cot and lit his fine cigar. "New York, you say? Never made it up there. Real big place, I hear. Very modern and all that. A sailor fellow I shared a beer with a couple of years back in Mobile told me of this new humongous building in New York called The Crystal Palace. He said it was as big as fifteen barns and the whole thing was made of glass and cast iron. Imagine that? I'd have liked to have seen that, yes I would." He took a puff, exhaled, and then drank from his tin coffee cup. "Well, maybe my ghost can make the trip up there."

After that, he sat on his bed and used the chair bottom for support as he wrote out his goodbye letter to his mother. It took a while, maybe sixty minutes, and I spied it as taking up roughly three-quarters of the page's length. He told me the address and said there was a coin or two in his overcoat that should cover the postage if I'd be so kind to mail it for him. I said I would.

"Bill, would you care for anything special to eat? Breakfast fare or maybe a steak and potatoes?" I offered.

"No, nothing special. Two eggs, two strips of bacon, and some bread, yeast roll or cornbread, doesn't matter," he replied as he enjoyed his Havana smoke. "What the Hell, make it three eggs and four strips of bacon," he tacked on and grinned my way.

"You got it, Bill," I said as jovial as I could. I made my way to the front sidewalk of the jail and asked Harvey to walk down to the hotel and pick up Campbell's breakfast. Then, back inside, I thought about how things would be changing very soon. Campbell would talk to me only when we were alone. Shortly, there'd be others in the room and no chance for our one-on-one talks. I took a shot. "You got your letter done, your cigar, and your spiked coffee, right? I'd like to know a thing or two, okay? I need to talk seriously-like with you."

He nodded but didn't look directly at me. He was wary of talking turkey to a man with a star on his chest, I assumed. It wouldn't hurt to try, so I took my shot.

"A little bit after you came to light in this jail, a mysterious man, saying he was a judge, came into town intent on seeing you in private. What do you know about that? Sheriff Smith and I smelled a rat and sent him packing. Did you have a false judge in your gang, or did a fake impostor come and try to spring you?"

"That was none of my doing. If I had to guess, I'd say it was Harmon's widow, Fanny, and McTimmons's widow, Janie. They've come to depend on me right heavily. I feed them, supply them their liquor, and even take care of their needs after the lamps are all out. Shoot, I never wanted to be married, and dang if I didn't end up with two needy women. That's my best guess, anyway. You know, I never had rye in my coffee before. Tried bourbon there a few times and liked it. This ain't half bad. You ought to try it sometime, sheriff."

Here he was, less than six hours from death, and talking as if he hadn't a care in the world, making small talk like we all do, just to keep the air moving. "Might have to take you up on that Bill," I replied. I tried to think of any other questions I could ask before the room became overcrowded and he clammed up.

"Say things had turned out somewhat different? Let's say you didn't go to the shoot-out with Mays. Instead, you went to Catahoula Swamp and dug up all the money. Then what would have been in store for Bill Campbell? Besides being the richest man in the state, of course."

"Oh, I'd have been well down the list of richest men in Mississippi, way down. There's a cotton planter out of Natchez named Duncan, I hear rakes in a million in a good year, half of one in a bad."

"Quit joshin' me, are you serious? A million dollars? In one year?"

"Makes me look like a pauper, don't he?"

"How, I mean how...how does a man spend that? How?"

"Now you've done it, sheriff. You've got me kicking myself for not going over to Natchez and separating Mr. Duncan from a million or two," Campbell said with a wistful voice.

I couldn't tell for sure how much of a joking nature Campbell was in, so decided to get off that subject. "All right, so you're a free man with $70,000 in your possession. What's the next move for Bill Campbell?"

"I'm just speculating of course, but I do like to read the newspapers and periodicals, to expand on what they say, so here goes. Now hold onto your hat, but I think slavery has run its course. The prices are just too damn high for everyone, except them like Duncan over in Natchez. I say that to say this: I'd invest in the coming freedom of the darkies. Oh, mark my words, that day is coming, and it ain't all that far off. The darkies will be free, and they'll be needing jobs. Where are the darkies, why down here, of course. So if I had money, I'd invest in non-agricultural jobs for them. Factory jobs. And lots of them. Instead of picking cotton, they'll be weaving it into clothes, they'll be fabricating iron, they'll be cutting timber and making it into lumber, they'll be learning to read and write, so some of them will need to be teachers for their own schools. Heck fire, anything we've got going in the white world, you name it, they'll need it for theirs, too. So, I'd answer your question by saying I'd used the $70,000 to open a big factory, a gigantic textile mill, and have them weave clothes. Yea, that's what I'd do."

He had me taken aback by that, and I went back to my desk and sat down. "You sure are a deep thinker, Bill," I said as I looked at the clock on the mantel over the fireplace. It read 7:30, giving Campbell four and one-half hours left to make outlandish statements like Negroes one day being free and going to school. Pshaw!

Harvey showed up with breakfast, and Campbell snuffed his cigar and quietly ate. It crossed my mind to leave him alone in the jail to be one with last thoughts. He might even pray if I wasn't around. Might, but probably not. No, I had to have my eyes on him at all times. It was my career at stake if anything happened. I recalled hearing from Sheriff Smith about a murderer sentenced to die in Adams County a few years ago. The inmate took his own life with his suspenders and hung himself a mere hour before he was due on the gallows, robbing the state and the victim's family of the opportunity to see justice dealt, as prescribed by law. I could see Campbell doing that, one last big fat middle finger to the world. I looked up from my desk to see Campbell's arm outstretched through the bars, patiently holding his tin cup. He asked for another coffee and rye, and I obliged his request.

Neither Campbell nor I spoke for the better part of two hours. He stared out of the cell window, sipping his spiked coffee, and I remained at my desk, faithfully watching him do next to nothing. Without turning around, he broke the silence. "Here's Deputy Daniels, so it must be 9:30. Leaves me with two and a half hours."

"That's right, Bill. Anything I can get you? Something more to eat or drink? Did you decide if you wanted to meet the newspaperman?"

"Bring him in, but if he says the wrong thing, it'll be the shortest newspaper article he's ever written. Oh, and I'll have another spiked coffee, as you call it."

I summoned Mr. Sullen and then asked Deputy Daniels to spell me for an outhouse visit. When I got back, it was only Campbell and Daniels in the room. I inquired as to Mr. Sullens's whereabouts, and after a long pause, Daniels finally answered that the newspaperman started off with a question Campbell didn't cotton to and was told to leave.

"What did he ask you, Bill?" I inquired as I moved back to my chair.

Campbell kept his back to both of us, and in an angry voice, said, "he wanted to know where I'd hidden my stolen money. After he introduced himself, the first thing out of his mouth was about money. 'Where's the gold, where's the money, what about the gold?' So I told him it was under Mrs. Sullens's side of the bed. Then I said 'Sullens, you're a mangy dog, get out,' because I wasn't talking anymore."

Deputy Daniels and I both shot each other a side glance. We were both grinning.

"Well, I guess we can all agree he won't be adding that gem to his article, will he?" I asked in Daniels's direction.

In a low voice, I reviewed the official procedure with Deputy Daniels. I'd lead Campbell to the gallows and Daniels would follow with a shotgun in hand. Roy, Pete, and Harvey would form a triangle around the gallows, each man facing the crowd and not the event. Reverend McClure would briefly speak, not so much for Campbell's soul, but as a learning experience for the younger crowd in attendance. Campbell and I would walk the thirteen steps up to the hanging area. I would read the death warrant aloud and grant Campbell an opportunity to say any last words. I'd step back and let Sgt. Micah Bailey perform his duty, on behalf of the state of Mississippi. After a specific amount of time has lapsed, Dr. Boudreaux would inspect the now-lowered body and officially pronounce William Wallace Campbell as deceased. I would ask if there was anyone present to claim the body, of which Campbell had led me to believe there would not be, then as part of Harvey and Pete's supplemental deputy pay, they'd take Campbell away for burial. It would be over, I assumed.

I asked the deputy to spell Pete McGinnis outside the back door and he started to leave. Daniels paused at the door, turned around, and said goodbye to Campbell, who returned the phrase, and he left. I did not know if it naturally happened or if it was arranged, but over the next five minutes, Roy, Harvey, and Pete all came into the jail and said goodbye to Campbell, who returned the salutation to each.

CHAPTER TWENTY ONE

The End Moves Forward

"I finished my Cuban. It was really fine," Campbell said when we were alone again. "Guess I'll go out smoking what I smoked as a lad, the Old Powder Keg brand." He lit up a fresh one and looked at me. "I could use something liquid; my throat is parched. How about another spiked coffee, but hold the coffee? Please, Sheriff Bacot."

"It'd be my pleasure, Mr. Campbell," I said, pulling the liquor drawer open once more. After filling his cup, I said at the deputy's desk where my writings were kept. "Are we all done? Your story, I'm talking about."

"Much obliged for the rum. And yes, I'd say we are done. I've come up to the point of my life where you know it as well as I—the trial for killing a man I didn't kill. Waiting in prison for the appeal, losing the appeal, more waiting, then you rode down and picked me up and brought me to this fine establishment, the Perrine County hotel—I mean jail. So, you know all that's happened since then, and…" he stopped mid-sentence.

There had been activity on the street for the past hour, but not so much more than the normal weekday traffic. Suddenly, many more horses, carts, wagons, and people were walking down Main Street, speaking in loud tones and with lots of laughter as they passed the jail, toward the gallows. Campbell half-turned and shot me a fearful look before he dropped his gaze. It had hit home. His death would not be away from the public eye, behind closed doors, or in the middle of nowhere on some dusty road. His death would be a gay attraction, an opportunity for a family to take the day off from normal life, come to town, eat and drink, and see a famous outlaw die. It wasn't much different from the Fourth of July or having politicians come in for a debate during elections. These people were *celebrating*.

Some unknown local yelled through the cell window bars on his way past, exclaiming, "Necktie social in one hour, Mr. Bill Campbell, and you're invited!"

"We got us a right nice day, Bill. Well…good for us, not so much for you, ha!" another bellowed.

"Bill, you tell that no-good-scoundrel partner of yours, James Harmon, when you see him in hell, that the Ashburn family opened a bottle of champagne when they heard of his death," another unknown shouted.

"Davis Summers, architect from Leakesville. Me and my wife are here, Mr. Campbell, to see your last hour on earth. I say my wife, my wife, you coward. Good riddance we say."

Taking cues from the others, a man close to Campbell's age approached the window. "Mr. Campbell, or Mr. J. Williams, as you are known sometimes. I've trekked seventy miles from Jackson, Alabama to see you hang. My name is Perry Hawn. You once sold me a bogus note for horses from Mr. Duplechain in New Orleans. You, sir, are no gentleman. You're a brigand and a freebooter. I second the gentleman's opinion of yours being indeed a good riddance."

Campbell turned away from the window and his eyes no longer showed fear, but anger. I could feel his rage seething. He flexed his fingers and the veins on his neck and forehead swelled, red. Campbell wouldn't need a gun or knife to wreak havoc on those insulting him. No, he'd want it personal, where he could lay hands on them and break their necks with pleasure. I'd have to deny any further request for alcohol with his turbulent and stormy mood.

I moved to the jail's front sidewalk and instructed Harvey to close the exterior shutters of the cell window. It seemed to help; Campbell stopped his frantic pacing and settled down. Eventually, he sat down in the chair, sipped his rum, and smoked his cigar. After nearly ten minutes of silence, he spoke.

"Sheriff, how much time do I have?"

"It's 11:20 now. We'll begin our procession to the gallows at 11:50. There are a few things we have to do before the noon hour."

GALLOWS RECKONING

The outlaw nodded and kept his gaze down. It was weighing heavy on him. I thought I had a duty to fulfill before the hanging. Campbell and Harmon's Beaver Creek gang had acquired a bevy of unscrupulous politicians, lawmen, judges, and businessmen all over South Mississippi. Their support of the gang and willingness to accept bribes marked them as slimy men under a rock, needing to be exposed. I moved back to the deputy's desk and withdrew my pencil and pad of paper.

"Bill, I hope you know I did my best to accommodate you while you were here, but now I need to be serious. The state needs to know the names of your Chieftains. What they did was wrong, and I can't abide by that. I need names and locations—their town of residence. Will you help me, Bill?"

Campbell looked at me with a hard stare. I waited in silence. He tried to wait me out. He blew a stream of blue smoke in my direction, and as his face was obscured by the cloud, he answered. "I guess I can give you a few names. It won't be their whole name, just their initials, and I won't give you their occupation, just the town or the county."

Settling in, I took a pencil in hand and wrote as he spoke. Campbell spoke quickly, hoping I couldn't keep up, I surmised. He'd say a Mr. DHS in Raleigh, or DDJ in Meadville. After he listed around two dozen, he stopped, went back to his cigar, and re-lit. I didn't say anything. With only initials, and not knowing their field of employment, I knew my work was cut out for me. Pinpointing who was a Chieftain and who wasn't off this information would be difficult.

Finally, Campbell felt obligated to explain. "I took that oath never to divulge clan secrets and that's one thing I can say I held true on. Might have just bent it a little by saying what I just said, but never did break the oath."

I couldn't tell if he was looking for congratulations or praise so I quickly changed the subject. I asked him if there was anything he wanted, like possibly the Bible. Instead, he shoved an empty cup through the bars. His fit of rage was well behind him, so I mixed a 25/75 ratio of rum-to-water and placed it on the floor near his door.

Surprisingly, Campbell then spoke up and asked for a mirror, a cup of water, scissors, and a comb, saying he was going to trim his beard and fix his hair. I obliged and silently watched as he took about two inches off his beard, combed his wet hair straight back, and then tucked the longer strands behind his ears. He then announced that he was finished and slid all the items back through the bars for me to collect. "Just in case my inherited wives, Janie and Fanny, show up, I'll look right handsome for them," he said with a laugh.

He then asked the time. I paused to consider, and instead of saying 11:47, just said, "it's that time, Bill."

He tilted his cup back and drained the contents quickly—commented on how quickly this morning had passed. I agreed as I moved to the front door and called all my helpers inside. I produced a two-foot-long rope and instructed Daniels to go in the cell and tie Campbell's hands together behind his back.

"Bill, I know you won't like this, but I have to tie your hands behind you. All right, here comes the deputy, so take it easy and we'll just all get through this together," I instructed firmly.

"Fine. I'm not going to put up a fight at this late point of things. Don't worry, I give my word. Come do what you've got to."

Those were the last words spoken by any of us inside the jailhouse. I placed my hand on Campbell's left shoulder and guided him outside. The day was sunny and bright, and both Campbell and I squinted in the glare. I glanced up and down Main Street, looking for any obvious threats, such as men on horseback wearing out-of-season coats to hide their shotguns and rifles. I saw none. We made a left turn and stayed on the board sidewalk. Pete and Harvey led the way—Daniels was right behind Campbell and Roy, about ten feet further back.

The gathered crowd saw us approach, and the insults, jeers, and laughs began again. I tuned them out as best I could and concentrated on scanning the crowd for anyone making a threatening move toward Campbell or law enforcement. Pete and Harvey used their gun barrels to part the crowd, and just like that, we were at the gallows. Sgt. Micah Bailey was already atop the gallows and I shot him a glance. For some reason, I had imagined he might be wearing a hood or a mask to hide his face, but he didn't seem concerned about that at all—his face was visible for all to see. He made a slight hand motion for me to come up the steps, probably thinking it was safer for me to not be in such proximity to the large crowd.

It was time.

I gave Campbell's shoulder a slight push and he took the first of the thirteen steps upward. My throat tightened a bit. I believed Campbell. I believed he was innocent of killing Harvey Mays. Yet his jury, the first judge, and the appellate judge did not know that fact. He is going to die for killing the likes of the Mexican *vaquero*, Mr. Hand's servant, and the Natchez Trace traveler—all innocent lives taken by his hand—plus the others he believed needed killing.

Soon Reverend McClure joined us atop the scaffold. The crowd was rowdy until the reverend held two hands up high, one with the Good Book, at which point they quieted down. Previously, I'd told the reverend to say his words of prayer after I read the state's case and death warrant, but he forgot and went straight into preaching.

"Hebrews. 4:12. Says 'for the word of God is alive and active, sharper than any double-edged sword, it penetrates even to dividing soul and spirit.'"

I tuned the preacher out.

Two men were riding up the south end of Main Street. I motioned Daniels to come halfway up the steps for a better view. I looked at the men and saw nothing suspicious. They weren't even armed, likely just farmers from the county. I then made eye contact with Pete, Harvey, and Roy to see if they had anything to report. I continued to watch the crowd who were all staring at Campbell. The preacher wound his talk up about repenting for one's sins, raised his hands again, and closed his Bible. He then moved over closer to Campbell and, in a low whisper, asked if Campbell wanted to say anything to God, his Maker. Campbell shook his head and the reverend moved to the far corner of the scaffold.

The crowd hurled a few angry epithets and slurs Campbell's way, but upon sensing what was about to happen, they quickly died down. The crowd was quiet. I had placed myself nearly directly behind Campbell on the gallows and so I moved up to be equal with him on his right side. As I did, Sgt. Bailey, noose in hand, moved square to Campbell's left side.

I caught myself sneaking a peek at the noose. I'd never seen one before. It was an ugly knot, big and thick, and the rope was new, with splayed frays shooting off in all directions. I then recalled I was a player on this tragic stage. Now was my big part.

"Good people gathered here, citizens of Batson, and the county, and others in attendance. I am sheriff of Perrine County, Lawrence Bacot, here today to conduct my appointed duty." I withdrew the letter from the Mississippi Circuit Court, which denied Campbell's appeal and gave the precise language to be read at his hanging.

I cleared my throat and began. "By the death warrant from the state of Mississippi, I, Sheriff of Perrine County, whereas on the date of June 28, 1852, the Circuit Court rejected all appeals of William Wallace Campbell, fully convicted for the murder of Harley Mays, by a verdict of a jury chosen and sworn between the parties, and was sentenced to be hanged by the neck on this date, September 9, in the year of our Lord 18 and 52, at this place upon the noon hour, as appointed by law. And he shall be hanged by the neck until dead, dead, dead. Given this under my hand, and seal number 7 by order number 191, signed Wm. H. H. Sharp, Judge."

As soon as the word 'judge' passed my lips, Bailey slipped the noose over Campbell's head and cinched it up tight, positioned under his left ear. In a voice louder than I thought necessary, Bailey asked Campbell if he had any last words. Campbell said he did.

"These people sicken me," Campbell said in a low voice, where only those on the scaffold could hear, then he cleared his throat and started again. "Cowards die many times before their deaths. The valiant taste of death but once. Of all the wonders that I yet have heard, it seems to me most strange that men should fear it, seeing that death is a necessary end and will come when it will come. That was from *Julius Caesar* by William Shakespeare."

Campbell stopped and beamed a wide smile, knowing most of those attending expected him to plead for his life, or at least make a last-minute pact with God to save his soul. No, instead he showed off. Beg for his life? Not Bill Campbell. Cross over to religion? Not Bill Campbell. This was exactly his way. And that's how he did it.

Under his breath, Bailey asked Campbell if he wanted a blindfold, to which Campbell told Bailey to go to hell. I stepped back to stand near the reverend and took my pocket watch from my vest. It read 12:00p.m. Bailey took Campbell by the shoulders and slightly moved him forward a few inches, to be positioned directly over the trapdoor. Bailey then took four steps over to his left and placed his hand upon the lever mechanism, which would spring the door wide.

An audible gasp came from the mouths of half the women in attendance. Another half bent over to shield and cover the eyes of their younger children. Bailey paused and looked over at me briefly, causing me to wonder if something had gone wrong with the trapdoor. What then?

"Larry?" Campbell said softly. "That letter was from McTimmons's widow, Janie, she said she gave birth to my baby, a boy she named Norby, but I won't tell you the last name she—"

We all heard the spring popping open to release the door. The notorious outlaw fell through the trap door, the sound of the uncoiling rope hissing like a snake. He hit bottom and the scaffold shook and quivered. A second, louder gasp came from the crowd and a few more insults were thrown his way. A small group yelled for him to try and rest in peace in hell.

Everyone was silent as Campbell fought it, pulling his legs up and down and kicking his feet so hard one of his boots came loose and fell to the ground, landing perfectly upright. Many of the children started to cry and were led away from the spectacle by their mothers. A few women screamed. Campbell's momentum then caused his body to spin, and if I looked down through the trapdoor, I could see him. I felt lucky that I could not see his face, only the top of his head. With his powerful arms and shoulders, he somehow managed to free his hands and they immediately went to his neck, where he tried to break free from the noose. His kicking began to slow down. A weak kick. Then half of a kick. Then nothing. Just after a pause, it started back again as fiercely as when it began with more kicking. I even heard a long, sucking grab for air from Campbell. So did the crowd, and another gasp arose from the people. One small kid yelled "he's dancing, Mama, he's dancing!"

No one laughed. I shot a glance toward Bailey, but he was staring straight ahead, not down toward Campbell. The kicking slowed once more, paused, and came back again with more violence than the last. Some in the crowd began to leave or wander toward the back, to put some distance between themselves and the grotesque pirouette. Still, it continued.

I looked at my pocket watch again—12:04, then five after. Campbell wasn't hung, he was being slowly strangled. Once more, I shot a look toward Bailey, who now had a worried look on his face. He knew he'd done a terrible job.

"Mercy!" someone yelled from the crowd.

"Shoot him in the heart!" another said.

"End it, Sheriff, end it now!" yet another voice cried above the din.

Most of the crowd had done an about-face on their wishes to see a hanging. I ran through the possible scenarios. Should I take my pistol and shoot Campbell at close range in the heart? Should Bailey do that? Instead, we all did nothing in silence and just watched.

It was 12:06 when Campbell stopped moving entirely. His arms, which had been up around his neck, flailing and pulling on the rope during most of this ordeal, now hung limp. The crowd was deathly silent now, and they moved back en masse to put some distance between themselves and the dead Campbell.

Sgt. Bailey finally looked my way and spoke. "Let's wait another two minutes, and then I'll let him down."

We did, and then Dr. Boudreaux approached and withdrew an ear trumpet from his bag. He placed the wide end on Campbell's chest and the thin end to his ear. After half of a minute, he stopped and placed two fingers on Campbell's wrist. He leaned in even closer and placed a small glass slide under Campbell's nostrils. After a minute, he rose and faced the crowd. "The prisoner has ceased to exist. The prescription of the death warrant has been fulfilled," the doctor said, a little more dramatically than I had hoped for.

He moved off and I spoke, announcing that should anyone present wish to claim the body, to come forward and see me. As he predicted, no one came up to claim Campbell's lifeless body. I descended the steps and had my first look at Campbell's corpse.

There was no peace on his face, his top lip seemed contorted, and his eyes held that wild look he sometimes exhibited when in a rage. I bent over him and noticed the vivid blue was gone from his dead eyes, so I closed his eyelids and placed a penny atop each, then looked at his face. The words from my reading of the death warrant came bellowing back at me. Fully convicted for the murder of Harley Mays. The words were true, but in the same breath, they were false. I was 100 percent fully certain Harley Mays was shot and killed by Campbell's brother, not him.

My law group then formed a semi-circle between Campbell's body and the retreating crowd. Once more, I assumed it was over. The crowd was now fifty or more yards back, and the festive mood seemed to return as a small group of musicians—a guitar player, two fiddlers, and a banjo player—struck up a song, *Old Dog Tray,* a popular Stephen Foster tune. I knew the tune, as Mrs. Smith had played it on the piano for the sheriff and me when I went to dinner at their home, almost two weeks ago. That pleasant night now seemed like an entire lifetime ago.

Sgt. Bailey came by and said he'd meet me in my office, as he had a form I needed to sign before he left town. My blood rose. I wanted to lash into Bailey here and now. He had caused a great deal of anguish on everyone here at these proceedings, not the least of which to his primary objective, Bill Campbell. I held my tongue for now, and instead answered, "yes, I do want to see you in private before you go."

Bailey gave me a knowing look. He knew—we both knew—that he should find another position in life as he was not suited for this one.

Then the day took an unexpected turn. Reverend McClure and our town mayor, Walter Landis, said they wanted to see me alone. We retreated under the gallows and into the shade.

"Sheriff, I wanted you to know the body of Bill Campbell will not be accepted into either of our town's church cemeteries," McClure said sternly.

"Well, Reverend, it was never my intention to ask that," I replied, equally firm.

Mayor Landis then moved directly in front of me. "The townspeople, really, the non-churchgoers, that is, petitioned me not to allow Campbell's grave in the Batson Common Cemetery, either. I agree with them, and for two reasons. First, this notorious outlaw doesn't deserve to rest next to good law-abiding folk, and second, and I've seen this happen, his notoriety will bring unwanted attention from curious folk and they will walk and trample over the graves of our dearly departed. And that's just the least they will do. I've heard some even dig up dirt and take it with them as a memento. We can't have that, sheriff, we can't."

"Well, those are the only three burial sites we have, gentlemen," I replied.

"I can only suggest you bury him somewhere not easy to access," the mayor said. "If you ask me, I'd put him down in the Leaf, not in the water mind you, but on a sandbar in the river. Yes, it would be a chore, but that way, when that day arrives and some curious hound wants to see Campbell's grave, we can just point to the river," he concluded.

"And it wouldn't be a lie," the pastor chimed in. "I agree with our mayor. He should be buried where it won't offend any living relatives of our town, and the river is the solution. Tourists wanting to see his grave would send the wrong message to the youth of Batson. A river sandbar burial solves that issue, too."

I looked at both men in silence. My years working beside Sheriff Smith came in handy. I would not win this fight. The secular members of the town were behind the mayor and the church-going public was behind the pastor. Even protesting would cause friction between the two most powerful men in town and myself. Sheriff Smith wouldn't fight this battle, and neither would I. Without responding directly to them, I turned to Harvey and Pete. I instructed them to go get their shovels and bury Campbell at the first sandbar they found in the Leaf River and not to worry about any grave marker. I added they should use the town cart and go out Main Street to the north, away from the crowd. They heeded my instructions and were off.

I headed to my office and my meeting with Sgt. Bailey. He was awaiting my arrival and pacing the floor when I walked in. Glancing left, I saw his grip packed, ready to hop aboard the Jackson-bound stagecoach within the half hour. I curbed my anger and let him speak first.

"Sheriff, I have to confess. I lied. When Campbell asked me if I'd ever hung a man before, well, to make him feel better I said that I had. That was a lie. Today, that...that was my first time," Bailey said in a low tone of embarrassment.

"Sergeant, I think and pray it should also be your last," I interjected.

We stared at each other from five feet away for a tense moment. I extended my hand, and he gave me the official state document I was required to sign, which I did. He exited the jail without any other verbal exchange.

CHAPTER TWENTY TWO

Tables Turned

The following day, after I left the post office from mailing Campbell's goodbye letter to his parents in Texas, I noticed the mayor and a couple of county officials gathered at the base of the gallows steps. This same small group, along with Sheriff Smith, had decided where to build the gallows and all agreed its presence would serve as a reminder and deterrent to crime in Batson. Now, after they'd all watched Campbell's grisly and gut-wrenching public strangulation, the mood was quite different.

I approached and tipped my hat, to which all three responded and then filled me in on their conversation. Tearing down the gallows would be a waste. Who knew, it may be needed again in just a couple of months. However, it could not remain here on Main Street, either. There was a copse of hardwood trees, ironically just behind the sawmill. If the two town carpenters could build a sled and secure the gallows, a team of oxen could drag it out of everyday sight. If they did need it again, the oxen could drag it back. I threw in that I liked their idea and started back to the jailhouse.

Just as I was about to enter my place of work, the Widow Smith, Ella, met me at the door. She was dressed all in black and her face was veiled, naturally, as she was in mourning. I opened the door and let her enter first, as she held a small basket in her hands. I offered her a cup of coffee, but she declined.

"Sheriff, I've heard around town that you had a very troubling last few days and that you practically lived here at the jail to keep watch over the prisoner. I know you probably weren't eating right, so I fried a young hen for you. Here, please accept this." She pushed the basket into my hands and took a step back. "I do so hope you enjoy it and get some nourishment."

"My gracious, Mrs. Smith, this is so very nice of you. I guess, having been married to a sheriff, you know the pressure he feels when an important prisoner is under his responsibility. You are very kind to bring me this chicken. It smells wonderful. Thank you."

"Oh, and there's a bit of onion and squash from the last bit of it growing in my garden. I must say, I'm surprised I was able to get squash this year lasting into September. It was Junius's little experiment to plant one short row, late, about the first week of July, if I recall."

"He always did have a green thumb. I'm going to enjoy some fresh squash. Haven't eaten any in over a month."

"Now sheriff, don't be afraid that I'm raising one-legged and one-winged chickens when you open the basket. I'll confess, the aroma got to me somewhat, and I had to sample the bird to make sure it was up to my cooking standards," she said coyly.

Her confession made me laugh and we locked eyes for a moment. The widow said her goodbyes and I settled in to devour a delicious meal. It was at that moment I realized I'd never thought of Ella Smith as anything other than the wife of my boss. But Junius Smith was dead and gone, and Ella was much closer in age to me than her deceased spouse. With her in mourning, there would be a two-year minimum wait to call on Ella, but she would be worth it.

After finishing my meal, I pulled out my notes of Campbell's life. That funny feeling hit again. I'd no longer be listening and writing the words from a famous outlaw's mouth. From here on, it would be my thoughts only. Recalling my attempt to gain the knowledge of all the gang's insider help from the Chieftains, I flipped back through my writing.

I know he named a few of them by their full name and where they lived. After a minute, I had three of them: Sam Adamlee of Paulding, Judge Runnels of Woodville, and Bob Troutt of Quitman. All right, there they were, but what to do with this information? They were all outside Perrine County, my jurisdiction. How could I move on these men? What if I approached the sheriff of Jasper County, where Paulding is located, but Sam Adamlee has control over the sheriff's department, one that I know nothing of, and I go whistling in saying Adamlee is a corrupt man? Would I be putting my life in danger? Very likely I would be, and these powerful men, willing to do business with murderous, thieving outlaws, would deal with me to protect their shady identity. Do they just take me out and shoot me right then and there? That could very well happen. Should I even get involved? Yes, but how involved?

I must tell the world, that's what I'll do, and let the public decide their fate. At the end of Campbell's life story, I'll add a section naming names where I can, and if all I have is Mr. X from County Y, then I'll put that in there. Maybe someone else can put those pieces together. I'm going to get this story out in book form. Right now, I don't know how, but I'll devote every hour I'm not working as sheriff to finding out how.

I did name names, and I paid the price.

Dear reader, you'll recall my opening paragraphs of this writing, that I cherished the "ka-chunk-chunk" sound of an iron cell door slamming as I was being freed. I was a two-year prisoner, a victim of my bold move—lifting that rock and exposing those shady businessmen who played their illegal game with Harmon and Bill Campbell.

Before my jail stint, my book was written, published, and then, on the eve of distribution, was destroyed by an arsonist. I would take up the fight again to have it re-published and distributed, but on my prison release day, all I could do was say thanks to God and revel in my freedom from the Jackson County jail. As my jailer led me outside the walls and the sun hit my face, I heard that mockingbird singing proud and loud. I squinted to see a single horse before a covered buggy. I stepped to one side to avoid the horse when a voice came from the deep shadow over the buggy.

"Sheriff Bacot? It's me, Ella Smith, from Batson. Hello!"

"Mrs. Smith? I'm pleasantly surprised. Hello, how did you know I'd be here?" I inquired.

She explained she'd been diligently writing and visiting every contact she had in the state law enforcement and judicial systems about my bogus conviction and sentence. Her deceased husband had quite a network of contacts and she used them. Most of those she contacted said that if I had been hired by Junius Smith, who was an expert on judging which men possessed first-rate admirable qualities, that was enough for them, and they agreed to help her free me. She then asked me about my plans.

"I don't have any plans. I just learned of my pardon from the governor, that I'd be set free two years early from my sentence, yesterday morning. I guess I'll go back to Batson and gather my things and see—"

Ella interrupted, "Mr. Bacot, you couldn't know, but Batson no longer exists. The Mobile and Jackson Railroad built a new line that bypassed Batson by nearly a dozen miles. Everyone in town left and started a new community further south on the Leaf River, where the tracks were laid. They call the new town Eden. Batson later burned. There's nothing there anymore. One of the last residents said lightning had hit the gallows, the same one Junius had built for the outlaw, Campbell. The gallows toppled over near the sawmill and all those mountains of wood shavings caught fire and spread, and pretty soon the entire town was engulfed."

"My goodness, that's terrible. I had no idea. How about you? Did you move to Eden?"

"I did not. I couldn't find any reason to go there, so I came south to Biloxi. I purchased a small bungalow on Bohn Street, just off Howard Avenue, where my sister and her family live. I teach piano and give singing lessons. Oh, and sewing, and it not only provides, but it keeps me busy."

My previous thoughts of calling on her returned, but I stayed away from that subject as well as the urge to ask if she was romantically involved. After all, she said her name was Ella Smith, so she was still using her married last name.

Much to my surprise, she announced she was here to give me a ride to wherever I needed and told me to get in the carriage. We started west, toward Biloxi, and after a two-hour ride, we decided I would sleep in her bungalow in Biloxi, and she would stay at her sister's place. I could make up my mind tomorrow about where I go next.

Ella came by her house the next morning around seven and asked if she could make us both some breakfast, to which I agreed. After she had gathered five eggs from her coop and come back inside, she asked if I had decided on a plan.

"My first step back into the legitimate world is to go to Jackson and seek an audience with the governor. His name is Petty, right?"

"Correct, John Paul Jones Petty, from one of our river port towns on the Mississippi. Rodney, maybe? Or is it Grand Gulf? What will you say to him?"

"First and foremost, he will receive my deepest gratitude, as you do as well, Mrs. Smith. From there, I will need something official from the office of the governor, stating I was pardoned and that my conviction for libel was overturned as erroneous. I can't expect to find a good job if my future employer thinks I went to jail legitimately."

"I entirely understand that thinking, Mr. Bacot. You will need proof of your pardon."

"I understand from my jailer that the bad men who rigged the system to railroad my libel trial also made sure every newspaper in the state ran headline stories about my conviction and sentence. It made sense on their part to publicize my guilt. My guilt equaled their innocence. Even though all my books burned, there were some who did manage to read it and some that had a part in publishing it. Surely a few people saw that list of names in the back of the book, that named names those in cahoots with the Beaver Creek Clan."

With that said we ate, and I wrote my letter to the governor's office seeking an audience, then walked the letter to the post office. That day set forth a string of good fortune in my life.

The governor saw me early in the year of 1857 and I officially received my pardon papers. Luckily, I met the president of the state senate as I was leaving the governor's mansion, an amiable man named Whiteside. I'd taken up smoking in my years in jail, as cigars were given out as rewards for good behavior. Whiteside asked me for a match, who I was, and why I was here, and then asked me to join him at Spengler's Corner for a mid-day meal.

Whiteside quizzed me about my background. After he found out about my connection to Sheriff Smith, he was excited and eager to help me. His engaging mind was able to put two and two together, with my deputy and sheriff experience and my upbringing in Simpson County's Westville. There were some vague connections like his brother-in-law was a second cousin to the current sheriff of Simpson County. This man had told Whiteside that he'd not be seeking re-election this coming fall but had not made his announcement public. Whiteside suggested I seek the office and I couldn't think of a reason to disagree. He even volunteered to take the train down from Jackson to Westville and help my campaign, possibly give a speech or two on my behalf. An old Mexican War buddy of his, Col. Daniel McLuney, was president of the bank in Westville and Whiteside volunteered to write a letter of recommendation for me to him, should I seek funds for the election. I gladly accepted and thanked my lucky stars for the chance to meet with the generous and influential Mr. Whiteside.

I moved back to Simpson County and bought a very inexpensive small house near the Old Hickory, to meet my residency requirement to run for office. I came up with the idea to travel the county selling firewood, like Bill Campbell's legitimate work. The pay was poor, but the idea was to meet and reacquaint myself with the people and to never accept any money from any widows I might come across. I also did some substitute preaching for a few churches when their regular pastor was not available and I was able to get my name in front of the people. In the evening on some nights, I began writing to Ella in Biloxi, and much to my wonder and joy, she began answering me. At first, they were just letters recounting the events of the past week or so, but things changed, and the letters became more about feeling than what we'd eaten for Sunday dinner. For my resolve, I decided should I win the election, I would not write her of my victory, but tell her in person, just before I proposed marriage.

DOUG WHITE

Sixteen months after I was released from jail for the phony libel conviction, my life was completely turned around. Each morning, I would kiss my beautiful wife, Ella, before heading to work at my dream job of protecting the good people of Simpson County, Mississippi. I shall end my story there. However, the story of Bill Campbell continued, even after his hanging.

The morning after Campbell's hanging, Pete, who had helped bury him, and I walked down to the west bank of the Leaf River to see the sandbar where they had deposited Campbell's corpse. September can be a dry month in Mississippi, and we could see the water was nowhere near Campbell's spot. It was high and dry. What was at Campbell's spot was a shock to us both.

His grave was not occupied. One could see, very plainly, the deliberate shovel strokes and markings, as well as the purposefully piled sand next to an empty hole. Batson had a grave robber.

I took no action, as I knew of none to take unless someone came forward with information, and then shortly thereafter, I was in jail. I certainly had no time to worry about the missing body of a dead outlaw.

Just because I did nothing, it did not mean I forgot about Campbell's whereabouts. I told myself some circus sideshow had probably mummified his head and was charging a nickel to see the infamous Bill Campbell. I surmised I would never see it, because if they had a lick of sense, they wouldn't show that around here. I would be proven wrong about the circus.

In 1882, a few years after my retirement as county sheriff, I received a call from a middle-aged man, about forty-five years old. Standing on my front porch was a tall, handsome fellow who said his name was Robert Dunbar and that he was a writer from New York, writing under the nom de plume of Asa Livings.

I invited him in, and Ella brought us both a cup of tea. He said he had recently finished writing books about the exploits of both Jesse James and Billy the Kid. I immediately said he'd picked a good subject, as most all had heard of them but did not know very many details. What he said next surprised me.

It was his opinion that if what he'd heard was true, Bill Campbell was right up there with them in the hall of dishonor, thievery, and murder. He wanted to interview me, as he'd heard I was the authority on Campbell's life but that my story and my book had been stifled. I said he was correct, that my attempts to have the book published a second time had never materialized, as I'd become sheriff and a married man with too many duties to pursue the book. He took out a pen and notebook, which reminded me so much of myself in 1852.

Dunbar said he was traveling by train a few days prior when the train stopped in the small village of Monroe, Mississippi, which is northwest of Eden. It was early in the day and the train engineer had become very ill, so they were forced to stop and wait for his replacement. It gave him time to explore the town. He said there was a commotion outside of a physician's office, as the front door had been kicked in and there had been a robbery. Dunbar said because of his interest in the lives of bad men, he stuck around to dig deeper.

The only lawman in Monroe, after the initial circus about the break-in, agreed to talk. The lawman said the building housed two businesses, both sharing one giant room. One side was the doctor's office, the other half was Willis & Crozier Druggists and Sundries, and both had been around since the early 1850s. He immediately jumped to say crime, of any kind, was unheard of there in Monroe. Everybody knew everybody, and half of everybody was related, so a break-in was a rare occurrence. There were valuable items that a regular crook would love to steal, but none of those were missing.

The only thing missing was a full human skeleton, suspended from wires, and the stand on which it was supported.

A standing skeleton had some value, $5 or $10 at most A single bottle of morphine or any piece of the doctor's equipment was equal to that. The thief also neglected to steal any cosmetics, perfumes, or tonics. The robbery piqued his interest. The lawman had no real information about the skeleton, except that it was the bones of a famous outlaw, whose name escaped him. Dunbar thanked him and returned to the pharmacy.

Mr. Crozier, it seemed, had recently passed away, but Mr. Willis could spare five minutes. Willis said the skeleton was here when they bought the building. Before it was their pharmacy, it was a meeting house owned by a Mr. Shoemaker, an out-of-towner. The skeleton had a wire metal frame surrounding it, for support, and stood on its own. The doctor used it frequently to explain ailments to patients and it was indeed famous.

Those were the bones of the notorious outlaw Bill Campbell. Shoemaker had told Crozier that he'd had one of his slaves steal the body out of a sandbar on the Leaf River, where it was taken to a skilled surgeon in Columbia, who removed the flesh, strung the bones together with wire, and then built the stand. The contract for Shoemaker's agreement to sell, besides a normal real estate transaction, had three stipulations. First, the skeleton would remain forever, as part of the building. Second, it had to be in the open, able to be seen, not stashed away in some closet. Third, if a man named John Campbell ever came by, they would not sell the skeleton for any price. If they sold to John Campbell, Shoemaker said he'd use all his considerable wealth to ruin Willis & Crozier and the doctor.

Willis said they agreed to his odd terms, and after a while, welcomed the bones, as it drew in customers who might not have otherwise entered their establishment. When the only lawman in Monroe asked Mr. Willis if he'd noticed any strangers milling about the store the day before, he answered with an affirmative. He said a muscular young man, of about thirty years of age, was in his store. He didn't seem to be shopping, so Willis thought he may be here to meet someone, and he introduced himself. Willis said he spoke first to the stranger, gave his name, and extended his hand. Oddly, the stranger did not extend a hand in return and only gave a one-word response for his name, Norby. When he asked if he could help him find something to buy, he declined and left. Dunbar explained that his interest was piqued even more.

GALLOWS RECKONING

It was time to delve into the identity of Bill Campbell and why no one had heard of him outside of a few counties in South Mississippi.

That was why Dunbar knocked on my door. After a full day and a half, with me talking and him listening and taking notes, he had his story of Bill Campbell. Dunbar considered himself somewhat of an expert on outlaws like Jesse James and Billy the Kid. He decided that it was time for the world to know the story of the outlaw that was every bit as bad as them: William Wallace Campbell.

Me? I couldn't agree more, yet I still think Campbell would have avoided it all if he'd just been punished and reformed at thirteen years old. Therein is the lesson of his life, and hopefully some other teenager will learn from it and not go down a wayward and destructive path. One that ends with him standing atop the gallows and awaiting the end, by way of the hangman's rope.

ABOUT THE AUTHOR

Recently retired banker. Fifth-generation Mississippian that long ago studied (stifle laugh here) at Ole Miss and finished at Alabama. Has three children, six grandkids, plus three step-children and six step-grandkids. Routinely found at the gym, mostly gabbing, according to my wife. Will watch TV from Labor Day to New Years Day. Enjoys reading, almost exclusively Southern history and discovering little-known minutiae found therein.

ABOUT THE PUBLISHER

Creative Texts is a boutique independent publishing house devoted to high quality content that readers enjoy. We publish best-selling authors such as Dulee Carmel, N.C. Reed, Sean Liscom, Jared McVay, Laurence Dahners, and many more. Our audiobook performers are among the best in the business including Hollywood legends like Barry Corbin and top talent like Christopher Lane, Alyssa Bresnaham, Erin Moon and Graham Hallstead.

Whether its juvenile fiction, post-apocalyptic or dystopian fiction, biography, history, true crime science fiction, thrillers, or even classic westerns, our goal is to produce highly rated customer preferred content. If there is anything we can do to enhance your reader experience, please contact us directly at info@creativetexts.com. As always, we do appreciate your reviews on your book seller's website.

Finally, if you would like to find more great books like this one, please search for us by name in your favorite search engine or on your bookseller's website to see books by all Creative Texts authors.

Thank you for reading!